THE CAGE OF ZEUS

SAYURI UEDA

THE CAGE OF ZEUS

SAYURI UEDA

TRANSLATED BY TAKAMI NIEDA

SAN FRANCISCO

The Cage of Zeus

© 2004 by Sayuri Ueda

Originally published in Japan by Kadokawa Haruki Corporation.

All rights reserved.

Cover illustration by Tatsuyuki Tanaka

English translation © 2011 VIZ Media, LLC

HAIKASORU

Published by VIZ Media, LLC

295 Bay Street

San Francisco, CA 94133

www.haikasoru.com

Library of Congress Cataloging-in-Publication Data

Ueda, Sayuri, 1964-

  [Zeusu no ori. English]

The cage of Zeus / Sayuri Ueda ; translated by Takami Nieda.

    p. cm. -- (Haikasoru)

  ISBN 978-1-4215-4003-0

1. Outer space--Fiction. I. Nieda, Takami. II. Title.

  PL876.5.E33Z4413 2011

  895.6'36--dc23

                  2011022601

The rights of the author of the work in this publication to be so identified have been asserted in accordance with the Copyright, Designs and Patents Act 1988. A CIP catalogue record for this book is available from the British Library.

Printed in the U.S.A.

First printing, September 2011

TRANSLATOR'S NOTE

In order to reflect the bigender state of the Rounds, this English-language translation of *The Cage of Zeus* employs Spivak pronouns—a set of gender-neutral pronouns devised by mathematician Michael Spivak—to refer to the Round characters. Spivak pronouns are formed by dropping the *th* from the plural pronouns "they," "them," "their," etc. Although gender-specific pronouns exist in Japanese, they are used less frequently, making it easier in Japanese to avoid using pronouns that specify gender.

I

1

ALTHOUGH IT WAS the weekend, Cryse University on Mars buzzed with activity. The walkways and cafés were alive with the chatter of students and scholars visiting from Earth and the Moon, while the staff, rushing to prepare for the next lectures and presentations, remained on high alert. A symposium of leading bioscientists was the target of radical groups demonstrating in the name of human rights. Any lapse in security and something terrible was liable to happen.

Ever since a clash decades ago that left many injured and even resulted in a few fatalities, it had become customary to exercise the utmost security precautions at any symposium. That people had died at a gathering to preserve the sanctity of life was deplorable, but the violence also indicated just how far bioscientific technology had advanced after the twenty-first century. Today marked the final day of the symposium hosted by the Planetary Bioethics Association, and a reception was scheduled for later in the evening. The five-day symposium was a major event that took place biannually on Mars, during which research presentations, reevaluation of bioethical measures, and all manner of political maneuvering took place.

David Lobe glanced across the lush lawn of the campus and felt horribly out of place. Although he had come dressed as Eddie Morgan had instructed, he found it hard to believe he blended in, even as he tried to pass himself off as a security team member or guest speaker.

"You were born on Mars, weren't you?" Morgan asked, as they walked down the path toward the courtyard.

"Yes," Lobe answered.

"Bring back memories, this place?"

"Well, no. I never went to college."

"No?"

"I moved to Asteroid City as soon as I finished my schooling."

Asteroid City was a space city orbiting within the asteroid belt between Mars and Jupiter. Originally built as a waystation between the two planets, it developed into an industry town that mined and processed mineral resources for export. The city was comprised of not only factories but housing for workers as well. Because most of the labor was automated, Asteroid City wasn't large as far as cities go, but was an industrial space city nevertheless. Lobe had worked there for ten years.

"One thing led to another and I ended up on Earth, with this job."

Morgan decided to drop the subject. He muttered, "The gravitational difference feels strange."

"Oh?"

"This is my first time on Mars. Even if a molecular machine can help to control the body's fluidic circulation, this strange lightness takes some getting used to."

"It's like jet lag. You'll get used to it soon enough," Lobe answered. "I wonder if she's actually going to show."

"If she's sure she won't get made. No one's made contact with her in almost twenty years. Most people don't even know she's alive."

"She might run at the first sign something's not right. People like her have a nose for sniffing out danger."

"If that happens, you go after her. Don't come back until you find out where she's been hiding," Morgan said.

They sat down on a bench in front of a fountain emblazoned with the university insignia's design. A steady stream poured forth from it. A landscaped lawn surrounded the bench, and there was a rose garden in full bloom, flowers as large and brilliant as the sun, on the side. All of the plants on campus were bioengineered to boost photosynthetic efficiency, thereby playing a role in supplying Cryse City with oxygen.

Lobe sat back and stared up at the man-made sky projected onto the interior of the canopy.

This was his first time visiting Mars in quite a while. There used to be only one orbital elevator when he was a kid, but three more elevators had been built along the equator since then and banded together with rings. The two moons that had once orbited Mars, Phobos and Deimos, had been completely consumed for resources during the construction of the elevators. But no one on Mars paid any notice when the two moons disappeared from the night sky. Then again, there was no way they could notice, living as they did inside the canopy.

Hearing footsteps, Lobe lowered his gaze. A woman in a lavender-colored suit was approaching.

Morgan stood up and shook the woman's hand. "I appreciate your taking the time to see me."

"Not at all. Thank you for making the trip from Earth," the woman said.

"Tickets are cheaper during symposium season, so it was no trouble at all."

Morgan showed her to the bench. "We can talk here, where it's quiet and private."

Lobe got up and stood behind the bench. The woman furrowed her brow and eyed him suspiciously. "My assistant," Morgan said. "It's all right, he's young. He won't mind standing for a while."

"But…"

"I'd hate for you to be uncomfortable."

"Then why don't we go to the café? We can sit, have a drink and talk there."

"I prefer to have our talk here, Ms. Karina," Morgan said.

A smile crept across the woman's face. "You must have me mistaken for someone else. My name isn't—"

"And while we're at it, I'm not a professor from Stanford. Merely an excuse to get you to agree to see me. You wouldn't have come otherwise."

The woman turned to leave, but Morgan grabbed her arm. "We know your history. You'll only make things worse by running now."

"I don't know what you're talking about."

"If you don't want to be turned over to the police, you'll sit down. We're here about a job. Not a bad job either. You'll be compensated generously."

"Let go of me."

"You'll lose your job, is that what you want?" Morgan said. "Everything you've worked to build over the last twenty years. I'm capable of destroying it all in an instant."

"Then do it," the woman said coldly. "I knew a scumbag like you would come and try to threaten me someday. I was ready for it. If you want to inform the police, be my guest. I'll find a way to survive."

"We've taken something you treasure above everything else hostage. If you refuse the job, the hostage will die."

"I have no family or friends that can be taken hostage."

"You're wrong. There's one thing you refuse to abandon. Something you'd give your own life to protect." Morgan whispered the name of the hostage. He explained just how he would kill the hostage if she refused the job.

Suddenly, the look on her face turned fierce. The woman shook off Morgan's hand and shoved him against the bench. She jammed a knee against his chest, stopping his fall from the bench, and wrapped both hands around his neck. His head thrown back, Morgan wheezed and struggled to break free of the chokehold.

Lobe ran around the bench, drew his gun, and pressed the muzzle down against the top of the woman's head.

Calmly, she cast her eyes upward. Lobe recognized the sneering confidence in her eyes and shuddered. At that instant, he realized idle threats would be useless against her. She was ruled only by arrogant pride and an iron will. People like her refused to submit under any circumstances.

"Go on. I dare you to shoot," she said, tightening her grip around Morgan's neck. "Do it and I'll break the boss's neck."

Lobe silently kept his gun trained on her head. Though he was armed, he felt his knees might start to tremble. One false move, and she would kill not only Morgan but him too. Her fingers might take out his eyes even before he got off a shot. She might punch his nasal bone clear into his brain. Or slip behind him and snap his cervical vertebrae.

"Lower the gun," Morgan said, gasping for air.

"But, sir—"

"Just do it."

Feeling relieved but feigning reluctance nonetheless, Lobe lowered his gun.

"The hostage will die whether we come back alive or not, " Morgan rasped. "And using us to bargain with our superiors will get you nowhere. We're nothing but pawns here. We're not afraid to die. Think about this rationally. Accepting the job is the only way to save the hostage."

The woman removed her knee from Morgan's chest. She fixed the hem of her skirt and shot him a wicked glare.

Morgan finally sat up, rubbing his throat. "The job is simple," he said, as if to mollify her. "You carry a package into a designated location, open it, and leave immediately. There's nothing to it."

"Don't lie to me. If you've gone to all this trouble to enlist me, there has to be more. What are you plotting? Just who are you people anyway?"

"A group fighting to protect the sanctity of life. If we succeed, our name will go down in history as heroes. As the ones who led humankind back from its errant path."

"I have no interest in money or glory," muttered the woman. "Look, I'm in my mid-thirties. I no longer have the drive or stamina. And I'm tired of killing. If I have to kill again, I'd rather kill myself right now and be done with it."

"The hostage will die even if you refuse the job via suicide. Simply put, you have no choice but to take it."

"You sons of bitches."

"Say what you will. But we desperately need your services." Morgan shot her a piercing gaze. "So you'll accept?"

2

WHEN HIS DAUGHTER Rui asked for help with her homework, Koichiro Hasukawa looked up from his enewspaper. He stared at his daughter, a bit nonplussed.

"I'm learning about the history of Mars," she said. "Tell me about when you were little, Daddy."

Rui was six. She was old enough to have mastered a computer terminal.

When Hasukawa suggested she access the database from the Mars Museum and look it up herself, Rui replied in a high-pitched whine, "But the teacher said we have to ask our mommies and daddies."

This appeared to be not just an assignment but also the Ministry of Education's attempt to investigate the home lives of their students. Are the students communicating with their parents? Any distortions in student character development? Warning signs of criminal behavior? It was an education program aimed at detecting the first signs of trouble by observing children via a sociomedical perspective. There were also assignments involving scans of the children's brain activity. Hasukawa recalled having to make a "brain album," compiling records of data, as a kid.

By profession, Hasukawa believed these efforts to be meaningless. Plenty of people raised in positive home environments went wrong, while others endured unimaginable hardship in their youth and grew up to be great men and women. People continued to change over a lifetime, for better or for worse.

When he called out to his wife, Kyoko, she gently admonished him. "You look after Rui once in a while. You'll collapse the way you've been working lately."

Hasukawa relented. He couldn't remember having a proper conversation with his wife or daughter in the last month.

Ever since the assassination attempt of a Martian government official in Pavonis City, Hasukawa had been obsessed with tracking down the terrorist group claiming responsibility for the crime. He belonged to the Special Security Division, the antiterror units, of the Mars Police Department. As captain, he was charged with overseeing day-to-day operations of the entire division.

He had little field experience. After completing his specialized training as a cadet, he had been assigned to a command post in a regional city and, after having gained some experience, returned to the capital city. He was one of those who'd chosen a conventional path straight to the top.

The SSD had narrowed its investigation by sorting through the voluminous reports coming into headquarters, but the suspect had escaped just as they were moving to make an arrest. There had been a leak from the inside. Although the Central Intelligence Bureau had launched an internal investigation, the leak's source had yet to be discovered. Either someone had hacked into the network or the SSD had a rat. He had yet to receive any reports on the matter. After watching Hasukawa chew his fingernails to the quick over the investigation, his boss had finally urged him to take some R&R.

As much as Hasukawa wanted to redeem himself as quickly as possible, he also knew that getting needlessly wound up would not force luck to fall his way. He accepted the offer and decided to take a two-day leave. He asked to be notified at home if there was any movement.

But he could hardly unwind at home. He was far more preoccupied with reading the incoming news on his tablet than talking with his family. Kyoko was right to scold him. Possessed by work as he was, he was liable to forget he even had a family.

Hasukawa took Rui into the living room. The little girl sat on the sofa and, after pressing "record" on the tablet, gazed up at her father with expectant eyes.

Hasukawa sat back and searched for a distant memory of when he was a child on Mars. Around the time he was born, several cities had already sprung up on the planet. The orbital elevator's entrance was located on the volcano Pavonis Mons, at the foot of which was Pavonis City, covered by an enormous canopy. With Pavonis as the hub, a transportation network was being built in every direction across the plains region, expanding the infrastructure daily.

Work was done around the clock to change the climate on Mars. Methane hydrate was extracted from the ground to create a methane layer in Mars's atmosphere, thereby raising the planet's temperature by way of the greenhouse effect. The seeds sown in the crimson wasteland had sprouted and were beginning to grow.

Ice from both the polar caps and the permafrost beneath the surface was being melted with massive reflective mirrors in order to transform shallow gullies and valleys into lakes. Settlers gravitated toward water sources, like they would an oasis in the desert, and there a city was born. The canopy protected the lake and the entire city, so the restored water did not evaporate into the atmosphere.

Hasukawa had heard about plans to submerge Marineris Canyon entirely under water, so as to create an ocean. But such plans had not gone forward as of yet.

"Let's see," he said to his daughter. "When I was little, Mars still had a moon. There used to be a moon, shaped like a potato, called Phobos that went around the planet."

"How fast did it go?" Rui asked.

"At first, it took seven hours and forty minutes to make one revolution around Mars, but then the orbital path was changed so it wouldn't get in the way of the elevator. Its traveling speed was decelerated at the same time. But when more elevators had to be built, the moon was consumed as a resource. Oh, and the sunset on Mars used to be blue."

"Why?"

"Because of the thin atmosphere and the sand particles flying around, the red-colored light waves are scattered, while only the blue-colored light waves reach our eyes, making the sunset look blue. Back then, people used to travel outside the canopy in sealed land rovers just so they could see the real sky. On Mars, the real sky is red during the day and turns blue at night. Tourists traveled outside the canopy because they got a kick out of seeing the sky in colors opposite of what they saw on Earth."

"How did you go from city to city? Did you have highways like we do now?"

"Road taxes used to be very high. It cost an arm and a leg just to get anywhere. But as the planet became more prosperous, public services grew more affordable, and Mars gradually became a better place to live. That's because the Earthian government encouraged people to relocate to attract people who could help Mars's development. The hardships your grandfather faced in his time became just a little bit better during my time. And by the time you grow up, Mars will be an even better place to live. Maybe the atmosphere will be denser and the cities won't need to be under canopies anymore."

Once the space program built cities with residential districts in both Earth's orbit and on the Moon and living off-Earth became more commonplace, human advance into space accelerated with every passing day. Even before the colonization of the Moon was complete, the program began colonizing Mars and, even before that was complete, launched the construction of Asteroid City. The farther humanity got from Earth, the greater the momentum to reach deep space grew. Just as humans had once emerged from some corner of the continent and spread across the Earth, they had begun to scatter their seed across the infinite black universe.

And now they were knocking on Jupiter's door. A staff of a hundred researchers and engineers was stationed at each of three space stations or experimental cities built in proximity to Europa, Ganymede, and Callisto, Jupiter's largest moons.

The staff was mainly engaged with two areas of research. One involved the environment surrounding Jupiter, including an exploratory study of the planet and landing missions on its moons. Biologists had also discovered microorganisms and crustaceans in the oceans beneath the layers of ice on Europa and Ganymede, attracting the attention of not just the scientific community but the general public. Images and reports released with each discovery spurred interest in further exploration. Scientists also confirmed the existence of a melted layer of ice beneath the surface of Callisto and were currently in the midst of conducting meticulous research on the ocean discovered under the thick ice crust. Data on the volcanic activity on Io and on the lightning discharge activity on Jupiter were also steadily being collected.

The other research area involved gathering experimental data having to do with space medicine. The biggest problems humanity encountered in space were the health impairments posed by living in environments completely different from that of Earth. Impairments from prolonged exposure to low-gravity environments and space radiation, as well as the effects of stress caused by living for extended periods in cramped residential quarters, were the primary concerns of the researchers. With an even harsher environment than that of Mars, Jupiter was an ideal planet to gather the best medical data. Researchers conducted experiments on not only animals but on human subjects too, drawing the ire of bioethics groups, but a special inspection agency stepped in to ensure no unlawful experiments were being conducted.

"What did the people that first came to Mars eat? What did they do when they got sick? Did they have TV and movies?"

As Rui continued to ask one question after the next, Hasu-kawa's wearable bleeped. It was John Prescott, chief of operations.

"Sorry to bother you at home, but there's been a development."

"Do we have the assailant?"

"Yeah, we're talking to him to now. But there's another matter we need to discuss. Can you get over here?"

"Of course."

"Sorry."

"No—" Hasukawa stopped himself from telling Prescott that he'd been bored anyway, remembering his daughter sitting in front of him. After telling Rui to ask her mother to tell her the rest, Hasukawa got up to grab his coat.

When Hasukawa arrived at Mars Police Headquarters, the media hounds were already camped out front. The moment he got out of his car, they swarmed him, sticking their recorders in his face, but Hasukawa managed to push past them and entered the building without saying a word.

Prescott was the only one waiting for him in the division office. "I've got someone else on the press conference about the assailant. You and I are going to a briefing."

"Did we receive a new terror warning?"

"There's another terrorist group, unrelated to the assassination attempt, on the move. I don't know the particulars, but we have to take the threat seriously considering their target."

"What are they targeting? Some sort of government residence?"

"Jupiter. Seems they're after the space station."

"All three of them?"

"Just one. Jupiter-I. The special district to be exact."

"Where did the intel come from?"

"Central Intelligence."

"Do they have somebody on the inside?"

"Probably, seeing how they gave us a name. The Vessel of Life," Prescott said.

Hasukawa grimaced. The Vessel of Life was an extremist group espousing a rigid bioethical ideology that had perpetrated countless acts of terror in the past. They frequently targeted bioscience corporations, research facilities, and hospitals and opposed the use of scientific technology to manipulate the human body and other species.

With regard to matters of bioethics, an organization called the Planetary Bioethics Association kept a close watch over the settlements between Earth and Jupiter. It was a legitimate organization, an international agency with the goal of advocating a "happy marriage" between human life and the technologies of genetic engineering. Denouncing the association's policies as soft, an antigovernment group emerged to form the Vessel of Life.

But their continued acts of extremism made Hasukawa question whether the group really wanted to protect bioethical principles at all. In addition to engaging in demonstrations, public denouncements, and harassment, they even resorted to bombing the facilities of organizations whose activities they wanted to stop. For this reason, the true goal of the Vessel of Life was rumored to be the incitement of political and economic turmoil from behind the cover of ideology.

On the other hand, Vessel members were also active in respectable endeavors such as publishing scholarly books on bioethics and exposing medical malpractice in gene therapy, winning them praise as champions of human rights. Thus, the Vessel of Life was not so much a monolithic organization as a global network of people and factions with disparate motives. Which complicated matters all the more. It was for this reason that many people believed the Vessel of Life was created to take up the mantle for bioethics in ways the Planetary Bioethics Association could not.

"Their aim is to stop the experiments on Jupiter-I," said Prescott. "The doctors there are conducting some cutting-edge space medicine and reproductive technology experiments."

"But the Planetary Bioethics Association approved those experiments on Jupiter-I. Why now?"

"The group was against these experiments from the start. They must've been waiting to act until they could get together the necessary funds and manpower," Prescott said. "But to think they'd actually go to Jupiter. It's hard to believe they'll stir up much publicity worth their trouble. I hope to hell it all turns out to be a hoax."

"If they're prepared to go to Jupiter to carry out their plan, they must think they've got a pretty good shot at succeeding. If they haven't at least come up with a way to penetrate Jupiter-I's omnidirectional warning system, they wouldn't even bother to devise a plan of attack."

"Sorry to cut your vacation short," Prescott said.

"Please," said Hasukawa. "You're going to be holed up here at headquarters for a while yourself, Chief."

"Better that than the pain of being at home. My niece is having a wedding party I just can't bring myself to go to. I used the job to beg out of going."

"Something the matter with the groom?"

"That's just it. My niece isn't marrying a man."

So it was a lesbian wedding. "That's allowed just about anywhere you go nowadays."

"Yeah, but here's where it gets complicated. The woman she's marrying is also a transgender."

"She used to be a man?"

"Yeah. She had gender reassignment—became a woman. Yet, she wanted to marry another woman instead of a man and chose my niece as her partner. My niece is fine with it. In fact, she said that if her partner even wanted to go back to being a man, she'd be fine with that too. She even said that she might want to try being a man herself one day."

"She was joking, right? I know artificial organ transplants have come a long way, but switching sexes on a whim…"

"I hear people change their gender like they change their clothes lately. They go from being a woman to a man and back again and again over a lifetime. Fluid transgenders, they're called.

I don't know what the kids these days are thinking," Prescott said. "Are humans starting to choose their sex depending on their circumstances the way clownfish do? If that's what's happening, I don't know if I can handle it."

"Is that why you decided not to go to the wedding?" Hasukawa said.

"What conversation could I have that doesn't end with me insulting my niece's partner? My head hurts just thinking about it. Of course, her friends are going to be there. Look, I understand in theory. This isn't the twentieth century. The law guarantees the rights of those who call themselves sexual minorities and queer. Discrimination is wrong. Absolutely, positively wrong, I tell you. And anyone that openly shows their disgust, no matter what they may be thinking, is just being a jackass. But actually interacting with one of them is exhausting to people like me who were raised on traditional values. You must think I'm a coward."

"Of course not."

"Tell me, how old is your daughter now?"

"She's six," Hasukawa said.

"Then brace yourself. Your little girl won't necessarily stay a girl forever."

Hasukawa lost his first wife to illness. The Planetary Bioethics Association had informed him then that since he had no children, Hasukawa had the right to inseminate synthetic eggs containing his dead wife's DNA with his own sperm, have an artificial womb carry the child to term, and register that child as his own.

Hasukawa had declined.

He couldn't imagine raising the child himself and continuing to work at the same time. He could have hired a babysitter, but what would have been the point if he'd simply let the sitter raise the child? That would have been the same as having a convenient pet. If that were the case, he would have been much better off remaining a widower and throwing himself into his work.

Even so, he ended up remarrying in his forties, having suc-
cumbed to loneliness.

Rui was born to Hasukawa and his second wife, Kyoko. By
the time his daughter would be old enough to marry, Hasukawa
would be over sixty. When that time came, there was no guarantee
that she would still be a woman, according to Prescott.

As much as such a thing would sadden him as a father, Hasukawa was also resigned to the fact that children grew up. He
wanted Rui to go on being a girl, of course, but if she were to declare herself a fluid transsexual, Hasukawa didn't have the right
to reject her even if he might protest. The Planetary Bioethics
Association had done away with such restrictive sociopolitical
paradigms and established laws to guarantee one's gender and
sexual identities. The individual's choice to change one's gender
however many times and to marry someone of any gender was
now protected by law.

There was only one choice forbidden on Earth and Mars, and
that was the bioengineering of an intersex human having both
male and female reproductive organs and then actually registering
that person as *intersex*.

Of course not everyone chose to live as a fluid transgender, even
while that right was guaranteed by law. Fluids were a minority,
and an overwhelming majority still held prejudices and bigoted
views on such a lifestyle.

"When I was a kid," Prescott continued, "I imagined the
future and going to space to be something more—you know,
spectacular. Sure, we succeeded in making many dreams come
true: the lunar cities have grown, the Martian cities are more
accessible, the mysteries surrounding Jupiter were solved, our
life expectancy is longer thanks to advances in space medicine,
and we can even prevent senile dementia. Humanity is on the
verge of sweeping across the entire solar system. And yet, we
haven't been able to eliminate the fighting and killing and terrorism on Earth, or the Moon or on Mars. I used to believe

that the farther we got from Earth, the more enlightened we would become about how small we are in relation to the universe and therefore become more humble, more peaceful. But the reality was different. We're still burdened by the intrinsic parts of ourselves that kept us earthbound. And why is that? We refuse to change our Earthian ways no matter how far we've come. As long as we insist on clinging to our bodies, we'll have to go on changing the space environment rather than adapt to it. We've yet to become 'Martians' or 'Jovians' even now. We're all still 'Earthians' living on Mars and Jupiter. We're imprisoned by this body. This body hinders our psychological growth, like a cage."

"By that logic, that would mean humans are capable of changing their psyches by altering their physical bodies."

"And that's exactly what they're researching on Jupiter. The experiments are beyond what I'm personally able to tolerate, but they're working on ways to improve human nature—that much I know. That's why we have to protect Jupiter-I. For the future of humanity. If anyone has a problem with the experiments, they can ask to discuss it or negotiate the issues. There are any number of peaceful ways to get it done. But if any fringe elements would rather solve this with guns and bombs, we have to stop them with deadly force."

The two men waited for the top brass from the Mars Police Department and the Central Intelligence Bureau to gather in the meeting room. Once they'd arrived, Hasukawa and Prescott took their seats at the far end of the table.

"According to the communiqué from the agent we have on the inside, the Vessel of Life will attack Jupiter-I within a month," said the director of the CIB. "We don't have time to send in reinforcements from Earth or Mars. The threat will have to be put down by whatever personnel we already have at the space station. How many do we have stationed there right now?"

"Just the usual complement of twenty," answered Prescott.

"But there's another team on a vessel headed there now to relieve the team stationed there. They'll be able to work together to secure the space station. I'll notify the commander of the relief team immediately."

"That makes forty. Will it be enough?"

"The Vessel of Life may be an extremist group, but they don't have the necessary cash flow to mobilize an army to Jupiter. Not to mention, that would require a large transportation vessel, increasing the risk of their being picked up on Jupiter-I's omnidirectional warning system. It's likely they'll send in a small but elite team to carry out the attack, in which case they'll try to come in on a cargo or research vessel. Our security teams are adequately equipped to neutralize the threat."

The director nodded, satisfied. The members of the police department, on the other hand, were red-faced, choking back the words that came to mind. Why hadn't they been alerted sooner? What the hell good was having someone on the inside? This last-minute warning limited their counterstrategy severely. What the hell had the CIB been doing?

"Who are the commanders in charge?" the director asked.

"The commander in charge of the first unit, the team on the space station, is Jeff Harding. Shogo Shirosaki commands the fifth unit, the relief team heading there now."

"The composition of the teams?"

"All of the members of both teams are from Mars, although there's some ethnic imbalance," Prescott said.

"How do you mean?"

"Harding's team has a good ethnic mix, but Shirosaki's team is comprised mostly of Japanese members."

"How did that happen?" asked the CIB director.

"With some recent transfers, the team just happened to stack up that way. But the members are quite used to working on a multiethnic team."

"Any experience working with Harding's team on a joint mission?"

"No, sir, but I believe both men are capable of executing the mission," Prescott said. "Would you like to have a look at their files?"

"Please."

Several hours later, Hasukawa compiled a report detailing the action to be taken.

He transmitted the information to Jupiter-I and the spaceship carrying Shogo Shirosaki's twenty-member security team.

This was where Hasukawa's job as an administrator ended.

After this, any amount of worrying was pointless. The voyage from Mars to Jupiter took several months. He would only receive reports and images, and whatever happened on Jupiter from here on out, Hasukawa would have no way to get a direct read of the situation.

Prescott had told him that he would not hesitate to use deadly force for the future of humanity. He was right, of course, but Prescott was only thinking in terms of the end result. Neither Hasukawa nor Prescott had ever been witness to any sort of bloodshed on the job. The only information that ever reached them came in the form of data and reports from which Hasukawa could sense nothing. Such reports contained only condensed fragments of the truth.

It would be Shirosaki and Harding in the field who would have to bear the burden of this mission.

II

1

THE FIRST THING he sensed was the smell of summer grass. A pungent smell, as though someone had just finished cutting the grass only moments before.

A feeling not so much nostalgia as restlessness came over him. Shirosaki recalled the summers he had spent as a boy on Earth. The lush vegetation overflowing from the conservatory. The thick, sweet smell of overripened fruit tickling the nose like spices.

The memories came flooding back. The odd shape of a caterpillar wriggling between the leaves. Candy-colored ants marching up a tree single file. Butterflies with wings like metallic plates flitting around the orchids. Richly colored birds and the chattering of squirrels. The Summer Dome of his youth fraught with excitement.

In his daydream, Shirosaki was a boy of ten. Even as he remembered the Summer Dome at forty, his point of view was that of a small child.

When he was ten, the trees inside the conservatory looked to him like monsters lurching toward him with outstretched limbs.

The humid air was stifling.

The winding path was free of traffic. Unlike the energy inside the dome, a comfortable stillness pervaded the indoor area before dusk.

Shirosaki caught something moving out of the corner of his eye and stopped.

He worked his way through the brush to find a little girl standing atop a stone wall.

She looked to be about six or seven. She was standing precariously on her toes, reaching for a mango on a tree.

Shirosaki held his breath and looked on. The girl pulled the mango closer, branch and all, then twisted the yellow fruit off the branch.

The leaves rustled as the branch snapped back. The girl cuddled the fruit in her arms and caressed it tenderly. Shirosaki blushed as if she were caressing him.

The girl turned in his direction. Her black eyes growing wide, she jumped up like a spring-action doll.

"Do you like mangoes?" he blurted out.

The girl did not speak and stood stiffly on the stone wall. He approached the girl and quietly clambered up the wall so as not to scare her. He looked around to make sure no adults were about. He began to pick one fruit after the next and toss them into her arms. He continued to pluck the fruit from the branches until the girl's face grew cloudy. "Stop, that's enough."

Looking down, he noticed the mountain of mangoes in the girl's arms. He worried that he'd upset her, but she began to giggle. She giggled so hard it made him wonder what was so funny. He smiled sheepishly.

The girl pointed to a tree farther away. "Can you climb that tree?" she asked. "Can you get that one?" He said, "Sure, I can," and jumped off the wall onto the path with the girl. The girl's hand clasped naturally in his felt soft.

Suddenly Shirosaki was overcome with an aching sadness. He didn't know whether he was feeling the ten-year-old's intoxication or the sentimentality of a forty-year-old.

The scene began to waver as if the signal were breaking up. The picture grew hazy.

Shirosaki moaned, nauseated by the feeling of being torn away from the world. The smell of the vegetation and fruit quickly faded.

Shogo Shirosaki lay inside the hibernation chamber and winced.

His breathing was erratic. His heart raced. He wondered why the hibernation system had summoned this particular memory. Wasn't it too sentimental to be used as a trigger to wake him? What was the point of rousing a space traveler's nostalgia in this way?

A yellow ambient light illuminated the chamber.

Shirosaki steadied his breathing.

The real world smelled faintly of his body odor and sterilized fabric. The smell of summer grass from his dream faded like a vision.

Like a caterpillar, Shirosaki waited for the lid of the cocoon-shaped hibernation chamber to open automatically.

Hibernating mammals have a gene that produces a hibernation-peculiar protein—HP—in the body. Human DNA contains a similar type of gene. By raising the HP level in the blood, humans can fall into a hibernatory state.

The hibernation chamber maintained a passenger's life functions during deep sleep. Required aboard all vessels capable of long-term trips, the system greatly reduced the amount of food and oxygen supplies needed for interplanetary voyages.

As the scheduled passenger-waking day approached, the system injected the passenger with a shot to lower the HP level in the blood, stimulating the brain into wakefulness. This triggered a memory, facilitating the transition into the waking state. Although in Shirosaki's case, it was not a terribly pleasant way to wake up.

The lid opened, and Shirosaki sat up in the chamber.

He grabbed hold of the edge with both hands and propelled himself out of the chamber with his arms and legs.

The gravity onboard was maintained at zero so passengers wouldn't feel the strain of locomotion after months of sleep.

After passengers underwent about a week of rehabilitation to work the muscles back to their original strength, the gravity onboard was adjusted to 0.3 G, the same gravity as on Mars. Since all of the passengers on his voyage were from Mars, maintaining a

1.0 G environment wasn't necessary.

Shirosaki was a field officer of an antiterror unit assigned to the Special Security Division of the Mars Police Department. Though his usual duties entailed maintaining security on Mars, his team was occasionally loaned out for special extramartian missions. The security details on Asteroid City and on Jupiter-I were part of teleplanetary duty rotation for his team.

Since none of the hibernation chambers containing the other members were open, Shirosaki checked the control panel. The display indicated he was the only one to have regained wakefulness.

Maybe he had received an emergency message for his eyes only.

Shirosaki slid into the seat in front of the terminal and activated the communications system. He entered his ID number to access the unread messages. There were two. One was a private transmission; the other contained orders addressed to the entire team.

He opened the private transmission. The face of Special Security Division Captain Hasukawa appeared onscreen.

"By the time you receive this transmission, you will be a week out of Jupiter-I. How are you feeling, Commander? I trust the hibernation chamber awakened you with a pleasant dream?"

Hasukawa smiled amiably as if he were seeing the man he was addressing.

"Yeah, thanks," Shirosaki muttered.

Although Hasukawa belonged to the Special Security Division, someone of his rank was rarely seen in the field. He would never make an appearance in the field on Mars, much less during a teleplanetary assignment. The figure of Hasukawa in a suit, leaning back in his chair, resembled a corporate manager more than a security officer. While Shirosaki certainly wasn't envious, he was made to realize the gulf between his home on Mars and his current location all the more.

"There's been a change of plans. Rather than relieving the security team stationed on Jupiter-I, you'll be joining their team to guard the space station. The security detail on the space station is being doubled. Do you understand what that means?"

Shirosaki felt his entire body tense.

Hasukawa continued:

"We received a communiqué from a CIB operative that terrorists are planning an attack on Jupiter-I. Find them and neutralize the threat. No arrests. Take every last one of them out."

Shirosaki knitted his brows. He was a member of the special security unit, not the military. While he had the authority to kill in extreme cases, wouldn't it be more prudent to make an arrest and try to extract more information about the group they were dealing with?

"The terrorists call themselves the Vessel of Life. We believe they're targeting the research facilities and the special district on Jupiter-I. We won't get anywhere negotiating with them or learn anything by making an arrest. Your orders are to eliminate them."

Hasukawa leaned forward and seemed to look Shirosaki directly in the eye.

"They're spending a pretty penny to get to Jupiter, so they must believe they have a chance of succeeding. They shouldn't pose too big of a threat considering their numbers, but be careful. Don't let your guard down."

Shirosaki closed the message file and let out a sigh.

He recalled what a colleague had told him before he left Mars.

You can look at the blue of the earth all you want and there's no harm in it. Whether you were born on the Moon or Mars, even if Earth is not your home planet, that blueness has the power to heal. There's no explaining why. It arouses something instinctual in humans. It's not exactly nostalgia but a kind of relief—that there is water on that planet—that soothes people's souls. But you better not look too long at the face of Jupiter. You'll go crazy if you stare at the Great Red Spot for too long. It's the eye of God, the eye of Zeus—the eye of a supreme being sending us a warning, trying to break the will of humanity from venturing out into deep space.

Being stationed on Jupiter-I had made Shirosaki's colleague ill. Unable to bear the idle days in the space station where nothing ever happened, the officer broke down before his assignment had ended.

As he stared at the Great Red Spot to help pass the time, he had become possessed by the eye of Jupiter.

The Great Red Spot was an enormous cloud swirling in Jupiter's atmosphere consisting of hydrogen and helium. The vortex was elliptical, measuring twelve thousand kilometers at its minor axis and twenty-five thousand kilometers at its major axis, making it large enough to consume two Earths. If you stared at it long enough, it might very well drive you mad.

The size of Jupiter, to someone only familiar with Earth, the Moon, and Mars, was an imposing sight. The equatorial diameter of Jupiter was 142,984 kilometers; you could lay eleven planets the size of Earth on it from end to end.

Jupiter. The planet named for the Roman version of the great god Zeus. This planet, shrouded in gasses and comprised of a rock core said to be about fifteen times the mass of Earth, completed one rotation in an astounding 9.925 hours, and ever threatened to swallow the space station and its residents with its sinister eye.

Unless you were fascinated by astronomy, the scale of Jupiter was usually a source of stress for humans—a species just starting to venture out into deep space.

In addition, Jupiter produced an intense magnetic field and radiation waves. The magnetic field expanded to trap sixty-three satellites into its orbit and was twenty thousand times the intensity of Earth's. The magnetic field contained high-energy particles, which emitted strong radio waves. One of Jupiter's satellites, Io, continued to be the most geologically active in the solar system. Its volcanoes dispersed sulfur and other chemical substances into space, triggering electrical discharges of three million amps. This created a storm around Jupiter's atmosphere, triggering an enormous aurora at Jupiter's polar regions that could cover the span of three Earths.

Were it not for the powerful defense mechanisms protecting spacecraft and the station, humans would die instantly in such an unforgiving environment. Without the medicines and metabolic molec machines to periodically restore their cells and DNA, humans would surely have a shorter life expectancy in the Jovian system.

Shirosaki was also required to undergo this restoration treatment. The same went for the staff living on the three stations near Europa, Ganymede, and Callisto. They were just barely able to survive, sufficiently shielded by all sorts of defensive measures and receiving the necessary preventative medicine.

In the Jovian system, humans were like bacteria clinging to the tiniest puddle of moisture. But these bacteria had both skill and smarts. They were gradually expanding their habitat into the depths of space. While they were only able to reach Jupiter now, surely they would eventually see what was beyond the solar system.

Shirosaki's colleague had an outstanding service record on Mars. He had prided himself in running headfirst into danger. He was a hero who'd captured and disposed of countless terrorists and succeeded in carrying out death-defying rescue operations. He had thrived on defeating the enemy. But when he transferred to the security detail on Jupiter-I in the twilight of his career, he began to erode like a sand castle on the shore.

Perhaps the toll of his aggressive approach to the job had finally caught up to him on Jupiter-I. He returned to Mars and immediately submitted his resignation. The man was forty-five. With a wife and kids. Now he had a sedentary job watching surveillance cameras in an office building in Cryse City.

What about himself, Shirosaki wondered. Idle days on Jupiter-I. A security detail where nothing happened. Fine by him. As a matter of fact, he'd been looking for just that kind of place.

Shirosaki had taken the job because the rotating assignment would eventually come around to him sooner or later. He was also becoming less enamored with going out in the field. He was growing tired of the routine of going in, taking control of the scene, and taking down the enemy. Since he'd chosen this job as his profession, he had no problem with going in to neutralize a threat with guns blazing. But the job did little more than treat the symptom. Unless society underwent some sort of drastic change, terrorism would continue to exist. It frustrated him to know that what was plainly obvious to everyone couldn't be accomplished without the right people and government departments working to effect that change.

They were only stalling for time. Unless something happened to transform society, the job would continue without end. But Shirosaki had misplaced his priorities.

He had hoped going to Jupiter would offer him some relief. He knew he was running away. But he was also aware that running would be the best medicine for him now. Cushy assignment or not, he was still going to get paid. At forty, Shirosaki had a wife and child to look after, and without any commendations to speak of, he couldn't very well resign. The Jupiter assignment was a godsend even if it meant spending months apart from his family.

Of course, that had all been dependent on nothing happening on Jupiter-I. It was a moot point now that he was likely to see action there.

One by one, the members of Shirosaki's team began to wake from the hibernation chambers. Shirosaki played Hasukawa's message intended for his team on the ship's screen.

The message's tone had been calculated to neither flame their fears nor put them on edge, but to rally and boost the team's morale. Nevertheless, the nineteen members instantly sensed the gravity of Hasukawa's message. The mood grew tense, as though they might draw their guns at any moment.

Shirosaki assured the team that they would not see action very soon after they arrived, and that as this was a joint mission, they had more than enough manpower to overwhelm the attackers. They were to recondition their bodies back to full strength before docking at Jupiter-I. Shirosaki told them that he would have more concrete directions after meeting with the supervisors of the station. Then he dismissed the staff. As the security members dispersed throughout the ship to begin their reconditioning, Shirosaki called over his second-in-command Naoki Arino and discussed plans for their arrival.

A week later, the ship carrying the relief team arrived at Station No. 1 Jupiter-I.

Jupiter-I was a cylindrical space station on one of the Jupiter-Europa Lagrange points. Its center was hollow, much like a pineapple after being cored.

The station was three hundred meters in diameter and eight hundred meters long. A central axis, running straight through the hollow center, housed the gravitational control system. The axis rotated the alloy pineapple-shaped station, creating a 0.3 G atmosphere in the residential district.

The central axis was connected to the outer shell by a series of spokelike support shafts, inside of which were high-velocity elevators running at a thousand meters per minute. A separate network of elevators running along the length of the outer shell was used to travel from one end of the space station to the other.

The central axis, which was longer than the space station itself, protruded at one end. The docking bays were located there. All vessels entered the cylindrical structure at the tip of the axis and were required to pass a security check. Anything suspicious, and the passengers were forbidden to disembark. If everything turned up green, on the other hand, they proceeded from the docking bays to the corridor where one of the high-velocity elevators carried them away to the residential district. Unmanned vessels were transported by an automated system from the docking bays to a designated mooring inside the core.

The docking bays were kept apart from the rest of the station as a safety precaution against collisions. The docking bays had been designed to disconnect from the rest of the station in the event of a fire or explosion caused by a docking accident. In this way, the protruding tip of the axis was like a lizard's tail, able to be cut away from the body by disengaging the lock.

Of course, this was also one of several measures to protect the station from terrorist attacks. Even if an explosives-laden vessel were to enter, the docking bays would be separated in order to protect the residential district.

Upon entering the docking bay, Shirosaki's vessel passed through security, and they were authorized to disembark. Shirosaki and the nineteen security personnel under his command proceeded through the double doors and down the corridor, and boarded the elevators leading up to the central axis.

Once there, they boarded another elevator traveling through the support shaft and arrived at the entrance of the residential district in about five to six minutes.

Standing at the entrance of the residential district, which was maintained at 0.3 G, were three men and a woman.

The woman, who appeared to be in her late forties, lithely stepped forward and spoke in English. "Welcome to Jupiter-I. I'm Liezel Kline, the supervisor of Jupiter-I."

Shirosaki shook her hand and introduced himself as the commander of the relief team.

Kline smiled. "We can use all the help you can give. We're grateful you're here."

A man older than Kline spoke next. "Dan Preda, assistant supervisor."

"Pleased to meet you," said Shirosaki. He proceeded to explain that his team would be procuring their food and oxygen from the stores that had been brought with them to resupply the space station. But he assured them that a supply vessel had left Mars soon after these orders had been handed down and would arrive before the station's supply was exhausted.

Preda nodded. "No worries, we always keep a reserve supply on hand."

A man about Shirosaki's age came forward next. He was

wearing the special security uniform. He shook Shirosaki's hand, stone-faced. "Commander Jeff Harding. If it weren't for these damn threats, my team would be back home on Mars by now."

The man standing next to Harding also held out a hand and flashed a smile. "Sub-commander Larry Miles. Nice to meet you."

Since the cargo had automatically been unloaded and transported to the residential district, Shirosaki ordered the team to deliver the cargo to the appropriate destinations. With his sub-commander Arino in tow, Shirosaki followed Kline and the rest of the welcome party to the meeting room.

When they arrived, another staff member was waiting for Shirosaki.

The figure that stood before him was in eir early thirties with spindly arms and legs and slight features. Eir silken hair, cut evenly at the chin, shone as it moved. Although difficult to guess eir ethnic origin and not exactly beautiful, ey had strangely magnetic eyes.

"My name is Tei," ey said. "My people don't use family names, so please call me by my given name. Or Doctor, if you prefer. I'm in charge of medical matters on the station."

Shirosaki exchanged greetings with the doctor, despite wondering what a doctor was doing at a strategy meeting.

"A female doctor," Arino said, cracking a smile. "Nice to see I'll be in good hands if I'm wounded."

A faint smile came across Tei's pink lips. Shirosaki moved to caution Arino, sensing that the smile on the doctor's face was one of cynicism rather than delight, but Tei spoke first. "I'm not a woman, Sub-commander Arino."

Arino's cheek twitched. "My apologies."

"And incidentally, I'm not a man either," Tei added. "I'm a human from the special district that you've come to guard. I've come as a representative of the special district."

"By a human from the special district, you mean…"

Preda noticed Arino's appalled look and let out a chuckle

that sounded like a purr. "Forgive me, I should explain. The doctor is a Round born in the special district—a bigender. Do you understand what that means?"

"The doctor is male and female at the same time," Shirosaki said. "Yes, I read the report."

"Unlike what our society calls intersex, Rounds are absolute hermaphrodites possessing functioning genitalia of both sexes. They are a new type of human born on Jupiter-I. Dr. Tei acts as an intermediary of sorts between the special district and the rest of the station, which is why we requested the doctor's presence here today. Since the Rounds don't ever leave the special district, they communicate with those on the outside through an intermediary as necessary."

Suddenly looking indignant, Arino glared at Preda for with-holding this information as if he'd been testing them. Shirosaki, wanting to avoid an altercation from the outset, used his implant communicator to send a message directly to Arino's inner ear. "*Take it easy, Arino.*"

"*We're here risking our necks on this mission,*" Arino answered through his communicator, "*and they're mocking us.*"

"*We're only familiar with their society from what we've read. And they only know us through the data they have on us. They're just trying to feel us out. Don't let him get to you.*"

"*I had no idea hermaphrodites looked so feminine. Do you think everyone in the special district looks like that?*"

"*We'll find out soon enough. Just get back to the meeting.*"

"Ms. Kline," Preda continued, "perhaps we ought to explain to Commander Shirosaki about the culture inside the special district. About why the Rounds were created and how they came to be absolute hermaphrodites."

"Let's not start with a lecture," Harding interrupted. "What we should be discussing now is how we stop the terrorists. We don't have time for cultural lessons."

"Gruff as usual, I see." Preda flashed a sardonic smile. "The relief team is seeing a Round for the first time. We should be able to afford a little time to explain."

"If I thought it would help us to come up with a strategy, I'd be all for it, but I don't."

Harding looked at Shirosaki. "Well, what do you have to say? Do you want to sit around and listen to a cultural lecture? Or would you rather get to work and talk about how we deal with the terrorists?"

Shirosaki answered, "I'd like us to discuss strategy. Maybe we can talk about the special district another time."

Preda shrugged, but Harding remained expressionless, not acknowledging Preda with so much as a smile or frown.

"Why don't we all sit down?" Kline said, frowning. "We won't come to any decision while we're standing."

"Indeed." Preda nodded. "We may be here a while," he said, pulling up a chair.

After everyone took their seats, Kline began the discussion. "According to the data sent to us from Captain Hasukawa, it's likely the terrorists will be coming in on a research vessel from one of the Jovian satellites or a cargo vessel from Asteroid City. The research vessel has a particular route; it picks up specimens and materials from the experiments conducted on each of the satellites. The vessel from Asteroid City transports mineral resources and the water necessary to keep Jupiter-I operating. In order to enter this space station, the terrorists will likely have to come in on one of the spacecraft. They may have commandeered an unmanned ship, and we can't rule out the possibility that the terrorists have taken hostages."

"When will the next ship arrive?" asked Shirosaki.

"In two weeks."

"Then we ramp up security at the docking bays. We check all of the cargo there in the presence of guards. If a fight were to break out, it'd probably happen in the cargo bay. Of course, the terrorists have probably thought of that." Shirosaki asked Kline, "Where are the research facilities and special district located? Those are the two terrorist targets. They're sure to head there first."

Kline nodded. She punched a button on the control panel on the table and a three-dimensional schematic display of the station appeared. "Jupiter-I rotates with one cylindrical end facing the surface of Jupiter. The station has defensive walls that, when activated, can seal off each section of the station in an emergency."

The schematic showed partitions being lowered. Each of the sections were now highlighted in different colors. "The areas highlighted in blue are the research facilities, the orange area is the residential district for the staff, the green areas are the administrative facilities, and the red area is the residential district for the Rounds—the special district. There is a zero-gravity laboratory and a factory in the central axis area, along with a relaxation room."

Next, a glowing grid was superimposed over the entire station. "And this?" Shirosaki asked.

"The network of maintenance shafts used to maintain the outer shell of Jupiter-I. The defense shield to resist the radiation and magnetic field around the Jovian system is installed on the inside of the outer shell. A thick composite layer made of materials such as high-density tungsten, water, and ferromagnetic metals with a high relative magnetic permeability covers the entire space station. The maintenance system constantly monitors the shield and sends a signal to the control center when it's in need of repairs or periodic maintenance."

"What are the dimensions of the shaft?"

"About as high and wide for five to six adults to walk through holding hands."

"The security inside the maintenance shafts?"

"It's possible to load a security system onto a repair robot. But you can't enter and exit the shaft just anywhere," Kline said. "Access is restricted. The access points are only located in the control center and residential district for the staff. The special district can't be accessed through the maintenance shafts."

"But once someone is in the shaft, can't they cut their way out through the ceiling?"

"Not likely. The shaft isn't made of anything so vulnerable. Even if someone were able to cut their way out, the noise alone would alert the Rounds in the special district. Not to mention the intruders would be picked up by the heat and vibration sensors."

The special district was located on the Jupiter end of the station, farthest away from the docking bays. It had been built there deliberately to keep intruders at bay.

"What about the possibility of their breaking in from the Jupiter side?"

"Jupiter-I is equipped with a surveillance system. We're capable of destroying any spacecraft that tries to approach us."

"Looks like the special district also has an air lock." Shirosaki pointed to the schematic. "What are these capsules along the walls here?"

"Emergency shuttles. There are also four shuttles dedicated to the special district."

"Its capacity?"

"Eighty. The shuttles are fully equipped to fly to Asteroid City."

"How many people are on this station now, including the Rounds in the special district?"

"Exactly one hundred staff members, forty task force members, and one hundred fifty-eight Rounds, which makes two hundred ninety-eight."

"Then all we need to do is guard the docking bays," Shirosaki said.

"In theory, yes."

The task force was forty strong—more than the number necessary to monitor the ships coming in to dock.

"The Vessel of Life has two goals: to stop the bioscientific experiments going on at the station and to destroy the facilities and existing data. The fact that they're coming out here rather than inciting demonstrations on Earth and on Mars seems to indicate that they think they have a fighting chance. We can't take this threat lightly."

"Is there any chance the terrorists will simply give up? That they'll turn around and head back after realizing the security precautions we've taken?" Kline asked.

"That's certainly possible if they realize we're onto them," Shirosaki said. "But I'm willing to bet it wasn't cheap to put a team together and send them out here. Now that the plan's been set in motion, they won't give up so easily. There'll probably only be a few of them, just the necessary manpower to destroy the station's facilities."

"Then what we need to do is clear." Harding looked at the faces around him. "We intercept them at the docking bays and end them there. But we keep the walls between each section lowered in case they're able to penetrate our defenses. Station some officers at the walls separating the special district from the rest of Jupiter-I for good measure."

"To think that a group standing up for bioethical principles would resort to bloodshed." Preda let slip a cynical smile. "Just who is being inhumane here? Those of us conducting medical experiments or the fringe group unashamed to commit acts of terrorism?"

After parting ways with the station staff outside the meeting room, Shirosaki and Arino headed for the quarters assigned to the security team with Harding and Miles.

As they walked down the corridor, Harding said to Shirosaki, "They're a bunch of fruitloops, right?"

"Who are you talking about?"

"All of them. Preda is a stuck-up government toad, and Kline is infatuated with Round culture. She's convinced the Rounds are an ideal incarnation of humanity. And the doctor? The doctor isn't even human."

"Is something the matter, Commander?"

"You're not disgusted? You don't feel anything looking at someone so—ambiguous?"

"I barely know anything about, uh, them to feel *anything*, much less disgust," Shirosaki said.

"*Them* is fine. Just don't get caught calling them *him* or *her*. They'll call you out for using that language."

Of course gendered pronouns are discriminatory in the bigender world, Shirosaki thought. *So there are tricky issues of discrimination here just as there are in the planetary cities.* "We've been briefed about the special district. We also have some knowledge about the Rounds. But our orders are to protect the special district and the Rounds. As long as those orders stand, our job is to guard them whether they're human or lab animals."

Harding stared at Shirosaki with a look of contempt. "Have you ever seen sea hares mating?"

"No."

"They're simultaneous hermaphrodites whose male sex organs are exterior, while the posterior holds the female. When the sea hares mate, they form this long link. One puts its male organ in the female organ of the sea hare in front of it, while its own female organ is entered by the male organ of the sea hare from behind. Scientists call that a 'mating chain.' Snails mate in a similar way, only they have to face each other to insert the male organ in the other's female organ. Same goes for the Rounds. With a single act of intercourse, they can love as a man and be loved as a woman at the same time. I'm telling you, that's not right. A group that doesn't have any scruples about doing shit like that don't deserve to call themselves human."

"You paint a pretty vivid picture," Shirosaki said. "You didn't ask to watch, now did you?"

Harding glared. "You stay cooped up here long enough, you start to hear things."

Shirosaki fell silent.

"They're not like the intersex people in our society. They're the same as sea hares and snails, with the ability to inseminate and be inseminated at the same time. And do you want to know what they call us? Monaurals."

"Meaning what?"

"We're called Monaurals because each of us can only be one sex. From a bigender perspective, we're monosexual—Monoaurals. Something's become fundamentally different about them."

"But they're also living beings. In that sense, they're no different than we are," Shirosaki said.

"You're a broad-minded one. I don't have it in me to be so tolerant."

"Hey, give it a rest," Miles said lazily. "Criticizing the Rounds' existence doesn't make our job any easier. We should just think of them as our protectees, like Shirosaki said. As strange as this may sound, the Rounds' existence is why we're getting paid."

"Not me." Harding shook his head. "Just looking at them makes my skin crawl."

"I can't say that I don't know what you're feeling," Arino said, sighing. "You can't disown what you feel."

"Don't worry about it so much," Miles said. "When we finish the job here on Jupiter-I and are back home on Mars, we'll forget all about the Rounds."

2

TEI ALLOWED THE lukewarm water spraying from every direction of the tiny shower room to wash over eir entire body. White foam streamed down, tracing the contours of eir body, and swirled down the drain. The wastewater went to a recycling facility to be treated and reclaimed as nonpotable water. Such was the way Tei existed, within a perfectly cyclic system—vital to living near Jupiter.

In order for humans to embark on a long-term journey outside of the solar system, better recycling facilities were needed. Traveling for decades and centuries in an environment without solar energy was no easy feat. Space was an endlessly unforgiving place.

But every time Tei thought about it, ey felt something like

intoxication welling up from within. What lay beyond the solar system? Just how far could we go? *How many generations will it be before we're able to see the countless galaxies and black holes firsthand, as we see Jupiter today?* There were times Tei desperately wished for immortality. Rather than entrust the dream to someone else, Tei wanted to see everything with eir own eyes. Tei wanted to see and appreciate galaxies colliding, the birth of stars, hot Jupiters expelling bright gases near the stars from a distance close enough to touch. It was because of this desire that Tei could bear living here.

Tei continued to shower, caressing eir body with both hands. The roundness of eir breasts, though not glamorous by Monaural standards. The smooth and supple skin. The subtle curve of eir waist. The visibly bony figure. The firmness of eir joints. The tautness of eir muscles. Tei's fingers slid from the swell of eir breasts down past the torso to between eir legs where both genitalia were tucked away. Ey fondled the soft flesh.

A moist slit and a copulatory organ protected by a thin sensitive skin. A Round possessed both sexual organs similar to those that female and male Monaurals had. Tei was no different. The twenty-third chromosome pair of Rounds like Tei, known as the sex chromosome, was neither XX nor XY, but a synthetic chromosome, double-I—a pair of I chromosomes resembling two sticks. The remaining twenty-two chromosome pairs contained the genetic sequencing making the Rounds perfect hermaphrodites and produced peptides that sent commands to the subcerebral lobe, an organ unique to Rounds located next to the pituitary gland.

Back when Tei still spent the majority of eir time in the special district, ey had no doubts about the way eir body was formed. They had been told that all of the Rounds in the special district were built the same way, though different from the humans that lived outside the special district. Tei had entered adolescence suspecting nothing. When ey had tried to make love with another Round—more as a way of communicating than for the purpose of procreating—ey had realized that ey was built a bit differently from the others.

It was a trivial distinction, posing no problem to engaging in the sex act itself. Rounds were capable of impregnating and being impregnated at the same time. Tei possessed the reproductive organs to do just that. There was, however, one difference. This distinction alone had saddled Tei with a deep feeling of alienation.

The Rounds were a special existence to those living outside the special district. Tei was an even more special case among the Rounds. Naïve as Tei was in her adolescence, ey had been assailed with unbearable doubt and feelings of inferiority.

Why am I different from the others?

I am not a Monaural. But I'm also not a Round.

Then what am I?

Tei had rushed to the infirmary, where the station's supervisor, Kline, gently informed em that such things happened all the time. Dr. Wagi, the chief of medicine, pulled up piles of data to logically explain to Tei how ey had come to be this way.

Dr. Wagi's explanation had been a persuasive one. He had ended by telling Tei that a simple operation would solve the problem.

But Tei had refused. Tei didn't want to think of eir own body as so peculiar that ey required surgery. Doing so would have denied how ey had lived up until now. Doing so would also mean condemning the children who would come into this world built like Tei. Deformed. That was unacceptable to Tei.

Tei simply learned to accept that ey was different from the other Rounds and resolved to live an exemplary life that would blaze a trail for the next generation.

That was when Kline had asked Tei to serve as an intermediary. "If you focus on a job with responsibilities, you'll forget your problems," she told Tei. "Fortia and Album are in charge of the special district now and their tenures won't end for a while. If you want to do something comparable, the ambassadorship will be perfect for you."

Tei had accepted the offer immediately.

Ey didn't want to go on wallowing in self-isolation over something so trivial as a physical aberration.

Tei also aspired to be on equal footing with the Monaurals. The feeling of inferiority that surfaced among the Rounds when they encountered people from outside the special district, despite being the newer generation of human, had always troubled Tei.

Tei resolved to be equal. To live on equal terms with the Monaurals.

Having been born on Jupiter-I, Tei had no concept of racial discrimination, and such antiquated feelings were similarly alien to the supervisors of the space station.

Tei got along with the station staff immediately. Owing to eir burgeoning medical knowledge and skill, Tei earned the trust and honest respect of the staff with each achievement.

As ey became more used to eir duties, Tei also grew to enjoy having sex with other Rounds as a means of social interaction.

Adolescence was short for the Rounds, who matured three times faster than Monaurals.

Tei quickly became an adult and was approaching middle age.

Having lost the tendency to dwell on eir differences as ey did when ey was younger, Tei became a doctor and also a counselor to the younger generation.

And yet, there were times Tei still felt a void.

A feeling that something was missing.

That the universe was incomplete.

A nagging matter that no one could empathize with.

Tei, closing eir eyes, tilted eir head upward into the shower stream and rubbed eir face with both hands.

Ey recalled the meeting when ey was mistaken for a woman by the new security team member.

A smile escaped eir lips.

The security team members that came to Jupiter-I were always only able to recognize Tei as having one sex. The male officers mistook Tei for female. The female officers mistook Tei for male. To Tei, nothing was as inconvenient or as baffling as the Monaural concept of gender. The Monaurals were callow beings held captive by outdated values.

On the other hand, at times Tei found emself envying them. That they operated under a gender binary system seemed to intensify their romantic feelings. The passion with which Monaurals lusted after what they lacked was a quality that a sexually uniform race like the Rounds did not have.

Of course, love was ultimately an interpersonal fantasy and so wasn't something that blossomed exclusively between two sexes. In that sense, Rounds and Monaurals were no different.

Even so...

Tei was amazed by the Monaurals' unflagging fixation with sex. In certain cases, they couldn't help violating the objects of their affection. Just how were they driven to such madness?

Tei yearned to know with the same curiosity that sparked eir desire to gaze at the end of the universe.

III

1

SHIROSAKI DECIDED TO get a lay of the land in the two weeks before the first cargo vessel arrived at Jupiter-I. After ordering the security team members to familiarize themselves with every inch of the station, he inspected each of the facilities himself with Kline.

First they visited the residential district for the station staff and the administrative facilities.

The area was further subdivided into smaller sections and looked much like a floor in an ordinary office building. Because the walls of the corridors obstructed his view at fixed intervals as Shirosaki walked, he hardly noticed the curved contours of the cylindrical station.

The inside of the administrative facilities was pleasant enough to make Shirosaki forget that outside its confines was the Jovian system.

Located in this section were the control rooms for each of the station's systems, the research facilities, food factories, health and wellness facilities, storehouse, mess, recreation center, infirmary, the control center, meeting room, and the staff quarters.

Upon entering each department, Shirosaki and Kline were greeted courteously by the staff.

The staff was racially diverse. Shirosaki had also imagined the staff at the front lines of Jovian space to be emboldened with an intrepid frontier mentality, but they were nothing if not composed. They went about their daily duties as if they were on the planets.

Inside the observation room, an omnidirectional screen displayed images from outside the station: Jupiter, Io, Europa, Ganymede, Callisto, as well as Earth, the Moon, Mars, and the Sun. Images from Saturn and beyond the solar system.

Shirosaki felt Jupiter bearing down on him and shuddered. "Do people come here often?"

Kline nodded. "After all, we can't go out there to see Jupiter for ourselves."

"I know it's just an image, but I feel as if I'm about to be crushed."

"Perhaps you'd like to sit down. You'll feel better."

In the center of the room were tables surrounded by a sofa on each side. The sofas, arranged back-to-back, faced the tables and the screen.

Kline tapped her wearable, and the entire floor became a screen displaying a million stars at Shirosaki's feet.

Suddenly, Shirosaki felt as if he were plummeting through space and had to keep himself from shouting. "I'm sorry, but would you mind turning off the floor screen?"

"Don't members of the security team receive any space training?"

"Yes, but most of my duties keep me on the planets."

"Oh, I'm sorry. This must be disorienting for you."

Kline turned off the floor screen.

Shirosaki let out a sigh of relief. "You aren't bothered by it?"

"When you've lived here for over twenty years you get used to it."

"I didn't realize you've been stationed here so long."

"I was one of the first staff to come here." Kline then asked, "Do you know why the special district was created on Jupiter-I?"

"Yes, I read about it in the report. Though as an outsider, I may not have an accurate understanding of many things."

"What did you think of Dr. Tei?"

"I found em appealing," said Shirosaki, using the gender-neutral pronouns he'd learned after his conversation with Harding.

"Even after you found out ey's a Round?"

"My impression of bigenders was that they would look more synthetic—like they were entirely different beings. I had no idea they would be so much like us."

"The doctor may be similar to us because ey works with humans outside the special district as an intermediary."

"Are the Rounds in the special district different?" Shirosaki asked.

"Their sensibilities are gradually deviating from ours, since their contact with the staff has decreased of late. They have an air about them that's uniquely their own."

"Do you encounter any difference of opinions as a result of their bigender state?"

"The Rounds are a branch of the human evolutionary tree—one possibility of humanity's progression. We should regard them as partners and must not pressure them with any undue expectations. We must think of them neither as an ideal form of humanity nor a new breed of human reigning over us, but as a new subspecies coexisting with us. Although I realize this is difficult to understand for outsiders."

Harding had said that Kline believed the Rounds to be an ideal incarnation of humanity, but apparently that wasn't exactly the case.

"I'd like to hear more about the Rounds. Things I won't find in the files."

"That might take a while."

"That's all right. I consider it a part of the job."

Kline nodded and began slowly. "How much does your generation study about sexology?"

"Just that human sexuality is comprised of three elements: physical sex, psychological sex, and sexual orientation."

"Then you know the difference between gender and sexuality?"

"Gender is a socially constructed concept that defines femininity and masculinity," Shirosaki said. "People's ideas of what it means to be feminine and masculine differ according to the social environment in which they live. Even within a single society, those ideas change along with the changing times. Sexuality is a term used to consider biological differences between the sexes as well as one's sexual preference."

"That's the correct textbook answer. Has your department ever encountered any issues with regard to gender and sexuality?"

"Nothing that's been made public at least."

"Not even employment discrimination?"

"I wouldn't know, as I'm not involved with the hiring process and practices."

Kline smiled. "Sexual minorities have been an issue in Earthian society since the latter half of the twentieth century. While the term *sexual minority* may be recognized as a pejorative now, it was still commonly used during the twentieth and twenty-first centuries. True to their name, there were few sexual minorities back then. For example, the homosexual population numbered only ten percent of Earth's total population. There were fewer lesbians than gay men and even fewer bisexuals. These so-called sexual minorities experienced great difficulty combating the prejudices of the majority."

In the field of sexology, human sexuality encompassed three components: biological sex, psychological sex, and sexual orientation.

Biological sex was the vector of gender biology—male, female, intersex, including those with chromosomal and genital anomalies.

Psychological sex or gender identity was a matter of individual identification—the cisgenders identified with their biological sex and transgenders identified with some sex other than their biological sex. It was a matter of which gender you identified with and whether or not that was consistent with your biological sex.

Sexual orientation was the vector of heterosexuality, homosexuality, and bisexuality. Sexual orientation had to do with the sex you were attracted to. All three of these components were not at all static but extremely fluid, forming more potential combinations than there were names for them.

"Gay, lesbian, bisexual, transgender. These groups were treated as mentally ill. They were criminalized and marginalized by society until they began to form their own communities and began to demand recognition and rights. By the end of the twentieth century, homosexuality was removed from the list of psychological disorders. Although the majority's prejudicial attitudes remained, in the process of changing the laws as a result of hard-won court battles, sexual minorities forced the majority to recognize that they were not sick, that being a member of a minority was nothing more than a part of one's identity, and that biological sex, psychological sex, and sexual orientation were not to be forced upon anyone but rather practiced freely by the individual.

"The end of the twentieth century also saw advances in life manipulation technology such as in genetic diagnosis, gene therapy, prenatal diagnosis, organ transplantation, and artificial organ manufacturing. Sexual minorities were inevitably affected.

"By the end of the twentieth century, sex reassignment surgery was recognized as a way to treat gender identity disorder. At the start of the twenty-first, scientists made breakthroughs in manufacturing artificial organs using stem cells. Fierce debates raged over the ethics of their actual use, but in the end, stem cells were allowed for treatment purposes. This decision paved the way to making possible the manufacture of reproductive organs, which had been perhaps the greatest obstacle standing before sexual minorities. Do you understand why this was so significant?"

"It became possible to transplant artificial reproductive organs that weren't merely cosmetic but actually functioned," Shirosaki said.

"That's right. As news of successful transplants of artificial livers and kidneys made from stem cells spread, the thinking that the transsexual issue could be solved medically began to take root. This marked a big shift in values. With sexual reassignment surgery technology still nascent, complications weren't all that rare. Failed surgeries plagued patients with chronic pain; even with successful surgeries, they had to continue to take hormone pills to maintain their new bodies. Long-term drug use also caused problems with the liver and other parts of the body. As a result, many people elected not to have sexual reassignment surgery altogether rather than risk their lives to maintain their sex. Intersex surgeries were also far from perfect."

An intersex person was someone born with both male and female reproductive organs. Since being intersex was thought to be a deformity at the time, it wasn't uncommon for the reproductive organs of one sex to be removed from the child. With the surgery not yet perfected, sometimes the chosen sexual organs did not function when the child entered puberty. Other times, in cases where the parents had decided their intersex child's sex based on their outward appearance alone without telling that child, the child flew into a panic when the other sexual organs developed during puberty.

I thought I was a man, but they told me I have ovaries and a uterus. Does that make me a woman? Do I have to dress like a woman from now on and marry a man and have kids of my own?

I thought I was a woman, but they told me I have testicles. Does that make me a man? Do I have to dress like a man from now on and marry a woman and make babies with her?

"Toward the end of the twentieth century, intersex people started to protest that parents and doctors were selecting and surgically assigning the sex of their intersex child without the child's consent," Kline explained. "Many people came to believe that only the intersex children themselves had the right to determine their sex and that they should be recognized as a third gender that was neither male or female until they were ready to decide for themselves. At the same time, people began to advocate for the right to not choose either sex at adulthood and to remain intersex.

"But once synthetic sex hormones became possible, the thinking that transgender people should automatically 'fix' their problem surgically began to spread among the majority, while those who did not were thought to be abnormal. Because of these medical advances, people's once diversified concept of gender at the end of the twentieth century began to revert to the gender binary classification with a clear delineation between male and female."

"Something like a shift back to traditional values? I wonder if they began to feel nostalgic for the old days as a reaction to the sexual diversity they perceived had gone too far," Shirosaki said.

"Perhaps. One segment of the population strongly resisted. For those that viewed male and female on a spectrum without drawing sexual and gender lines, such twentieth century binary thinking had become impossible to accept. Artificial organ transplantation techniques furthered progressive thinking. Single-sex people began to want intersex bodies.

"At the time, organ transplantation was thought to be an answer for the transgender population. A solution to the problem of how to reconcile one's biological sex with one's psychological sex. But once the technology was perfected, another trend emerged. Some people expressed a desire to have the reproductive organs of both sexes and began to claim that right. Such thinking was inevitable once we diversified our concept of gender. The thinking that you can only be male or female went out with the twentieth century. Since bigenderism exists as a choice, it's hardly a surprise that someone had the idea to integrate both sexes into one body. When you sit down and think about it, there's no reason why humans have to go on being one sex or the other."

"But as perfect as the artificial organs are, do the organs of both sexes function together inside the same body?" Shirosaki asked. "Aren't hormones responsible for initiating the reproductive functions? The body requires male sex hormones to produce sperm and an abundance of female sex hormones to nurture an ovum in the uterus. It's hard to believe that both sex hormones can act upon the same body."

"Yes, that posed the biggest problem. Our endocrine system

can't stimulate the organs of both sexes to function despite having them transplanted in our body. Both men and women have gonadotropin-releasing hormones that stimulate the secretion of both female and male sex hormones. Even so, it isn't easy to stimulate the growth and maturation of both sex organs. With regard to the reproductive organs, one has to dominate the other," Kline said. "One person can be biologically intersex, be psychologically male or female, be heterosexual, homosexual, or bisexual with regard to sexual preference, and either have male or female sexual functions—the variations only increased. Far from restoring our concept of gender to the old gender binary, medical technology served to complicate it, and so too our choices. After all, this technology enables humans who are biologically and psychologically male to give birth."

"Is that something men even wanted?"

"At times, yes. That notion has existed since the twentieth century. By implanting the fertilized egg in the abdominal cavity, men can also become pregnant. It's basically the male variation of an ectopic pregnancy. Male pregnancies aren't rare in the natural world. Seahorses, for example."

"Human males are hardly the same as fish," Shirosaki said.

"I'm merely illustrating a point. That is to say, once this technology became a reality, the woman-equals-childbearing sex paradigm was completely destroyed."

"But a normal man wouldn't think of such a thing, much less desire it."

"What is *normal*, Commander Shirosaki? One person is biologically female but identifies as a male. And if that person accepts that contradiction rather than regard it as a gender disorder, is that person male or female?"

Shirosaki grimaced. "By your explanation, I suppose that's entirely up to the individual."

"Exactly. Sexual diversity means to no longer think of the disparity between one's sex and gender as a disorder. So if someone expresses a desire to bear children, we must acknowledge it regardless of sex or gender. We've already acquired the technology. The issue isn't with the number of surgeries already performed. Neither is it a matter of how many people support it. It's about somebody having an idea and all of humanity waiting for the technology to make that possible. That alone can give rise to an entirely new sex.

"Surprisingly, it wasn't the minority that fought for bigenderism. In fact, a good portion of the minority disdained the notion more fiercely than the majority."

"Then who wanted it?"

"People who belong to the gray zone."

"The gray zone?"

"A broad group that positions itself between the minority and majority," Kline said. "They live as part of the majority without ever revealing their allegiance to the minority. Well, not that they're part of the minority anyway. Straddling the line between both groups, the people of the gray zone empathize with the positions of both and yet do not openly declare where they stand. They're fascinated by the marginalized culture, even as they continue to live and have families in dominant society. They're usually the ones that, with a little push from behind, come upon a novel idea. And so it was the people of the gray zone that came at the idea of sexual diversity from a different perspective and made it real and commonplace."

"I don't think I quite understand."

"That's all right. You don't have to. In any case, the words *minority* and *majority* were soon deemed discriminatory, and such semantic distinctions ceased to exist. At last, people came to realize that such reductionist thinking was meaningless. That there was no exact delineation between the majority and minority. That the majority can always become a minority. That possibility was the essence of what it means to be human.

"And so intersexuality isn't so much a peculiar goal of people with peculiar ideas as it is a challenge we must face in order for human culture to mature. Although whether governments recognize the lifestyle is a different matter."

The world's progressives began to fight for the right for people to have both sexes. The conservative majority protested. To the conservatives, bioengineering hermaphrodites was nothing more than a vulgar hobby of freaks.

Although there was a storm of debate, in the end, society simply couldn't accept the idea of intersexuality. The media chased after the story for a while but soon stopped once the controversy died down.

But the progressives had not completely given up.

At the time, space medicine research was already being conducted on Jupiter-I—research that had continued since humanity established its first city on the Moon.

The path to the Jovian system was fraught with bigger obstacles than the paths to the Moon or Mars: the cosmic radiation, far greater than on the way to Mars, plus the gas giant's intense magnetic field. Humanity was faced with the challenge of increasing its ability to adapt to the space environment. Medication to restore the cell structure and DNA damaged by the radiation, a new model of molecular machine, overcoming the circulatory disturbance resulting from the zero-gravity environment, etc.

At some point, the data gathered from animal testing eventually had to be tested on humans.

That was what the progressives had put their finger on. They asked scientists to create a special community on Jupiter-I in exchange for offering up their bodies for experiments.

They requested approval for the creation of an exclusive dwelling for the bigender—the special district.

"The notion of body modification, which arose from the sexuality issue, presented us with the new challenge of figuring out how the sexual functions of both sexes could coexist in the same body. The only answer was to manipulate the sex chromosomes, but no one dared take on the risk on Earth. The strong opposition of the conservative majority was one reason. The issue of ethics was another. Once we recognize anyone having chromosomes other than X or Y as human, we begin to entertain the possibility of modifying the entire body. For example, improving the functionality of our arms and legs, improving our audio-visual faculties, being able to subsist on water, minerals, and light like plants. If we make radical alterations to the body in this way, how far can we go and still call ourselves human? Where do we stop in order to remain human? It was obvious that no one would be able to draw that line, which is why even researchers hesitated," Kline said. "Nevertheless, the people seeking to become bigender tried to overcome those hurdles. Humanity has to change—no, humanity must actively seek out change, they said. Through the issue of sexual diversity, they came to the conclusion that the human body must be and should be reinvented. If people's ways of thinking change along with the times, then it's only natural that the body do the same, they said. These people were an appealing opportunity to scientists. They had offered their bodies for experimentation just when scientists were in need of subjects."

"But on the condition that they would be made intersexuals and promised refuge in the special district," Shirosaki concluded.

"The International Space Probe Agency based on Earth, the Planetary Bioethics Association, and scientists on Jupiter-I came together to negotiate the terms of the experiments. And establish boundaries for what types of body alterations were allowed and not allowed to avoid any reckless behavior."

"How so?"

"First, the special district was officially designated as a sovereign state. The people of the special district are residents of a new country who acquired a family register upon moving to or being born in the special district. In other words, they were not to be treated like lab animals we can have our way with. The Rounds have the individual right to refuse to take part in any experiment.

The medical experiments can only proceed with the consent of the Rounds and the station staff; we can't force them to take part in any experiment they don't agree to."

"But you *can* try to convince them."

"Of course," Kline said. "The operating cost of the special district comes out of the International Space Probe Agency's budget. The grant element is set at zero percent, but since the agency profits from the data collected from the experiments, the Rounds aren't in the position to refuse every experiment. The district will stand to lose its operating budget. Rounds who simply can't participate in the experiments have no choice but to leave the district and live among Monaurals."

"Is that even possible?"

"It's rare, but some Rounds who are unable to adapt to the district's policies do leave. Since the Rounds aren't allowed to travel outside the Jovian system, however, they have no way of earning a living other than to become part of the station staff."

"I mean, are the Rounds capable of living in the space station among Monaurals outside of the special district?" Shirosaki asked.

"It requires considerable physical and psychological effort on their part, but it's not entirely impossible."

Kline went on to explain that the medical experiments adhered to specific guidelines. "The biggest rule is that the Rounds' appearance cannot deviate from the way Monaurals look. Their familiar appearance will reduce the psychological resistance others might feel toward the genetically different."

"On the other hand, prejudicial feelings may arise because they do look like us."

"But people may also find it easier to empathize with the Rounds. We can also avoid giving the false impression that we're conducting unnatural experiments. In addition, we clearly defined two purposes for creating bigenders," Kline said. "Officially, the Rounds are staff working on the frontier of space exploration. Only a small staff is dispatched to the frontier at first, limiting the choices of sexual partners. Under those circumstances, it simply isn't efficient to halve the gene pool by restricting the partnerships to between a man and a woman. The best method is to expand the choices by making everyone a possible sexual partner."

"The expectation to bear children seems to be an anachronism, wouldn't you say?"

"For the record, of course—it's a pretext to create bigenders."

"What if you take frozen eggs and sperm to the frontier? With a diverse supply, the staff can have as many children as they like from outside their gene pool," Shirosaki said.

"Of course, we're pursuing that avenue as we speak. Unfortunately, the success rate has been disappointing. Some technologies that prove effective on Earth oftentimes fail in the Jovian system. As the research continues, I do believe that method will eventually take root. But the human ability to propagate the species can't be undervalued. Our ability to bear and raise children in places without the aid of an artificial womb or incubation system is a tremendous advantage."

"And the second purpose?"

"To resolve the issues raised by gender differences. Our society has not been able to overcome gender discrimination with our laws and ethics alone. We're incapable of eliminating the conflicts stemming from the differences in sexes. And that's only natural. Our physiology is different. So are our hormonal cycles. There's no way to understand the other completely. That's fine, I suppose. You might say that such issues are what make humanity so fascinating and profound. But now as we've left the tiny confines of the solar system and are attempting to embark on a journey into the dark expanse, we can't afford to quibble over such trifling matters. Which is why we should dispense with the problems that can be resolved by reinventing the body. A society where we are equals, where only individual differences exist. That was the ideal scientists proposed, and it was largely because of these two goals that the creation of the Rounds was approved. And so strictly speaking, the term *Round* isn't the name of a new race but a word to describe a certain condition."

"How was that name derived?"

"It stands for *roundtrip gender*—a being constantly moving between masculinity and femininity. It was a word coined here on Jupiter-I."

"While we may be able to overcome gender differences, as long as individual differences continue to exist, I doubt we can eliminate interpersonal conflicts altogether," Shirosaki said.

"We certainly don't believe we can resolve all conflicts by ridding society of sexual distinctions alone," Kline responded. "But at the very least, eliminating physiological differences will free us from the *because he's a man* or *because she's a woman* mode of thinking. Are you familiar with the myth of the hermaphrodite from Plato's *Symposium*?"

"I'm afraid I'm not."

"According to Aristophanes, humans were once hermaphrodites with four arms and four legs. Wary of humanity's hubris and might, the gods tore the humans in two. This was the origin of men and women, each sex searching and desiring the other half ever since. I can't say that I believe in the myth, but the story has resonance, wouldn't you say?"

"And were the progressives satisfied by the creation of the Rounds?"

"Hardly. They mounted quite a protest. In a way, maybe the progressives had a better understanding of the implications of these experiments. The emergence of a society where one person has two sexes becomes commonplace. They realized that alone could jolt our values from their foundation. Perhaps the progressives intuited that changing just one aspect of our social universe could change our universe entirely."

"So how do they contain such a threat?"

"None of the data from the experiments can leave the Jovian

system," Kline said. "The Rounds can only be created on the Jovian system. Rounds cannot travel to Earth or Mars. In short, they're absolutely forbidden to enter our society. Those were the terms of the agreement. Not a problem since the people who'd volunteered to be subjects had abandoned their homes on Earth and Mars. Thus, the special district was established. The first generation, called the pre-generation, acquired their bigender surgically. Though pre-gens weren't absolute hermaphrodites and thus couldn't procreate, a bigender society was born in the special district. Every one of its residents is both male and female. And every one of them is psychologically male and female. Their feelings develop not for the opposite sex but for the individual. During the experiments, they also began bearing children through artificial insemination. The fertilized eggs were injected with a synthetic gene called double-I instead of the sex chromosomes Monaurals possess. Those children were born as absolute hermaphrodites from the start. They represent the first generation of Rounds. Since then, a second and third generation have been born through traditional procreation methods."

"What became of the pre-generation?"

"They work and live among the station staff outside the special district. The pre-generation and first generation have completely different ways of thinking. As different as their physiology is, they might as well be different species. All the scientists did was eliminate sexual distinctions. But that change alone can transform human society—our lifestyles, value systems, our sense of humanity. What do you think?" Kline asked. "About our creating a race of bigenders?"

"I haven't had occasion to give it much thought."

"You're not the least bit interested?"

"I don't quite know what to think, as I'm perfectly satisfied being a man and a Monaural. I can appreciate the concept of a gender-free society. But a society that is free of sexual distinctions by changing the human physiology goes beyond what I'd consider ordinary."

"You'll get used to it. We all need time to adapt to a new value system."

Adapt to what? Shirosaki thought. *To the fact that humans are becoming absolute hermaphrodites? Or to the idea that I would grow accustomed to a society without sexual differences?* "Harding brought up the subject of language discrimination earlier. I understand there are words we shouldn't use in reference to the Rounds."

"There's no need to be overly sensitive. The Rounds are fully aware of their differences and they won't fault us for a slip or two. But there are some things you're better off not saying out of consideration for the Rounds. 'You look feminine for a Round' or 'You look masculine for a Round,' for example. Surely you must have assumed Dr. Tei to be a woman when you first saw em."

"Yes, I did," Shirosaki admitted.

"When we Monaurals see a Round, we tend to recognize traits of one gender over the other. Which is why we say a 'feminine Round' and a 'masculine Round.' For those of us accustomed to having gender differences, we can't help seeing the Rounds in those terms as well. And maybe we're projecting our desires upon them too. 'I hope that Round is feminine.' Or, 'That Round has to be masculine.' Nothing more than an illusion on our part. The Rounds have no awareness of being more one sex than the other. What exactly did you feel was feminine about the doctor? Eir slender proportions? Or eir features?"

"I suppose it was the voice," Shirosaki answered. "Ey looks like a woman, of course, but I detected a kindness in eir manner of speaking and timbre of eir voice that I perceived as distinctly feminine."

"That's all strictly according to your own definition. In your mind, you have some standards by which you distinguish the sexes. But those standards won't work with the Rounds."

"This is all so very confusing."

"There's no need to feel bad about yourself. Few of us have ever been in contact with the Rounds. It's natural to feel uncomfortable. Your thinking will change while you're here. By the time your assignment here is done, I promise you your views about sexuality will be completely transformed. Oh, and another thing—please don't call the Rounds 'sea hares' or 'snails.' The Rounds hate it when Harding calls them that."

Shirosaki and Kline exited the observatory and boarded the high-velocity elevator, which took them to the special district in mere seconds. Kline stood in front of the entrance where a biometric scanner worked its way up and down her entire body.

After the system finished reading her personal information, the door opened.

Shirosaki's eyes grew wide.

Lush greenery filled his field of vision. It was like an entrance to a botanical garden.

The special district lacked the subdivisions and corridors of the station staff's residential district. The entire space lay open like a magnificent garden. Not so much a garden but closer to a small cityscape. The ceiling was thirty feet high. The garden appeared to slope up into a sharp incline at both ends. Because the area was free of obstructions, unlike the Monaurals' residential district, Shirosaki could see the curvilinear shape of the cylindrical station.

A wide path snaked along the shape of the central axis, branching off into various areas of the district along the way.

Kline gestured toward the path, and they began to walk. Shirosaki felt as if he were being led through a garden made for pleasing tourists.

Suddenly the image that had triggered his wakefulness in the hibernation chamber came flooding back to life. The oppressive smell of greenery. The memory of the Summer Dome. A prophetic dream? Or coincidence?

Shirosaki asked Kline, "Is the entire district a plantation of some sort?"

"There's a separate garden elsewhere. These plants have been bioengineered. They constantly release oxygen and absorb CO_2 gases regardless of the availability of light energy. They take in the air and release just the oxygen back into the environment."

"Water and nutrients?"

"They don't require as much of either as normal plants."

"I see they bear fruit."

"Not edible, I'm afraid," Kline said. "They absorb just the carbon from the CO_2 gases. When they mature, they're harvested and processed for carbon fiber at the recycling plant."

Kline picked one of the fruit and handed it to Shirosaki. It had none of the fleshy elasticity of edible fruit. Shirosaki squeezed it and the fruit crumbled, leaving a powdery residue in his hand like pumice.

Shirosaki and Kline passed by several Rounds as they walked.

The Rounds wore flat shoes and long tunics, which resembled quarter-sleeved Chinese dresses with stand-up collars. The front of the lightweight cloth was decorated with embroidery from collar to chest. Since the tunics were identical, the embroidered designs alone seemed to reflect individual tastes. The children, scampering around the garden in sandals, were dressed more simply. All of the Rounds wore portable comm devices on their arms or chests.

"I feel as if I've wandered into an ancient civilization."

"When we considered the proper attire for a society without sexual distinctions, this was the design we came up with."

"It seems a bit more classical-looking than unisex. It's enough to make you forget this is a space station."

"Would you have preferred a different design? Such domestic matters tend to take a back seat here."

"Are the Rounds happy with it?" Shirosaki asked.

"They don't say either way. Although the embroidery was their idea."

None of the Rounds registered any emotion upon seeing Kline and Shirosaki.

Their oddly tranquil gaze as they walked past without so much as a smile reminded Shirosaki of Dr. Tei's light brown eyes.

"I have a feeling we're not welcome here."

"Don't let it bother you. It's a kind of etiquette here."

"How do you mean?"

"The Rounds have a different physiology and accordingly, they have different values. Disregarding the other is the most peaceful method of interaction," Kline explained.

"But you all live on the same station."

"This is the special district. It isn't like the other parts of the station. You musn't think of this place in the same way."

Residential units were scattered throughout the garden. The yellowish-ochre modules bunched together resembled an insect's nest.

"Those are the residential quarters," Kline explained.

"Does each of the quarters house only one Round?"

"There are units that accommodate one, and larger units that house five or six."

"Are they resistant to gunfire and explosions?"

"Not likely. Under fire they'd probably just fall into a heap in seconds."

Shirosaki stared at the clusters of units as he continued to walk. There were residences scattered all throughout the district. Impossible for an intruder to take many hostages at once. Most of the residents should be able to escape.

Since the plan was to neutralize any threat of an attack at the docking bays, it was unlikely anyone would penetrate the station this far.

A Round family was peering at Shirosaki from the window of a residential unit. Shirosaki smiled and waved as he would to his own child, but neither the adult nor children registered any response. Turning away, they disappeared from the window. Shirosaki lowered his hand and asked Kline, "Were those children third-generation?"

"Yes."

"They seem awfully big considering when these experiments began."

"The Rounds mature at a much faster rate than we do. They reach adulthood three times faster."

"Then they have a shorter life span?"

"Actually their rate of aging slows upon reaching adulthood. If you try to guess their age by our sensibilities, you'll find yourself mistaken. The Rounds have a growth calendar uniquely their own. One Round year is different from one Monaural year."

"How is that possible?"

"Through the miracle of space medicine, really," Kline said. "One of the advances in biogerontology. Mars and Earth have also pursued it, but the research on Jupiter-I is the most advanced. The technology has to do with controlling the secretion of growth hormones and telomerase synthesis. Given the need for good people to work on the cosmic frontier now, all the better if they mature faster and live longer. There's no need for a waiting period. We don't have the luxury of waiting eighteen or nineteen years like on Earth or Mars."

"So how are the Rounds different?"

"According to the Monaural growth calendar, our body secretes an enormous amount of growth hormones until we're six and begins to secrete gonadotropins at seven until maturation. Once we reach adulthood, the body secretes less gonadotropins and begins to produce telomerase."

Telomerase is an enzyme that acts upon a base sequence of DNA called telomeres, which limit the number of times the body's cells can divide and replicate. The number of telomeres decreases as cell division is repeated. Once the telomeres are completely gone, the cells cannot reproduce. The telomerase essentially acts to replenish the telomeres as they erode so the cells can live longer. Theoretically, the body's cells can go on replicating endlessly as long as the telomerase remains active. The body can continue to produce tissue, thereby slowing the aging process.

"The Rounds receive injections of telomerase genes, and T-antigen genes. Scientists also made modifications to the

Rounds' klotho genes, to mitigate the aging process as well as change the 5,178th base sequence of the mitochondrial DNA from cytosine to adenine. A nanomachine that replicates neurons is implanted in their brain. The Rounds are also much more resistant to cosmic radiation."

"Do you mean to tell me that we have the technology to make us immortal?"

"Oh, no. There's much more research to be done before we attain immortality. We may have succeeded in prolonging the life span of the Rounds, but the technology is far from perfect. We estimate the Rounds will continue to live healthy lives past two hundred, but the first generation has already begun to show signs of aging. Although they appear outwardly young, their blood test results tell another story."

"Still, they'll outlive us. Is that right?"

"Probably. Without ever experiencing senility or physical impairments."

Kline's gaze wandered and her face lit up. "Ah, we're in luck," she said. "That's the leader of the Rounds over there. I'll introduce you to em."

The Round was picking fruit from the bioengineered plants. Ey was tall with eir long straight hair behind em. Ey appeared to be a little older than Dr. Tei.

"I'm sorry to interrupt," Kline called out.

The Round turned around and looked at Shirosaki with placid eyes.

"This is Fortia, the superintendent of the special district," said Kline.

Fortia bowed eir head slightly and said, "Welcome to the special district," in fluent English. Ey spoke politely, but there was a chill in eir look. Unlike the other Rounds who'd remained expressionless, ey was clearly gazing at Shirosaki with a look of caution.

"*Fortia* is Latin for 'strength,'" Kline explained. "All Round names are derived from Latin words. The Monaural names are gender-specific. Lucy is a woman's name, Jim is a man's name, and so on. Since names connoting gender distinctions aren't appropriate for the Rounds, we decided to give them Latin names in the tradition of scientific names. The names come from nouns, verbs, and at times, adjectives. We came up with the names for how they sound, so please don't read too much into their original meaning."

Fortia twisted eir lip into a smile and asked Kline, "Is he part of the security staff?"

"There's no need to be alarmed. Not everyone on the security team is like Commander Harding."

Fortia appeared masculine to Shirosaki. Maybe it was eir build. Compared to Dr. Tei, ey was taller and had a much bonier physique.

If Shirosaki stared long enough, ey might have even looked like a strapping middle-aged woman or a life-weary mother. And yet, Shirosaki sensed something very masculine about Fortia. He didn't quite understand the standards by which he was projecting his own perceptions of masculinity and femininity onto the Round. Was it one's outward appearance and attire? The timbre of the voice? Mannerisms? None were factors that definitively distinguished one sex from the other.

People whose gender identity was incongruous with their biological sex were no longer a rarity even in Shirosaki's society. Sexuality was not determined by one's physiology alone. Then by what standard was he intuiting Fortia's sex? On what basis was he perceiving one sex more strongly than the other?

Fortia asked Kline, "Has something happened to prompt a visit from special security?"

"We've received word of a possible terrorist attack. We expect to contain the threat in the docking bays, but Commander Shirosaki is inspecting the layout of the facilities just in case."

"We should go inside. This isn't something we should be discussing here." With that, Fortia turned around and made eir way down the path.

The exterior of Fortia's residence was painted a light green, making it easier to pick out from among the others.

As soon as Shirosaki entered the room, he let out a cry of admiration. The interior was made of wood. For Shirosaki, who'd been born on Earth, it was nothing if not a nostalgic sight.

The polished boards were not poor imitations made of non-flammable synthetic materials or metals; they had been cut from real trees. From cedar and cypress trees no less. Where did they manage to procure this much wood? Wood panels covered the hall, ceiling, and the entire walls. The stairs leading up to the second floor were also made of cut logs. The rustic interior seemed entirely out of place on a space station responsible for developing the latest scientific technology.

"Does it interest you to see a house made of wood?" asked Fortia.

"More like nostalgia," answered Shirosaki. "Homes like these exist only on Earth now, and not everyone can afford to build a home from such expensive materials as wood."

"The materials here are from the trees grown in the special district. Wood is quite handy for maintaining the humidity and temperature."

"How do you manage to grow cedars and cypress trees in this space?"

"They're genetically engineered dwarf breeds, so they only grow to about six feet. The wood boards are laid over a framework built from synthetic materials."

"Are all of the units like this?"

"They're all designed a bit differently, but basically, yes. We Rounds don't have any experience living on the planets, so I can't speak to your feelings of nostalgia. We're only using the wood because it's a useful material. How nice you find it pleasing."

They stepped inside the living room and found another Round. When ey looked up from whatever ey was doing, Shirosaki instantly recognized eir masculine qualities. Ey appeared to be younger than Fortia. A young man. When Fortia asked em to make them some tea, ey nodded and disappeared into the kitchen. Fortia offered Kline and Shirosaki a seat on the sofa.

"My partner, Album. I suppose that makes us husband and wife in your society."

Having assumed they were siblings, Shirosaki replied flatly, "I see."

As estranged as the Rounds were from Monaural society, the interior and furnishings were completely Earth-inspired. Perhaps the Rounds had yet to come into their own in this aspect of culture or they simply accepted whatever tools were practical. Or perhaps they were deliberately being made to use these familiar items in order to minimize the differences between Rounds and Monaurals.

Shirosaki looked up at the ceiling. There was a skylight above the living room. He didn't exactly know why a house would need a skylight in a place where no sky existed, but maybe this too was another cultural influence adopted from Monaural society. No doubt the skylight had been incorporated into the design more as a novelty than for its functionality.

Album returned and placed several sealed containers of tea on the table. Although eir bony fingers were in no way delicate, after having heard the two were husband and wife, Shirosaki couldn't help but feel strangely attracted to them. He felt discomfited by the inescapable tendency to distinguish the Rounds by his own standards of gender. After thanking Album, he took one of the heated containers and opened the seal. He felt the warm tea go down his throat, along with the sensation that he had not quite caught up to the reality of the special district.

"Do you mind if Album joins us?" Fortia asked. "Ey is also an assistant superintendent of the special district."

"Of course not," Shirosaki replied. Then he proceeded to explain why the security staff was being doubled. How a terrorist group called the Vessel of Life was plotting to destroy the special district. How the terrorists would likely come in on one of the cargo vessels. How he and his security team were familiarizing themselves with the facilities in the event of a battle.

Fortia and Album listened without a hint of emotion.

Their non-reaction made Shirosaki uneasy. Isolated as they were in the special district, were they unable to understand how frightening a terrorist threat was? Perhaps they didn't comprehend how violent the humans on Mars and Earth were.

After Shirosaki warned them of the possibility of a shoot-out inside the docking bays, Fortia turned to Kline. "Isn't the construction of *Apertio* complete yet?"

"Not for another three years. There are also supplies to procure. We're not anywhere near launching it."

"It doesn't matter where, as long as we can get far enough away from the Monaurals. Maybe the terrorists will give up if we can somehow get as far as Saturn."

"Colonizing Saturn isn't possible yet. There's still so much data to collect and so many issues to resolve," Kline reminded em.

"What about Venus or Mercury?"

"Their environments are too severe."

"It's been three generations. We can't continue to depend on the Monaurals forever."

"Is there a plan to move the Rounds?" Shirosaki cut in reluctantly. "And what is *Apertio*?"

"The Rounds are preparing to participate in experiments to establish settlements beyond Jupiter," Kline answered. "As I explained earlier, the Rounds are, on the record, a race engineered for the express purpose of space exploration."

"Do you mean to tell me they're acting as human subjects in our place?"

"To put it bluntly, yes."

"But they must be terrified," Shirosaki said. "Or at least resistant."

Fortia laughed. "I'm proud to be a Round. I will be venturing into uncharted space before any Monaural, testing the limits of my skills to gather valuable data. That data will serve as the foundation for when the Monaurals are ready to journey farther into space. I have been entrusted with a wonderful and rewarding job. We're capable of doing the work no unmanned probe will be able to handle in your stead. We'll die satisfied, even if it means cutting short our lives. Didn't you Monaurals embark on space exploration with those same high aspirations all those many years ago? That's what we Rounds are trying to do now. For all of humanity."

Fortia spoke with unwavering conviction, eir voice revealing not even a hint of doubt.

Unlike Shirosaki, who'd return to Mars when his job here was done, the Rounds had only Jupiter-I and unexplored space. They had no home. They were like human probes, destined to travel deeper and deeper into space to gather data for as long as they lived.

"I'm willing to undergo any physical change to adapt to space. We may be nothing more than imitations of Monaurals now, but we don't have to be human if that's what it takes to adapt. A new being. I wouldn't mind that at all."

"The construction of a vessel is now under way on Asteroid City," explained Kline. "A supership capable of towing the special district—that's the *Apertio*."

"The special district *entirely*?"

"Jupiter-I is shaped like a cored pineapple before it's cut into round slices. The special district will be cut away from the rest of the space station, just like one of those slices, and will head for Saturn towed by the supership."

"I see. So the special district was designed to be part of a long-term exploration vessel from the start."

"One that can be cut loose by removing just a few screws. Or perhaps it's more like cutting it away with an enormous knife," Fortia said. "The current threat will not be the end of the Vessel of Life's activities. Eventually we will have to leave the space station."

"The people on Earth and Mars are afraid that the technology enabling us to become bigender will make its way into their societies," Album said. "They'll come after us as long as we're within reach. That's why we need to get out of here."

"But I thought there were laws forbidding this technology

from leaving the station."

"The Monaurals don't give a damn about that. All they feel is hate and repulsion. When I hear all of the horrible incidents happening on Earth and Mars, I can see there's no negotiating with them."

"If that were true, humanity would have perished long ago."

"All Monaurals are good at is preserving the status quo," Album said. "They only care about what's in it for them; they're not interested in discussing solutions."

"That's enough politics," Fortia said severely. "You're being rude to our guests."

Smiling crookedly, Album leaned back on the sofa and said nothing more.

"The people on Earth and Mars are afraid their next generation will be injected with the double-I chromosomes," said Kline. "With the inclusion of bigenders in their society, the old concepts of gender and sex will be completely destroyed. This is what the Vessel of Life fears most. The idea of one human possessing both sexes baffles them. At best, they may understand the concept of changing from one sex to another. To them, surgically transplanting sexual organs is nothing more than the act of a deviant, never mind switching XX and XY for double-I chromosomes."

"Isn't it your job to ensure that technology doesn't get leaked?"

"Any information that exists will eventually be leaked, as long as there is someone coveting it."

"Are you suggesting that people are after double-I for themselves even though the Vessel of Life opposes it?" Shirosaki asked.

"Naturally. Humans desire change even while they desire stasis. And generally speaking, they prefer to change physically before they do psychologically."

"But you didn't seem very shocked to see us, Commander Shirosaki," Fortia noted.

"Shocked enough, I assure you. I've been trained to control my emotions."

"Not everyone on the security team is like you."

"Are you talking about Harding?"

"I'm not speaking only of him. Usually Monaurals react oddly when they first see us, like they don't quite know where to look." Fortia continued, "Tell me something. If you were able, would you choose to be transplanted with double-I? Would you choose to change your sex chromosomes?"

"Thank you, but no. I'm perfectly satisfied being a man," Shirosaki said.

"It appears you're someone we can trust," Fortia said, smiling for the first time. "You're not like Commander Harding. You're not trying to understand us or seeking our friendship. And that's just fine. We don't need Monaurals to understand us. All you need to know is that we exist on Jupiter-I. We need you to protect us. There's absolutely no need for any sort of human interaction between the Rounds and Monaurals."

"What has Harding done? Why do you dislike him?"

"That's none of your concern." Fortia said nothing more.

Kline did not offer an answer. Album let slip a sneer.

Clearly something had happened that hadn't been reported to Captain Hasukawa. As much as this troubled Shirosaki, he kept silent. That no report had been filed no doubt spelled some sort of scandal best kept private. Although Harding seemed to dislike Kline and the Rounds, the problem seemed to stem from him.

Shirosaki left Fortia's residence with Kline without learning any more about the matter.

2

AS ARINO WENT through his workout routine in the training room, he thought back to his encounter with Tei in the meeting room. That cold smile. Had it been one of contempt? A ridiculing look the younger generation directed at the older set? The look of disdain the arrogant cast upon an inferior?

Biologically speaking, Arino understood how the Rounds were equipped and how they procreated. But as much as he understood intellectually, how he felt was another matter.

What was the Rounds' sexual orientation according to Monaural standards? Would they be considered homosexual since they all had the same physiology? Or would they be considered bisexual because they had intercourse as both sexes?

It was nothing he could understand. A concept beyond convention, and yet, one that might become commonplace in the future.

The unfamiliar had the power to both frighten and tantalize at the same time. People grew all the more drawn to what was taboo.

Tei looked just like them—like normal humans. Spoke English and dressed like them and ate like them. The difference lay in the sexual organs. But Arino was puzzled by the way that difference alone made Tei seem something other than human to him.

They had been the ones to create the Rounds. Had they been as scared when childbirth was made possible through artificial insemination? What about when the first humanoid robot was built? Why were they so discomfited and bewildered by the simple fact of gaining one sexual type?

After finishing his workout, Arino went into the locker room and showered.

He threw on some fresh clothes and dragged his sluggish body toward the residential district assigned to the security staff.

As spacious as Jupiter-I was, it was still only as large as a standard space station. Learning the layout of the station and visiting each of the facilities had taken all of three days. The security team's mission didn't begin in earnest until the first cargo vessel arrived. Thus far, their scheduled patrols had been strictly routine and did nothing more than demonstrate they were earning their keep.

In his boredom, Arino's thoughts wandered to the special district. Shirosaki's team had no active contact with Harding's team. Once the terrorist threat was put down, Harding's team would go back to

Mars, so the two teams had no reason to fraternize. They exchanged nothing more than a few pleasantries even when they bumped into each other in the mess, recreation room, or training room.

But because no one on Shirosaki's team aside from Shirosaki himself was allowed to enter the special district, their curiosity only intensified. Most of the members tried to learn as much about the Rounds as they could from the snatches of conversation with those on Harding's team.

But none of the members of Harding's team was very forth-coming on the subject. No matter how much they were questioned, they dodged the questions and inevitably said, "Look, if your commander's telling you to stay out of the special district, I'd listen. The Rounds aren't some animals you can gawk at. You can't stare at them. Another incident will only spell trouble for the station staff. After a while, you'll forget that the Rounds even exist."

None of this satisfied Shirosaki's team, however. Every time they gathered in the mess and the recreation room, they traded gossip and indulged in wild conjecture. After several members of Harding's team had given them both dirty looks and warnings, Shirosaki's team members took to speaking in Japanese, not just about the Rounds but on all matters. Although Arino didn't approve, he decided to monitor the situation until Shirosaki gave him a direct order to intercede.

After making several turns along the corridor, he came upon a mother carrying a baby walking from the other direction. Dressed in a quarter-sleeved one-piece dress, the woman had long blond hair that was tied in back.

Arino was surprised to see children on the space station. He smiled, remembering his own wife and daughter.

"Hey there," Arino called out. "She's a cute one," he said, peering in at the baby's face. "How old is she?"

A troubled look seeped across the woman's face. She averted her eyes from Arino's sunny face. "A little over three months."

"She's a big girl. I figured her for at least a year old."

"We grow much faster than you do. We mature three time faster."

"Oh, excuse me," Arino said. "You're from the special district."

"Yes."

Arino couldn't help eyeing the Round up and down. Ey frowned and glared.

The Round cradling eir baby was tall but looked like a Monaural woman. Ey appeared even more feminine than Dr. Tei. From the curvy silhouette of the body to the delicate white countenance, ey was the image of a woman in Arino's eyes.

"I have to go," the Round said irritably. "I'll be reprimanded for talking to you."

"Reprimanded? By whom?"

"By many people. By your people and mine."

"But that's silly. What's wrong with our just talking?"

"I'm sorry, I can't…"

"All right, I won't keep you any longer. But I meant what I said about your little one. I have a daughter who's three. She's back home on Mars with her mother, and so when I saw you with your child, I couldn't help saying something. I'm sorry to have troubled you. Forgive me."

The Round bowed without a word and continued on eir way past Arino, hastening eir steps back toward the special district.

Shirosaki had told him that access to the special district was prohibited. But Arino had no idea relations were such that a brief exchange in the corridor might warrant a reprimand.

What had soured the relationship between the Rounds and Monaurals on the space station? And why was Tei acting as intermediary?

Arino tilted his gaze up at the ceiling.

What if the surveillance system had recorded this exchange just now? Or someone had seen them talking?

It made Arino heartsick to imagine someone blaming that Round.

Shirosaki's team members Eiko Shiohara and Yuna Ogata were thoroughly displeased about their assignment on Jupiter-I. As much as they knew their turn would come sooner or later, they had pissed and moaned about everything that had to do with their detail on this godforsaken place.

They could hardly bear the boredom of doing nothing. Although a showdown with the terrorists was pending in two weeks' time, once that was done, the boredom would return. Considering the number of members on the detail, they couldn't lose. It would all be over in seconds. No thrill to be had. Perhaps they'd end up watching from the sidelines without being called into action.

As the two women walked the corridors on their scheduled patrol, Shiohara let out a groan. "I can't go back to the residential quarters. The thought of having to see the others' ugly mugs makes me sick."

"Wouldn't it be nice to visit the special district?" said Ogata.

"Yeah."

"I wonder if all of the Rounds are as handsome as the doctor."

"I'd sure like to find out," Shiohara said.

"We have to come up with some excuse to sneak in."

Dr. Tei, who looked female to the male members of the security team, appeared male to the team's two female members, Shiohara and Ogata.

Shirosaki had explained that perceptions were gendered; Tei looked male to them because Ogata and Shiohara were female. But that did nothing to satisfy their curiosity.

Just as their male counterparts chased Tei with their eyes as they would a woman, Shiohara and Ogata had regarded the doctor as a man. When they looked at Tei, they saw only a handsome man.

While the men were drawn to the female part of the Round on one hand, they were also put off by the male part. Whatever they felt about transgenders, the men couldn't reconcile the fact of two sexes coexisting in one body.

Shiohara and Ogata were different. They felt little resistance to a masculine Round existing inside a female physiology. In fact, it might have been what attracted them to Tei. Perhaps that was because they worked in a profession that demanded a dose of masculinity. Although the men they worked with were a rough and tumble bunch, Shiohara and Ogata knew all too well that machismo alone was not the measure of a man's appeal. A kind and sensitive man—a type that did not exist on the security team—was attractive. This was precisely the type of "man" Shiohara and Ogata believed Tei to be. Their service on Jupiter-I would last at least a year. They wanted to spend as much of that time as possible being entertained.

The two found themselves fantasizing about the kind of relationship they would have if they were to fall in love with a Round.

Would that count as a heterosexual relationship? Or a homosexual relationship?

"Maybe it's both," Ogata said. Even if they thought they were entering a heterosexual relationship, if the Round loved them from the standpoint of a woman the relationship would be a lesbian one.

Ogata remarked she wouldn't quite know what to feel, but that was part of the allure.

As the women continued down the corridor contemplating all the possible relationship patterns there might be, a shadow darted out from around the corner and nearly collided with them.

The slender figure stumbled, jostling the baby in her arms. Her handsome features twisted into a frightened look. Shiohara reached out with her arms and stopped the woman and the baby's fall. The woman grasped the baby tightly in her arms, her face still frozen in terror.

"Careful," Shiohara said sternly. "Watch where you're going."

"Sorry," the woman answered hastily and hurried on her way.

"Was that one of them?" Ogata asked.

"Really?" Shiohara turned around, but the Round was already gone. "I thought it was one of the station staff. She looked just like a woman."

"I guess the Rounds come in all types."

"Maybe they become more feminine after childbirth. Do you think the doctor looks like a man because he's still single?"

"She looked like she was in a hurry. I wonder if something's happened," Ogata said.

They resumed their patrol and ran into Arino farther down the corridor.

"Someone came from this direction in an awful hurry. Do you know anything about it?" Shiohara asked Arino.

"Forget it," Arino answered. "It was nothing."

"A woman with a child."

"No, that was a Round," Arino confessed.

"She looked like a normal woman."

"Took me by surprise too, but I guess some of the Rounds are like that," Arino said. "Hard to believe she's also a man at the same time."

"There are androgynous people like that in our society too, but in the case of the Rounds, they really are both sexes."

Shiohara caught a glimpse of Arino's conflicted face, which tickled her curiosity. "You're curious about the special district too, aren't you, Sub-commander?"

"Well, no—"

"I don't understand why only the commander is allowed access. Here we are living on the same station. Isn't it natural to be a little curious?" Shiohara said.

"Forget it. You heard the commander's orders. The special district is off-limits. And anyhow, the special district requires a security check to gain access."

"Then we can get someone to take us," Ogata said.

"Who are you thinking of?"

"Dr. Tei. Maybe we'll be allowed in if we're with the doctor on some official business."

Shiohara and Ogata arrived at the infirmary to find the doctor already entertaining visitors. Several of the men from Shirosaki's team were sitting on the infirmary beds chatting up the doctor seated on the examination chair.

So long as the special district was off-limits, the only Round they had contact with was Tei. Unable to learn anything from Shirosaki or from the members of Harding's team, they had given in to curiosity and naturally gravitated to Tei.

Despite the tactless questions they had likely asked, Tei was good-naturedly laughing along with the men. Seeing this, Shiohara was stung with jealousy.

When she asked the others to leave so she could talk to the doctor, the men scoffed. "Go right on ahead and talk. Or is it something you don't want us to hear?"

"That's right. A conversation between women."

"Well, you see, we're doing some male bonding here ourselves. Maybe you should come back another time."

"Dr. Tei isn't a man."

"Of course not. But the doctor isn't just a woman either."

Arino stuck his head inside from the corridor. "Do you mind giving us a few minutes?" he asked the men. "We need to discuss something with the doctor."

Realizing that Arino was with them, the men straightened up and hopped off the beds. "Sure thing, Sub-commander. Excuse us."

"Thanks, fellas," he said.

"Sir."

The men turned to Tei. "We'll be back. Or maybe you'll visit our quarters sometime. Maybe we can have a drink or two on your day off."

"I'm sorry, but I'm afraid I don't drink," Tei said. "We can't indulge in anything that damages the liver cells regulating our sex hormones."

"Some tea, then."

"Perhaps sometime in the mess. Thank you."

Shiohara scowled at the men as they trudged out of the room.

"You have to be careful, Doctor." Shiohara raised her voice once they were gone. "Don't let them fool you. You can never tell what men are thinking."

"It's all right. I'm only interacting with them as a man."

"Even so, they may have other plans."

"I'll bear that in mind. Now, what brings you here?"

"We have a favor to ask," Shiohara said.

"What is it?"

"We'd like to see the special district."

Tei chuckled. "You're just like the others. Did you discuss it with Commander Shirosaki?"

"No."

"As a general rule, any interaction with the Rounds is prohibited."

"Well, yes. But we're allowed to talk to you," Ogata said.

"That's because I'm an intermediary."

"Maybe we can tag along as your assistants. How about that?"

"I can't take you for no reason."

"So we'll make up a reason. Give us something to do," Shiohara said. "Please, Dr. Tei. We're bored to tears. At this rate, someone's bound to try to breach the security protocols to break into the special district."

Tei thought about it. After a moment, ey looked up as if ey'd come upon an idea and smiled. "I assume you can handle some heavy lifting?"

"Sure."

"There is something you can help us with. We could use some extra hands."

Arino, Shiohara, and Ogata were recruited to finish the interior construction of one of the Rounds' residential units. The work involved laying wood boards cut and processed from the garden inside a newly built residence.

After passing the security check with eir ID, Tei led the three visitors inside the special district.

Shiohara and Ogata were thrilled to learn that the district was an arcology in which bioengineered plants and trees supplied Rounds with much of their oxygen and raw materials. "I just knew a closely guarded place like this would have a wonderful secret," Shiohara said.

"I never expected to see such beautiful greenery out here on Jupiter. Can we take a look at the garden?" Ogata asked.

"I'm afraid not. A human presence would contaminate the garden."

They arrived at a finished residential unit, which only required the wood boards to be fitted into the floors, walls, and ceiling. The three volunteers laid the wood boards one by one into the framework made of nonflammable synthetic materials, transforming the unit into a remarkably warm and inviting space.

As hard as the work was, Shiohara and Ogata were elated to see the fruits of their labor.

Only Arino groused about his being roped into such grunt work. "Aren't there any robots for this sort of thing?"

"We try to use as few of them as possible to conserve energy."

"So then all of these units are—"

"Yes," Tigris, the owner of the home, said. "You learn to enjoy the work once you get used to it." Tigris was a second-generation Round with a sturdier build than Tei. Ey looked clearly male in Shiohara's and Ogata's eyes.

When Shiohara stole a moment to ask Arino of his impression of the Round, he answered, "Used to be a woman in my neighborhood who looked just like her." Tigris apparently had traits that men like Arino recognized as feminine, no matter how muscular eir build.

"Thank you. You're a great help," Tei announced to the crew.

"No worries," said Shiohara. "We were sitting around without anything to do. We're happy to have something to pass the time."

After they had made some progress, the five decided to take a break.

They took a walk to the assembly hall, where a Round named Calendula was waiting for them with tea packs and dessert.

Calendula was Tigris's partner. Slender in build, ey had a slightly higher-pitched voice than Tigris's. To Shiohara and Ogata, ey looked male. But Arino recognized more of the Round's feminine traits.

Their children, lying in a cradle next to them, outwardly looked just like Monaural babies. Shiohara and Ogata couldn't perceive any gender traits from them. Apparently, all babies were difficult to distinguish by sex no matter what their subspecies.

As Arino peered into the cradle and waved at the giggling babies, he asked, "They look alike and yet they don't. Are they fraternal twins?"

"They're not twins," Tigris answered. "We each gave birth to one."

"Each?"

"We can both be impregnated in a single act of intercourse."

"Oh, both of you…" Arino said, his face clouding. "Well then…"

"A Round couple can love as a man and be loved as a woman in a single act of intercourse. Not every act leads to pregnancy, of course, but repeated intercourse eventually stimulates the pituitary gland to secrete gonadotropic hormones. You are voluntary ovulatory animals. We, on the other hand, are reflex ovulatory animals."

"What is that?"

"Monaural women have a menstrual cycle," Tigris said. "Women ovulate once a month to prepare for pregnancy, whether they're sexually active or not. This is called voluntary ovulation. Reflex ovulation, on the other hand, is when ovulation is triggered by some physical stimulation to what Monaurals call the cervix. When that stimulus reaches the brain by way of the spinal nerves, the pituitary gland secretes gonadotropic hormones triggering ovulation. Hares and felines on Earth employ this method of ovulation."

Hares. Felines. Arino blinked in disbelief.

Tigris continued, matter-of-factly, "Just how long after the cervix is stimulated the body begins to ovulate differs depending on the animal. For example, it's ten hours for hares, but in the case of

Rounds, it's about a week after the copulatory act. When that act isn't entirely consensual, sometimes ovulation doesn't begin until a month later. Since the pituitary gland is vulnerable to psychological influences, stress can delay ovulation. But as we continue to have sex with a compatible partner, both Rounds experience synchronous ovulation, making possible dual pregnancy. That's why children are always born in pairs. On rare occasions, one Round may have twins, in which case one couple can have three children at once. Four if both Rounds have twins. Five or six in the case of triplets."

"So it's always two or more. That must be quite a strain financially," Arino said.

"But an efficient method of creating offspring. Our bodies have been engineered for that purpose. A Round's pregnancy lasts five months. Some give birth at four months. Everything from the efficient insemination method, the short gestation period, to the swift maturation rate is expressly engineered so we can adapt quickly to any nonplanetary environment. Adaptation is our lifestyle."

For Shiohara and Ogata, the figure of this attractive masculine-looking Round talking about ovulation and pregnancy as if it were his own experience was enough to give them goose bumps.

Ordinarily, men couldn't fathom what the sensations of ovulating and being pregnant felt like. It was a difference between the sexes that could not be bridged no matter how women might try to explain. There was nothing anyone could do about that.

Men simply couldn't experience the pain and agony associated with female reproductive functions in the way women like Shiohara and Ogata could, nor did women have the right to expect them to. The reality was that Shiohara and Ogata couldn't understand the troubles associated with the male body either.

Their understanding of sensations relating to male sexual function was limited to imagination.

But the Rounds were different.

One Round was capable of knowing what it was like to both impregnate and be impregnated. Not just for a limited period but for a lifetime. That alone was enough to transform the worldview of the Round.

From the perspective of the conservatives on Earth and Mars, the Rounds were indeed strange beings. But from the Rounds' perspective, the Monaurals were a far more strange and restrictive race. Absolute hermaphrodites such as snails and sea slugs existed in Earth's natural world, and fish that changed sex depending on their social environment, such as clownfish, were also not rare. The incubation temperature of the fertilized eggs determined the sex of a lizard called the red head agama. The ciliate known as *Euplotes crassus* was not necessarily sexually compatible with every mate. These ciliated protozoa had something resembling sexual distinctions—only the possible sexual types numbered thirty-eight.

Thus, the binary system in which one's sex was predetermined before birth and remained fixed for a lifetime was nothing more than one variation among many in the natural world.

Calendula picked up one of the babies from the cradle and looked at Arino. "Babies are sweet whatever their subspecies, no? Would you like to hold em?"

"May I?"

"You look like you might have a way with children."

Arino took the baby and held em in his arms like he would his own. "You're very perceptive. I have a family back home."

"You left your family to come here?"

"That goes for all of the security staff. Since the job demands discretion rather than bravery, the department doesn't hire anyone who is single. Their thinking is that we won't act recklessly with a family to think about. The antiterror task force selects its members in much the same way."

"Your family must be very worried."

"We train and sharpen our skills daily so nothing will happen," Arino said. He gazed at the child in his arms. "Ey really is very sweet. Makes me homesick for Mars."

Calendula took the baby from Arino and offered em to Shiohara. She happily cradled em in her arms, while Ogata beamed as she peered at the child's face.

"The regulations prohibit us from having kids until the interior of our house is completed, but it just sort of happened," Tigris said, a bit bashfully. "It's been difficult building the house and caring for the children at the same time. We were looking for some people to help us. We're grateful for your help."

"Don't you have anyone in the special district to help you?" Ogata asked.

"We were planning to ask some friends at first. But then the doctor mentioned ey had some people in mind."

"I wonder if our helping was a good idea. I hope we didn't ruffle any feathers."

"Don't worry," Calendula said. "Most of the Rounds would rather be spared the trouble. I have a feeling they're relieved not to have been asked."

"By the way," Arino said, changing the subject, "I've been meaning to ask."

"Yes?"

"The other day, I ran into someone who might have been a Round in the corridor outside the special district. Ey was tall and thin—someone who might pass for a Monaural woman—and ey had a baby with em. I spoke to em, thinking that ey might be one of the station staff, and scared em off. If it's possible, I'd like to see em again and apologize. Do you know who it might be?"

"If you saw em outside the special district, it's probably Veritas. Sometimes ey goes to the infirmary for a counseling session with the doctor," replied Tigris, speaking of Tei.

"Why the infirmary outside the special district?"

"I offer to see em here inside the special district, but Veritas won't listen. When ey's agitated about something, ey comes straight to the infirmary to see me. I don't discourage it since I don't want to aggravate eir condition."

"Ey was very frightened," Arino said. "Ey said that ey'd be reprimanded if any of the Rounds or staff saw em talking to me."

"Yes, Fortia is strict that way. While it's true Monaurals aren't allowed inside the special district, there's no rule forbidding the Rounds from leaving it. Fortia is the one who looks down upon it."

"Why is that?"

"It's complicated," said Tigris. "I can understand how you must feel, but it's best you don't see Veritas. Ey was separated from eir partner not too long ago and is raising a child on eir own. The separation has taken a harsh toll on em. Even we can't seem to console em, so I doubt you'll be able to help. Ey also had some trouble working with the station staff and has grown a little suspicious of Monaurals since."

"So that's why the doctor's been counseling em," Arino said.

"You have a family, so you must understand. Sometimes, it's best for outsiders to leave well enough alone."

"I didn't know there was such a thing as divorce in Round society," said Arino. "I understand. But please give em my regards."

"Thank you. I'll be sure to pass on your kind sentiments."

A moment later, the door of the assembly hall opened.

A Round whom the security staff did not recognize stood in the doorway. It was Fortia.

Fortia took one look at the scene and glowered. "Doctor, what is the meaning of this? I informed Commander Shirosaki that Monaurals are not to come here."

Tei stood and answered, "It was my decision to bring them here. I don't work for the commander. I am an intermediary and a staff member of this station. I don't take orders from anyone, even if that person is you."

Fortia fixed a stern look on Tigris and Calendula. "Why did you agree to such a thing without consulting me?"

"Since the doctor brought them here," Tigris said softly, "I assumed they were authorized to be here."

"I authorized nothing of the sort. I'll ask the Monaurals

to leave at once."

Tigris and Calendula looked each other in the eye. Tigris nodded as if to relent. But before Calendula could open eir mouth to protest, Shiohara spoke up.

"We won't stay where we're not welcome. We didn't come here to start any trouble."

"Then you'll leave here, now."

"You don't have to tell us twice."

Shiohara patted Tigris and Calendula on the shoulder. "I'm sorry we couldn't finish the interior with you."

"Please, you were a great help. Thank you."

"We enjoyed our time here," Arino said. "We hope to see you again."

"Perhaps we can visit you sometime," Calendula offered.

"It's all right," Ogata whispered. "Something tells me your leader won't approve."

The security members said their goodbyes and left the assembly hall.

After sending Tigris and Calendula back to their residence, Fortia confronted Tei.

"What were you thinking? You know as well as I do the Monaurals are not to enter the special district."

"It's unnatural for us to be living apart on this tiny space station. This physical distance does nothing but exacerbate everyone's stress. As a doctor, I've observed this firsthand. The human psyche isn't so strong as to be able to completely put out of mind something that it knows exists."

"By *human*, are you referring to the Monaurals or the Rounds?"

"Both, of course," Tei said. "I'm not saying we have to get along. But all of us should be able to come and go as we please, like it used to be."

Fortia's eyes narrowed. "Have you forgotten what happened to Veritas? Do you want something like that to happen again?"

"I haven't forgotten. Neither has anyone on the station. We're only pretending that we have."

"Precisely the reason for maintaining this separation," Fortia said.

"I know that. But this isn't working anymore. The new security team knows nothing about the incident. They should be able to repair the relationship with the Rounds without any preconceived notions."

"The station's supervisors were the ones to prohibit access to the special district. Everyone agreed to it. Why should we change that now?"

"Every rule needs changing after a while."

"Don't be ridiculous, Lanterna."

"Don't call me by that name," Tei muttered. "I am an intermediary. I have a different name now."

"In any case, this can't happen again. I'll look the other way this time, but if there is a next time, I'll have to take more drastic measures."

"What? Will you exile Calendula and me to Station 2?" Tei asked. "I suppose that's exactly what you would do as superintendent of the special district. That's how you tried to segregate me from the others when you found out that my body isn't *normal*."

"You're wrong. We were trying to consider your feelings."

"Living apart will only serve to deepen the rift. Monaurals will grow to hate the Rounds, and the Rounds will scorn the Monaurals even more. The only difference between us is our physiology. Whatever technology was used to create us, we are essentially *intelligent beings*. In that sense, we're no different from the Monaurals. It's absurd not to be able to communicate with them."

"We will eventually leave the solar system," Fortia said. "We're destined to sever ties with the Monaurals altogether. Communication is meaningless."

"They have a culture we don't have in our society. A culture sustained by thousands of years of history. There are countless things we can learn from the Monaurals."

"Meaningless. We have nothing to gain from their history of wars and bloodshed."

"I'm not saying we have to embrace everything about them," said Tei. "But forbidding people from interacting with one another is wrong. They should at least be free to know more about the other if that's what they want."

"Is that what you want? Do you want to befriend the Monaurals?"

"They have many things we lack. I am a Round. A new breed of human. But I also respect the Monaurals."

Fortia fell silent for a long moment. Then ey muttered, "It was a mistake to appoint you as an intermediary."

Tei did not answer. Ey gripped both arms with eir nails and bit down hard on eir lips.

3

UNLIKE THE OTHER security members, Shirosaki had been assigned to a room of his own, albeit a small one. The tiny space could barely accommodate a communication terminal, desk, and bed. Nevertheless, he was afforded a modicum of privacy that the members of his security team were not.

The communication terminal bleeped.

Shirosaki tapped on the control panel, and the image of Fortia appeared onscreen.

He was taken by surprise at the sight of em, having been informed of the restricted access to the special district.

"We have to talk," Fortia began abruptly.

"What is it?"

"I thought we agreed there is to be no contact between the Rounds and Monaurals. Some of your people have already violated that agreement."

"Someone on my team?"

"Do you mean to tell me you haven't heard?" A look of irritation crept across Fortia's face. "You're their leader. How is it you're not aware of what is going on under your command?"

"I'm not privy to what goes on during private hours."

"This isn't an issue of privacy. Just what did you tell them about the special district?"

"That they're not to go there. None of the members' information has been entered into the system, so they couldn't have accessed the special district on their own. Even I need an escort to get in," Shirosaki said. "They must have gotten someone to take them. Who was it?"

"Dr. Tei."

"I see. Then it seems to me the breach in protocol is on your end, not mine."

Fortia scowled indignantly.

"What happened?" asked Shirosaki, his tone calm.

"Three Monaurals on your team entered the special district and assisted with unit building."

"Unit building—what is that?"

"A task shared among the Rounds."

"Maybe they were just lending a hand."

"It's nothing for which we need Monaural assistance. I can't dispute the doctor's role in this, but your people must have coerced em into bringing them here."

"I'd appreciate some time to look into it."

"Spoken like a Monaural. You're covering for them."

"As their commander, I have an obligation to find out the truth."

"Have you heard about Commander Harding?" Fortia asked.

"What about him?"

"He is the reason why we've confined ourselves inside the special district. He disrupted the order on this station. I don't want your team to repeat his mistakes."

"What happened with Harding?"

"He very nearly killed one of my colleagues."

Shirosaki knitted his brows. Nearly killed a Round? Harding? Surely Captain Hasukawa would have mentioned it in the report if anything that serious had happened.

Fortia's face was ashen and tense.

Something terrible had apparently befallen one of the Rounds for some complicated reason.

"We're here to protect you," Shirosaki said. "Regardless of what happened here in the past, my team and I don't want any trouble, I assure you."

"It's too late for that. Since the doctor was also involved, I'll let you people off with a warning, but if we have another incident like this again, there will be a severe penalty."

"I'll talk to the doctor. I need to find out what exactly happened."

After ending the transmission, Shirosaki sat on the edge of the bed.

Damn it. They were here on a critical mission to stop a terrorist attack. Who the hell had pulled a stunt like this?

After mulling over his next move, Shirosaki threw on his uniform and left his quarters.

The infirmary, located in the residential district, was where doctors oversaw the physical conditions of all the staff and Rounds in shifts. Inside the busy station, the doctors were responsible not just for medical care, but had other duties as well. When the four doctors on staff were not seeing patients, they were involved with conducting generation and growth experiments on various organisms.

Shirosaki waited until Tei would be going on call to pay a visit to the infirmary.

There was no one in the room other than Tei.

Shirosaki said hello and stepped inside. "I received a transmission from Fortia," he began. "I understand some of my people put you in a difficult spot."

"It's all right," Tei answered. "It was my choice to take them."

"Fortia wasn't all too pleased."

"That's the way Fortia is—imposing order is all ey has in eir head. Isn't ey a bore?"

"I'm afraid my staff only wanted to visit the special district out of curiosity. If you'd known that I doubt you would have complied."

"Yes, I was quite aware. I am a man and a woman, after all."

Tei offered Shirosaki a seat.

Shirosaki sat down on one of the patient stools. "You act as an intermediary between the Round and Monaural communities. Why are you defying Fortia?"

"On the contrary. It's because I'm an intermediary that I refuse to take sides." Seeing Shirosaki furrow his brow, Tei continued. "This station is a cage."

"A cage?"

"A cage built for the purpose of imprisoning the Rounds. To separate and keep us at a distance, to appease the Monaurals with the illusion that we do not exist. While we were born out of the will and aspirations of Monaurals, conservative Monaurals regarded us as deviants from the moment we were born. Like we were dangerous animals. For the Rounds, Jupiter-I is indeed the cage of Zeus."

A cage guarded by the eye of Zeus.

The words of his colleague who'd been possessed by Jupiter's Great Red Spot floated across Shirosaki's mind.

"What about you?" Tei asked. "Do you hate us like Commander Harding does?"

"My feelings have nothing to do with my mission here."

"If there is a fight with the terrorists, you may very well die trying to protect us. Are you prepared to die for a group for whom you have no feelings? Do you even believe we're worth protecting?" Tei asked.

"Worth has nothing to do with it. We're here on a special security assignment. We're bound by our duty to ensure your safety."

"Don't you have the right to refuse an order that goes against your will?"

"As hard as it may be for you to understand living here, our society is complicated."

Tei stared at Shirosaki as if ey were looking at a complete oddity.

"I understand a Round got into some trouble with Harding's team," said Shirosaki.

"Where did you hear that?"

"From Fortia. Something about Harding nearly killing em."

"It was an unfortunate incident. But I don't believe that was the commander's intention."

"But Fortia indicated that Harding had almost killed em."

"Fortia is prone to exaggeration."

"This isn't something to joke about. Please tell me what happened."

"It isn't for me to say. You're better off asking Commander Harding directly."

"He's liable to deck me if I do," Shirosaki said.

"I'd think a problem such as this would best be resolved among Monaural men."

"Surely you can't be serious. If you are, you've got the men in our society all wrong."

"How do you mean?" Tei asked.

"Harding is a proud man. He would never willingly reveal his own weaknesses. I can't possibly ask him knowing that, and as a matter of decency."

"What strange values you have. Are all Monaural men that way?"

"Not all, but that's the type of man Harding is," Shirosaki said.

"I have a feeling Commander Harding was the one who was hurt most by that incident. But you're the only ones who are capable of understanding that. I may not be able to read the delicate workings of his mind, but perhaps you can." Tei looked at Shirosaki with tranquil eyes. "I'm a doctor. I'm also a qualified counselor. I know what sedatives will calm a patient down. But some people can't be saved by that kind of care alone."

"Did Harding seek treatment?"

"He refused from the start. He wouldn't even let me take his pulse, simply because I'm a Round. Didn't speak to any of the other doctors either. He was leery of anyone trying to figure out what was going on in his head on the pretense of treatment." Smiling, Tei said gently, "Sometimes, he's like child."

"Fortia said any contact between the Rounds and Monaurals

is strictly prohibited. That nothing good will come of it. Why do you defy em?"

"Because it's unnatural to eschew contact. We were created by Monaurals, yet we know nothing about you. Could anything be stranger?"

"Having been born on this station, you were raised knowing little of anything other than what's here. Maybe you're just curious about us."

"Perhaps you're right. But isn't that reason enough? There are other Rounds who feel the same way but say nothing because they don't want to stir up trouble with Fortia. My job as an intermediary is to speak for those who don't have a voice."

"Harding aside, I hope you'll at least tell me the names of the security staff you took inside."

"Please don't punish them," Tei said. "They wouldn't have gone if I hadn't agreed to take them."

"Sorry, but they're going to get a grilling for what they've done."

"So you're like Fortia."

"We share similar responsibilities. You ought to have a little more consideration for Fortia's feelings."

Shirosaki got up from the stool.

"Do you think what I'm doing is a mistake?" Tei asked.

"That's not for me to decide," answered Shirosaki. "Or anyone else for that matter. It's up to you, Doctor."

Shirosaki summoned Arino to his room to question him.

"You are the sub-commander of this unit. What were you thinking by taking Shiohara and Ogata to the special district?"

"I'm sorry. It was stupid of me, I know," Arino said.

"The special district was ordered off-limits. What possessed you to disobey those orders?"

"I was curious, sir."

"Your reason stinks, you know that?"

"Yes, but..." Arino looked up and said, "I couldn't control

these feelings."

"What are you talking about?

"You don't feel it, Commander?"

"Feel what?"

"The feeling of complete loss when you lay eyes on a Round? That desire to know more about them, to have an accurate understanding of who they are?"

Shirosaki shot him a pitying look.

"I'm sorry." Arino hung his head.

"What do you think we're doing here, Arino?"

"We're here on a security detail, sir."

"That's right. In a few days, the first cargo vessels will arrive. The terrorists may be on one of them. You think you're going to be of any use to me the way you are now?" Shirosaki said.

"No, sir."

"Look," said Shirosaki with a sigh. "I get why you want to know more about the Rounds. I get why you're curious. But this isn't some pleasure trip we're on. What do you hope to accomplish by getting friendly with them? We'll be going back to Mars in a year, and the Rounds will eventually head to the front lines of known space. Their job is to leave the solar system. They're on a completely opposite path from where we're headed. All you'll feel is sad for having gotten too close to them. Just as the Rounds have their own society, you have a place to get back to. You have a wife and kid waiting for you at home, am I right?"

Arino nodded.

"I understand what you're telling me. But I can't have my subcommander acting this way."

"Yes, sir."

"We're in a situation here, so I can't afford to suspend you," Shirosaki said. "You get three months no pay. Now go back to your quarters."

4

LATER THAT EVENING, Arino went to the mess alone. He took some bread and a pack of stew from the heated case, dropped them on the tray, and sat down at a table.

On a rational level, he understood what Shirosaki was telling him. In fact, Arino knew it from the start. And yet, there was nothing he could do to resist.

Arino knew where this fervent obsession with the Rounds was coming from.

The feeling was something akin to homesickness.

As Arino wiped the rest of the stew off his plate with a piece of bread, Eiko Shiohara came by and sat down next to him.

"I thought three months was a little harsh," Shiohara said. "I figured on a month and a half at most."

Arino stuffed the bread into his mouth. "Serves me right for listening to you and Ogata."

"Don't blame us. You were just as eager about going as we were," said Shiohara. "Too bad you couldn't see Veritas."

"Yeah."

"It would have been nice to talk to her—you know, to help her get over her fears."

"I wonder what went wrong." Arino peeled off the seal of the coffee pack. "Maybe someone on Harding's team harassed her."

"About that." Shiohara switched from English to Japanese and lowered her voice. "I've heard rumors."

"Yeah?"

"About a Round getting hurt not too long after Harding's team arrived on Jupiter-I."

"What, like an accident or something?"

"The details are pretty sketchy," Shiohara said. "But the Rounds blame the Monaurals for what happened."

"And Veritas was the Round that was hurt?"

"Apparently so. The special district wasn't closed off from the rest of the station until recently. People used to come and go freely between the two areas. That all ended with the incident involving Veritas."

"Something must have happened between the Rounds and Harding's team," Arino said.

"Seeing how everyone involved is still here, we may be able to find out what if we do a little digging—"

Suddenly, a fist slammed against the table.

Shiohara nearly jumped out of her seat.

Harding was standing next to them.

"Playing detective so soon after your arrival?" said Harding, his Japanese fluent.

"We were just talking," Arino answered in Japanese. "There's still so much to learn about this place. All part of the job."

"Including talking shit about my team?"

"That isn't what we were doing," Arino said.

"Shirosaki let you talk back to him like that?"

"You're not my commander," Shiohara shot back in English. "Besides, I don't recall saying anything I have to be sorry about."

"What did you say?" Harding menaced, his face growing redder by the second.

"You're the one who caused this falling-out with the Rounds, aren't you? You despise the Rounds. For all we know, maybe you're the one who did something to Veritas."

Pursing his lips, Harding slowly walked around to the other side of the table toward Shiohara.

Shiohara held her ground and glared up at Harding from where she sat. Arino stood up.

Having sensed the ominous mood from one corner of the mess, Miles rushed in and grabbed Harding's arm from behind to stop his advance. "That's enough!"

Harding smacked Arino aside with one swing of his free hand, sending him crashing into the security personnel sitting behind them.

The mood inside the room froze. The eyes of the diners turned toward Harding and Shiohara.

Shiohara got up from her chair. With both hands on her hips, she dug in her heels and thrust out her chest like a mother scolding a child.

Looking down at her, Harding said, "I wouldn't go flapping your mouth based on speculation."

"All's fair in love and war."

Harding reached out to grab her. Miles intervened, wrapping his arms around Harding's torso. "Don't be stupid!" he cried. "You're a commander on this station." Then he yelled at Arino, "Hey, don't just stand there! Hold her back!"

Snapping out of his stupor, Arino sprang up and grabbed Shiohara by the back of her uniform.

"Let me go!" she cried.

"Miles is right," Arino yelled in Shiohara's ear. "Think of who you're up against!"

Harding twisted around, trying to shake Miles off him. Unable to get free, he clasped both hands, raised them above his head, and dropped an elbow down on the back of Miles's neck.

Miles did not loosen his grip around Harding's middle despite the pain. Harding cursed and swung wildly, punching Miles in the ribs. Still Miles refused to let go.

"Get the hell off me!" Harding roared.

Harding twisted his body hard in one direction and flung Miles against the edge of the table.

Miles let out a groan and let go, falling against the table on both arms. Just as he looked up, gasping for air, Harding punched him in the face. Losing his balance, Miles fell on his back.

Three members of his team jumped on Harding and held him down.

Pressing a hand against his nose, Miles staggered to his feet. The blood dripped from between his fingers.

Shiohara pushed Arino away and rushed to Miles's side.

Miles refused the handkerchief Shiohara offered him with a wave of a hand and spat out the blood in his mouth. Looking down as he pinched the bridge of his nose, he said in a muffled voice, "It's nothing. It's just a bloody nose."

He took a handkerchief from his pocket and wiped his face.

"You should go to the infirmary," said Shiohara.

"Yeah."

"I'll go with you."

"Actually, as long as I'm going there I'd rather let Harding take me." Miles called out to Harding, who was still being restrained by his men. "Why don't you show me what kind of leader you are? All right with you?"

Harding stopped and after taking a deep breath to calm himself, he answered, "All right. Let's go."

Shiohara began to protest that he couldn't be trusted, but Miles jabbed her in the side with an elbow. "I know Harding better than anybody. Don't worry."

Shiohara nodded reluctantly.

Although Harding was scowling as usual, he appeared to have regained his calm.

Miles fell in line next to Harding, covering his nose with one hand and patting Harding's back with the other. He turned to the others and grinned. "Looks like I made a mess," he said referring to the blood spattered on the floor. "Do me a favor and get that cleaned up, will you?"

After the two men had left the mess, Shiohara muttered, "I can't help thinking Miles would make a better leader. I wonder why they don't make him the commander of the team."

Arino let out a sigh. "Do you have any idea the trouble you've caused? You're cleaning up this mess. Go find yourself a mop."

5

OUTSIDE THE MESS, Harding mumbled an apology to Miles.

"Look, don't beat yourself up," Miles reassured him. "Just be thankful you hit me and not the girl. Shiohara is sure to have registered a formal complaint if you had."

"She hit too close to the mark. I couldn't let it go."

After rubbing under his nose to make sure the bleeding had stopped, Miles took out a packet of wet wipes from his pocket. As he wiped the stickiness off his hands, he asked, "You sleeping all right?"

"Yeah."

"You still taking the pills the doctor gave you?"

"No, they don't do me any good anyway."

"You may see some side effects if you quit taking them too soon," Miles said.

"It's remembering that scares me," mumbled Harding. "There are memories all over this station. Where we met. Where we talked. Even now, every time I turn the corner, I think I might see her. Like back then."

"What you did may not have been admirable. But I would have probably done the same if I were in your shoes. Everyone on the team knows that, which is why no one blames you for what you did."

"They may be quiet about it, but they must think I'm a disgrace. That they're better off with you in charge. Listen to me, Miles. You should relieve me and take over command."

"Once you're back on Mars, everything will work itself out," Miles said. "You'll forget everything. About the special district, the Rounds, and about her."

"No—every time I see Jupiter, I'll remember. It was a mistake I'll regret for the rest of my life."

Miles stopped and rested both hands on Harding's shoulders. He drew closer and whispered in his ear, "No one blames you for what happened. And no one thinks you should be punished. Shirosaki's team is in the dark about all of this, so they may talk a lot of shit, but it's all speculation. That goes for what Shiohara said. Call it women's intuition—doesn't mean she knows the truth."

Harding looked up, his expression haggard. "I'm tired. I just want to go back to Mars."

"Then let's get this job over with and go home, man, and leave all of this behind."

"Hasukawa authorized the use of extreme force to put down the terrorist threat. Then let's do it," Harding said, nodding, as much to convince himself as anyone else. "Then we can get the hell off this station."

6

WHEN THE BULK of the day's work on the house was done, Calendula informed Tigris, "I'm going to check in on Veritas. Keep an eye on the kids."

"What for?"

"To talk to em about Arino and to see if ey might be interested in seeing him."

"Don't go stirring up trouble. You saw how angry Fortia was," Tigris said.

"I don't have any intention of bringing him here. We're just going to talk. No harm in that."

Calendula went outside and walked down the path winding through the Round-made garden.

The environmental lighting inside the district was shifting to evening mode. Veritas's child would be asleep by now—a perfect time for two parents to have a conversation.

When Calendula arrived at Veritas's home, ey had just put down eir baby for the night and was taking a break.

"I'm sorry to barge in."

"Good timing, actually," said Veritas, gesturing toward the sofa.

Calendula sat down and waited in the living room, while Veritas disappeared into the kitchen. Ey returned with two packs of herbal tea.

"How are you feeling?" asked Calendula.

"I'm better." Veritas sank down on the sofa, eir long legs dangling over the edge. "The doctor has been advising me, so I'm in better spirits."

"Do you remember the last time you went to see the doctor?"

"Two or three days ago. What about it?"

"You ran into a Monaural on your way back."

"Yes, he stopped me in the corridor and tried to touch me and my baby. I was terrified. I thought I was in danger again."

"He wanted to apologize for talking to you without knowing anything," Calendula explained. "He's a recent arrival and wasn't familiar with the rules of the station. He asked for your forgiveness."

Veritas's eyes grew wider. "You met him?"

"Yes."

"He's not here, is he?"

"Don't worry, he's gone. We spoke for a while. He seemed like a good man."

"How could you, Calendula?" The anger in Veritas's voice rose. "Have you forgotten how irrational they can be?"

"That's exactly what Fortia said, which is all the more reason why I want to have a normal conversation with the Monaurals. And besides, if we sever contact with them over this, aren't you going to be the saddest out of all of us?"

Veritas slammed eir tea pack down on the table. "You have no idea what I'm feeling! Why should we try to develop a friendship with the Monaurals? We'll only be courting more danger."

"Do you have any desire to meet with Arino at all? Maybe talking to him will help you see that there are some good people among them. He really seemed like a kindhearted man."

"No."

"Are you afraid?" Calendula asked.

"As difficult as this may be to understand, I'm terrified to put myself in that situation again. Monaural men are intensely drawn to Rounds of my type. The way they look at you with that strange glint in their eyes, like beasts. The way they mentally undress you. You know as well as I do what that's like."

"Yes, I'm aware we share the same characteristics."

"I don't have any desire to subject myself to that nastiness just to talk to him. If you want to see him, be my guest. But leave me out of it," Veritas said.

"But telling them how they make us feel is important too. If they hear what we have to say, the Monaurals will have to rethink their behavior."

"Go right on ahead, but don't involve me."

"All right, Veritas. I won't force you. I'm sorry I even brought it up."

Calendula got up from the sofa.

Veritas remained sitting as ey looked up at Calendula. "Why are you so interested in the Monaurals? They come and go every year. Once they leave, you'll never see them again."

"That's just it—because we can only get to know them while they're here. I'm curious to know the Monaurals in the same way I'm curious to unlock the secrets of deep space."

7

AFTER LEAVING SHIOHARA in the mess, Arino headed for the infirmary to look in on Miles.

But neither Miles nor Harding was anywhere to be found.

"They just left," said Tei, who was on call. "He had a bloody nose. He seemed fine, so I sent him back to his quarters."

"Were they fighting?"

"What? Hardly. Harding seemed terribly down about something, and Miles was trying to console him despite being the one that was hurt." Tei looked Arino in the eye. "Were you the one who hit him?"

"Well, no."

"By the way, I have a message from Calendula."

"For me?" Arino asked.

"As a matter of fact, I was just planning to pay you a visit. Calendula wanted me to ask you to come and see em in the relaxation room tomorrow at 20:00."

"Where do I find the relaxation room?"

"Inside the central axis. There's an elevator that will take you directly there from the residential district. But first, you'll need to check out a directional control device for when you go into the zero-G area. You'll find it difficult to get around without it."

Arino checked a map of the station on one of the terminals. Just as Tei had said, the relaxation room was inside the station's central axis and zero-G area.

The high-velocity elevator transported him there in a matter of seconds. He stepped off the elevator to find himself in a zero-gravity environment. He bounced down the hall encircling the central axis and upon finding the entrance, slid open the door and peered in.

A colorful pattern of tiles like stained glass came into view.

The room was dark, but the soft light filtering in from the colored tiles filled the area with a sobering solemnity.

Arino felt as though he'd entered a cathedral.

The world on the other side of the door had a wall but no floor. The diameter of the area inside the central axis measured ten meters. The wall was covered with multicolored tiles, and a thin pole traversed up and down the center of the room.

Although the tiles did not represent any particular design, their abstract arrangement seemed to conjure a variety of images.

Arino kicked away from the edge of the door and leapt toward the center of the room.

The door automatically closed behind him, shutting out the light from the hall.

It was quiet.

Apparently, neither music nor heated discussions were allowed inside the relaxation room.

Grabbing hold of the pole, Arino circled around it several times and stopped, the friction killing the kinetic energy. At this speed, he was able to stop without using the propulsion device strapped to his waist.

As he clung to the pole, he looked up and down the cylindrical room.

The height of the cylinder might have been about thirty meters. The ceiling and floor were painted black and decorated with tiny lights to simulate stars. Or perhaps the view from outside the station was being projected onto screens.

Several people floated above and below him. The center of the room was curiously empty. The people stuck close to the walls, perhaps feeling more at ease there.

One appeared to be napping in a fetal position. Another was meditating. Another seemed to be listening to music on a sound system only he could hear.

Arino searched high and low for Calendula.

Calendula entered from a door above him. Spotting Arino right away, ey floated toward him and nimbly came to a stop around the pole with one twirl.

"I tried, but I couldn't convince Veritas to come," Calendula said. "Ey's too afraid of you."

"Gee, was I that rude?"

"You looked em up and down."

"What?"

"That's what Monaurals do. You leer at us from top to bottom as if undressing us with your eyes."

"I don't recall being as bad as that. If I was staring, it wasn't out of malice. I was trying to be friendly."

"It's your insensitivity that offends us."

When Arino started to object, Calendula raised a hand. "You musn't make a scene here."

Calendula kicked away from the pole and moved to where it was more private. Arino followed, then stepped on one of the shock absorbers embedded in the tiled wall and came to a stop.

Calendula said, "We were born and raised within the confines of this station, so we're extremely sensitive to the eyes of others. In our society, staring at someone is considered very disrespectful. I know you have a habit of observing someone from afar on Earth and Mars where it's more spacious. But you can't do that here."

"No offense intended."

"Swear to me you'll never do it again."

"I swear. I won't," Arino said.

"And please tell the others. You're all going to be here for at least another year."

"I promise."

"Veritas is terrified of Monaurals. Because you don't understand our customs."

"I'm sorry."

"Only partners can gaze at each other like that in our society," Calendula said. "So when someone other than a partner stares at us, we're very uncomfortable. Do you understand?"

Arino nodded.

"Veritas was once in love with a Monaural man," Calendula said.

Arino blinked. *In love? A Round with a Monaural?* An image flashed across his mind that nearly made him yelp. *Could that Monaural be…?*

"But things ended badly with that Monaural. And because of what happened to Veritas, the Rounds have become wary of all Monaurals."

"Did the bastard do something to hurt em?"

"I can't say for certain. Veritas doesn't say much about the incident, and details of the inquiry were never made public."

Arino lowered his gaze. Given the incident, no wonder the Rounds were afraid of them.

"Why aren't you afraid of me, Calendula? The way Veritas is?"

"I suppose I'm more curious than afraid. We're all different, you know."

"Curious about what?"

"Why Monaurals are only capable of seeing us as one sex," Calendula said. "You have intersex people in your society. Then why do you think of having two sexes as abnormal? From our perspective, the Monaurals are a very inconvenient and peculiar people. You're restricted by one sex and possess the reproductive organs of only one sex. How does that affect the way your mind operates? How do sexual distinctions change your way of thinking? How does your society manage to maintain equilibrium despite all the disparities that arise between the sexes? How can a society with sexual differences manage to nurture the same unshakable solidarity as ours, which has no such differences? These are the things I'm curious about. Like solving the mysteries of the universe. Tell me, Sub-commander Arino. How do I look in your eyes? Do you see me as a man? Or a woman?"

The light trickling in from the colored tiles shimmered behind Calendula like a heat haze. Calendula, who'd only looked like a woman to Arino at first, was beginning to seem more male with every passing moment.

In the end, it all boiled down to perception. Whether Arino saw em as a man or woman did not change the fact that physically, ey was bigender. Ey was capable of simultaneously inseminating eir partner and being inseminated. Calendula didn't merely self-identify as bigender, nor had ey been born bigender via a chromosomal fluke. Ey was not an imaginary creation of some mystic or an angel that had conveniently transcended the sexes.

The Round standing before him was a proper biologically bigender being.

"Both," Arino answered. "Finally, I see you as both."

"Would you like this body? Would you like to be bigender yourself?"

A shiver running down his spine, Arino imagined his body with female reproductive organs.

A body with the ability to both impregnate and be impregnated at the same time.

What kind of person would he become if his body were to acquire both sexual functions? How would he think? What would his likes and dislikes be? And how would he act? The body creates the psyche, which in turn creates the body. Just what kind of being would he become as a result of both influences?

Arino was secretly shocked by the part of him that was considering the question. He'd been married to his wife for five years and had a three-year-old at home. His wife was a woman, biologically and psychologically, and also heterosexual. Not once had Arino questioned his sexuality until he'd come here.

Had he been deceiving himself all this time? Was one's sexuality so easily changed? Or was he merely getting carried away by this new encounter?

"Is that even possible?" Arino asked.

"Unfortunately, no. There are people on Earth and Mars who want to be injected with double-I, but switching out the sex chromosomes alone won't make you a Round."

Arino let out a sigh of relief.

"Disappointed?"

"Maybe a little."

Calendula smiled.

"If all the station staff were like you, none of us would have encountered as much difficulty as we have." Then ey muttered, "If only everyone would become Rounds. Then there would be fewer prejudices in this world."

8

OVER TWENTY YEARS had passed since Kline first came to Jupiter-I—about the time it took for Jupiter to make two revolutions around the sun.

When she'd first learned of the existence of the special district, she had been shocked and moved and felt an intense desire to protect it.

A subspecies both male and female. Not the fantasies of body modification fanatics or hermaphrodites with cosmetic genitalia made possible through artificial organ transplantation.

The Rounds were the kind of beings—having functioning genitalia of both genders—envisioned in Plato's *Symposium*.

No matter how progressive and extraordinary they were, the Rounds were seen as anomalies by Monaural society. In a society comprised entirely of absolute hermaphrodites, however, they would be the norm.

Indeed, the special district was an ideal community. If Kline could protect this haven, in time the Monaurals' value system would gradually change.

Having anticipated the station would become a target of Monaural terrorists from the start, Kline had been instrumental in pushing through the exorbitant budgetary expenditure required for the installation of Jupiter-I's omnidirectional warning system. She had also recognized the need to demonstrate that this was no defenseless paradise, but a fortress built to defend a new ideology.

Kline was prepared to crush any group knowingly threatening to breach the walls.

If it were possible, Kline would grab a gun and face the enemy herself. She had no scruples about killing if she could protect the Rounds.

Kline rested on a sofa in the observatory and sipped a glass of bourbon.

A million stars were displayed on the omnidirectional screen and the floor screen at her feet. Europa, one of Jupiter's moons, filled the screen directly in front of her.

Europa resembled an old marble marred by scratches. Or a glass orb striated with intricate cracks. Its color was clear blue from the thick layers of ice covering the surface and brown from the sulfide deposits seeping to the surface from within.

The dark cracks gashing the surface were the dull red of dried blood. The intricate fissures crisscrossing the entire surface reminded Kline of the chapped fingers of an overworked laborer.

Europa was approximately 3,138 kilometers in diameter, about the size of Earth's moon.

Hidden beneath the thick ice crust covering the globe lay a vast ocean one hundred kilometers deep, rich in sulfuric acid and magnesium sulfate, unlike the oceans of Earth.

Europa was a frozen moon with a daytime surface temperature of minus 130 degrees Celsius.

Scientists drilled the ice crust in search of microorganisms trapped inside. They also continued to probe for whether oceanic life-forms like those on Earth existed on Europa.

Jupiter-I served, in part, to support those activities. In time, scientists discovered a hot geyser along with organisms that relied on the sulfuric oxides contained within the geyser water to exist. What they had unearthed was a biotic community that had developed in much the same way as the biotic community discovered in the depths of Earth's oceans. Biologists also confirmed the existence of organisms living in a similar oceanic atmosphere on Ganymede. And now they were exploring Callisto's ocean, hoping to discover a third ecosystem in the Jovian system there.

Reports of life on the Jovian moons served to remind not only scientists but the public just how immeasurably profound and mysterious the universe was. The news inspired awe in the fierce resilience of life.

These life-forms on Europa and Ganymede lived regardless of human expectation and died quietly once they'd expended the life given them. They neither resisted nor surrendered to the environment they found themselves in, but simply used it to survive.

Kline could not help but feel awestruck and envious of the single-minded tenacity of life.

She heard a knock, snapping her out of her musings. Dan Preda walked into the observatory.

"Well, this is a rare sighting," said Kline as she set her glass down on the table.

"I like to have a drink or two under the stars from time to time." Preda sat down diagonally across from Kline, holding a glass of his own. "I daresay we have a real situation on our hands. To think, an actual terrorist threat."

"We don't know anything for certain yet. Even if the threat is real, the two security teams should have little problem defeating the terrorists."

"But with Harding commanding one of the teams…"

"Commander Shirosaki is a man we can trust. I'm sure he'll keep Commander Harding in check. Miles will be there too."

"Yes, I suppose we can only hope for the best." Preda sipped from his watered-down drink enriched with vitamin C.

The door opened again, and another visitor entered the observatory. "Oh, there you are."

Microbiologist Von Chaillot approached holding a bottle of Martian beer in one hand.

Von kissed Preda and Kline on the cheek and joined them. "Is it true we have a terrorist threat?"

"Well, it seems the whole station is abuzz about it," said Preda. "I hear some of the station staff have a little bet going."

"A bet? About what?" Kline asked.

"The time the security staff will need to neutralize the terrorist threat. They're trying to predict it down to the minute."

"What was the shortest time?"

"One minute. I think the longest was fifteen."

Smiling, Von held out a memory plate in Kline's direction. "I promised you this. Care to see it now?"

"Thank you. I think I will."

Kline inserted the plate in her wearable. After sending the commands remotely to the observatory's control system from her wearable, the stars on the omnidirectional display disappeared and the images contained in the memory plate came up on screen.

A constellation of a different kind filled the black screen.

Moving their tiny flagella, the luminescent bodies spun around busily like windmills.

"What do we have here?" Preda asked. "Your latest discovery?"

"Bioluminescent microorganisms found inhabiting the ocean beneath Europa's ice shell. We haven't determined why they emit light like they do. We think they might naturally give it off during metabolic activity, rather than for any particular purpose."

"Something like 'Europa sea fireflies.'"

"If that's what you'd like to call them. They haven't been given a scientific name yet."

"How about naming one of your discoveries after me?" Preda said. "All told, you've found thousands of marine microorganisms on Europa and Ganymede, haven't you?"

"I'll put in the request myself if you can send some funding our way."

"So even names can be bought for a price," Preda said.

"Anything to continue our research."

Kline tapped a button, and a larger spherical organism appeared onscreen.

"Now here's an odd one," said Von cheerfully. "This is a microbe colony, comprised of a single type of microbe that moves about in clusters like this one. The rate at which the microbes die and new ones are born in their place differs depending on where they exist in the colony. The outer microbes die faster than those on the inside."

"Why is that?"

"Maybe it's a defense mechanism against the elements contained in Europa's ocean, or perhaps it's due to the cold temperature or oxygen concentration. The outer microbes act like a kind of wall to protect the microbes on the inside and adapt to their environment through the repeated process of reproducing and dying off. They may be in the process of becoming multicellular organisms. In a couple hundred years, this colony may evolve into a single life-form."

Operating the screen from her own wearable device, Von brought up another image. "Not exactly my area of expertise, but here's a recently discovered species of crustacean. It even made the news on Earth and Mars."

"Looks like a crab," Preda said.

"Exactly right. It's called the *Europa crab*."

"I wonder how they taste boiled."

"I suppose that depends on their composition. If they contain high levels of ammonia, they won't be good for eating."

Von tapped a button, and a video of shimmering creatures came up onscreen. They resembled jellyfish on Earth, contracting and expanding their bell-shaped bodies as they drifted in the void.

"They really are soothing to look at," said Kline.

"You should come to Europa and see them with your own eyes."

"I think I will—just as soon as this is all over."

Von worked in the lab on Europa. Her job entailed exploring Europa's ocean in a research submarine to gather data on the water composition, current patterns, and marine life.

She and her assistant Ted visited Jupiter-I periodically to analyze specimens with equipment not available on Europa and to send reports back to Earth.

She and Kline had been friends for ten years.

Von had been twenty-seven when she first met Kline; she was thirty-seven now. Kline knew that Von had gone to college after having spent much of her youth working to earn tuition money, but she looked much younger than her actual age. People who did what they loved always seemed so youthful. Von's features reflected mixed Asian heritage. She did not have the cool, well-proportioned features of an actress or model, but a kind of beauty that seemed both familiar and nostalgic.

"Will you be checking what we bring from our labs in the docking bay too?" Von asked. "I'm not crazy about anyone going through our cargo. We'll be transporting organisms that need to be kept at controlled temperatures."

"It's a simple inspection, but I'll let the security teams know to take extra care with your specimens."

"I just don't want anything to happen to our precious samples. Besides, we don't have any suspicious types working in our labs. There's no way the terrorists will come here by way of Europa."

"Yes, but the cargo vessel coming from Europa is unmanned. It's possible they might commandeer it en route."

"En route? But that ship isn't equipped to accommodate passengers."

"We just don't know how the terrorists plan to infiltrate the station," said Kline. "Better to be safe than sorry."

Von asked to have the run of one of the labs, as she usually did, once the cargo vessel arrived, to which Kline readily agreed. "You can reserve a lab through the system. I'm sure no one will bother you."

"Thanks. I'll be holed up for a while, but I'll come up for air eventually."

"Just make sure you eat. I remember that one time you forgot to eat for three days."

"I lose all track of time when I'm working."

"Now listen. I'll arrange to have meals sent to the lab. You make sure Ted eats too. A man of his size won't survive, even if you can do without a meal or two."

"What about you?" Von asked Kline. "You look pale. Has something happened again?"

"Nothing new," Preda cut in before Kline could answer. "Some of the Rounds are complaining about intrastation relations."

"Tell me about it," Von said.

Kline recounted the goings on inside the space station to Von, embellishing some details to humorous effect as she usually did. About how members of Shirosaki's security team initiated friendly contact with the Rounds. And how that resulted in a quarrel.

"I see," Von said, with a single nod. "You remember what happened to Veritas."

"Well, yes."

"Then you can't allow this contact to continue. You're only asking for trouble if you do."

"I know. Fortia has repeatedly instructed the younger generation, so I assumed the Rounds understood. But some of them just can't seem to suppress their curiosity," Kline said. "And it's no help that the Monaurals, who are just as curious, are the ones that inevitably instigate trouble."

Von tried to stifle a laugh. "Maybe someone needs to do a better job of teaching the Rounds just how cruel and vicious the people outside the special district are."

"And tell them what—that the women are just as savage as the men?"

"Yes, and that even women can sexually threaten a Round. Isn't it your job to ensure the Rounds aren't reduced to Monaural playthings?"

"To tell you the truth, there's a part of me that's not so sure."

"About what?"

"Maybe the best way to get the rest of the world to accept the Rounds is to openly promote the fact that the Rounds get along with the Monaurals here."

"The people on Mars and Earth aren't stupid," Von said. "They're bound to see through such a transparent PR stunt. Isn't the reason why you had to come here in the first place because the Rounds and Monaurals couldn't coexist? If they were able to simply get along in the first instance, you would have been able to conduct your experiments anywhere. But you couldn't because you knew the two ideologies would collide."

"Yes, but—"

"Don't worry. The relief team and the Rounds are only engaged in a kind of play because, at the moment, they only recognize what's good about the other. In time, they'll lose interest and drift apart."

"Do you think so?"

"I can see you're overworked. You really should get away from the station sometime. You should come to Europa," Von offered. "I'll take you for a ride in the research submarine. One look at the ocean will help clear your mind right up."

"Thanks. I'm impressed you've lasted as long as you have on that frozen rock."

"Because of what's underneath," Von said. "When I think about all the life-forms yet to be discovered in that ocean, it gives me the chills. At times, I've even thought of all the creatures in that ocean as my children. Undiscovered, unnamed children. And I'm the one to find them and give them names. That's a job I'd gladly give my life to."

"You sound like you're married to Europa," Preda said teasingly.

"Yes, that's right," Von answered proudly. "We were betrothed after I fell head over heels in love with Europa's ocean. I much prefer her to human men. Always faithful."

"Indeed."

The image of the microorganisms onscreen lured Kline, now comfortably mellowed by the bourbon, into a moment of reverie.

Maybe I will go to Europa after this is all over, Kline thought. *Yes, I'll take a long break and forget all the station's troubles.*

9

THE ROUNDS MADE use of the central axis's zero-gravity environment in much the same way the station staff used the central axis area as a relaxation room. Children used it as a playground, while others meditated there as the Monaurals did. The space was subdivided into two sections—one for children and one for adults.

Mare, the special district's education supervisor, reported a fight in the zero-G zone to Fortia.

"At two years old, they like to roughhouse." Mare was frowning onscreen. "I thought you should know someone was injured."

"Any broken bones?" Fortia asked.

"Yes, but it wasn't a child. It was one of the adults who stepped in to stop them."

Mare had scolded them severely but wanted Fortia to reprimand the children as well so they would learn their lesson. Fortia agreed. Patrolling the residences and elsewhere in the special district was part of eir daily duties, and ey had been about to make the rounds anyway.

"Also, the second generation thinks it's about time we used implant communicators," Mare said.

"Like the Monaurals? Why would we need implants in a habitat as small as the special district? Our wearable devices suffice."

"When something like this happens again, with implants we can send messages directly into the children's ears."

"No amount of yelling in their ear is going to make a difference if no one is there to stop them."

"With the implants," Mare said, "we can send signals directly to the brain to temporarily freeze the children's motor functions."

"We would be resorting to mind control," Fortia said.

"I believe a sense of unity is critical, especially in as confined a society as ours."

"As much as we're in the position to supervise the district, we do not rule over it. We resolve our issues by talking. We have no need to rely on Monaural inventions."

The only means of distance communication inside the special district were the stationary terminals used to communicate with the station staff and the wearable devices for personal use—indeed obsolete technology. Implant devices, on the other hand, were standard issue among Monaural researchers and security staff and were used not only for conversation but to access databases.

The Rounds were not authorized to use implants because of the Rounds' role as medical test subjects. Doctors had decided that implants could skew the results of their experiments.

"Our databases are filling by the day," Mare pointed out. "We'll be able to increase search efficiency if we implement a neural connection system. The implants will also be useful for educating the children. If they develop a habit of looking up information anytime and anywhere for themselves, we can nurture and maintain their curiosity for knowledge."

"Can we wait awhile? Once we begin colonizing Saturn, we'll enter the second phase of experiments. We can submit a request to Kline for implants as a lifestyle modification then," said Fortia. "Right now, we still rely on the Monaurals to keep the special district running. But if we can make this place a sovereign state, not just in name but in reality, and become truly independent, we'll be able to change how we associate with the Monaurals."

Fortia spent the next several days checking up on the workings of the special district. Ey spoke to the engineers in charge of maintaining the bioengineered plants, inspected the harvest conditions of the garden, and checked the operations of the recycling plant. Ey also visited the astrometrics facilities as well as the laboratories where the Rounds were conducting some independent biological and engineering experiments.

Fortia then went around to all of the residential units and met with each of the Rounds of the first generation and second generation. In doing so, ey was able to get a record of the general mood of the 150-plus adults and children of the community.

There was one thing that worried Fortia. Was Tei the only one trying to repair the strained relations between the Rounds and Monaurals, or were there others? Did people like Calendula and Tigris support Tei? And if so, why had they kept silent about it to em, the leader of the special district? Ey intended to find answers by analyzing the audio data ey'd gathered from speaking with each of the Rounds.

Fortia also visited the zero-gravity area in the central axis.

The adults-only section was quiet; several Rounds were meditating, floating balled up in a fetal position inside the dimly lit room.

The children's section was also relatively quiet when Fortia peered in through the door. But when ey entered the room, the children swarmed around em and tugged at eir tunic. They whooped and hollered as they clung to and hung on eir arms.

Fortia's wearable bleeped almost instantly; Fortia answered it. On the other end was a Round who'd been surveilling the scene from a hidden camera in the children's section.

"I'm sorry. I'll be there immediately to quiet them."

"It's all right," Fortia said, gently patting the head of the tiny Round that had hurled emself at em in a bear hug. "Are they always like this?"

"Yes."

"The children of the second generation tended to be more shy. How long has this been going on?"

"It varies, but the two- and three-year-olds are very active."

"That's good to hear. I'll be there after I've played with them a little. Get your supervisors together."

Recalling the time eir own children were born, Fortia spent some time playing with the children. Ey told them eir name and title and encouraged them to visit em anytime they wanted to talk about life in the special district. Guileless as the children were, they groaned and clung to Fortia when ey started to leave. One child was even teary-eyed, and Fortia had to go around appeasing each of them before ey could leave the room.

At the meeting, the five members in charge of education, including Mare, gave Fortia an update on the schooling of the third generation. All of the Round children were given computerized interactive lessons, allowing them to learn at their own pace. The five educators then instructed them in areas that couldn't be covered online, such as socialization and interpersonal communication. Collaborative work, involving machine building and experiments and observations in the zero-G zone, was also part of those lessons.

Fortia didn't notice any conspicuous problems with the third generation's progress. While their academic achievements varied as might be expected, they were all satisfying the set standards.

The third generation encompassed a broad age group. The oldest Rounds were just short of adulthood, and the youngest were still babies. Since the Monaurals regulated the schedule of Round births, the Rounds could not procreate whenever and however they pleased. There were budgetary concerns to consider. The population could not be easily increased, owing in part to the limited availability of food, equipment, oxygen, and water in the special district.

The Rounds' education was based on Monaural curriculum, covering three areas: science, medicine, and language. The science curriculum included mathematics, physics, chemistry, astronautics, information engineering, astronomy, geology, and planetary biology. The medical curriculum was comprised of medicine, biochemistry, and reproductive science. The only language requirement was English, and the Latin names given to the children were merely taken from a dictionary in the databases. Since a comprehensive database of non-English languages was available, for the most part, the Rounds were able to communicate with the Monaurals by using a universal translator.

Because the Rounds matured three times faster than Monaurals, they began their education at an earlier age.

Between the ages of two and a half and six, they were taught the fundamentals of living in space and basic science, medicine, and English. Unlike the schools on the planets, there were no summer vacations or extended holidays for the Rounds, who knew nothing of the world outside the special district. With a constant schedule devoted to classes and play, they were quickly able to accumulate knowledge and develop their critical thinking skills.

After completing their primary education, the children chose a specialization according to their interests and began their studies and practical training in their chosen profession. To the Rounds, the special district was their world. Everyone had a job with specific appointed duties, and aside from periods devoted to raising children, no one was allowed to laze around doing nothing.

Every person was crucial and everything inside the special district had a reason for existing. Otherwise, anything or anyone thought to be a waste of resources and energy had to be evaluated and eliminated.

After finishing their report on the children's education, the supervisors moved on to the subject of the adult Rounds.

"I think we need to reeducate the second generation," one of them said. "Since they've had extensive communication with the station staff, they've been exposed to the written and visual works brought into the station by Monaurals. Monaural paintings, literature, and songs contain stories with sexual distinctions not reflective of our society."

"They insist they're fully cognizant of those differences, but in the long term, I think we need to be wary of Monaural influences on our culture," another added.

"Are you detecting any noticeable changes?" Fortia asked.

"Some have started to imitate the Monaurals and have begun to write stories and songs of their own. They've been writing love stories taking place in Round culture and composing songs about romantic relationships. Some of them describe relationships between Rounds and Monaurals. I hear these Rounds get together during their time off to share what they've written."

"I don't understand. Why would they create such things knowing what happened to Veritas?"

"Curiosity. Veritas was the only one hurt in the incident, and everyone else was a passive onlooker. Since any association with the Monaurals is forbidden, they're probably trying to live vicariously through the stories."

"What does Veritas say about all of this?" Fortia asked.

"Ey grins and bears it. Veritas doesn't say anything to stop it nor to encourage it. Ey said ey's grown used to being talked about. Anyone who wants to fantasize about associating with the Monaurals is free to go on doing so, ey said. What shall we do? Should we forbid their activities altogether or place restrictions on what they can write about?"

"Either way they'll likely continue behind closed doors."

"Yes."

"Then let them be," Fortia said. "We'll require the Monaurals' financial support for a while after we go to Saturn. If some of the Rounds are able to find some respite inside these stories, then so be it. Better that than to violate the rules and fraternize with the Monaurals in reality."

"What if the stories influence others to emulate Veritas?" one of the other educators asked.

"Then they'll have to learn the hard way by being hurt themselves."

"We believe that reeducating the second generation might inspire works of art unique to Round culture," another teacher said. "Stories and paintings and music for and by Rounds."

"Art isn't something to be bestowed. When the time is right, our society will naturally conceive an art free of Monaural influence. Have a little patience."

"So we won't take any action?"

"I think that's advisable," said Fortia. "But I'd like to know what all of you think."

After about four hours of discussions with the education committee, Fortia returned to eir residence.

Ey went straightaway to the bedroom, without dinner, and threw eir weary body on the bed.

Jupiter was displayed on the screen taking up most of one wall in the bedroom.

That gas giant, banded with streaks of color, was a sight Fortia never tired of seeing.

In fact, hearing that some Monaurals went mad from staring at it had shocked em. Ridiculous. What could be more inspiring than the eternal swirling clouds of Jupiter?

The Rounds were headed beyond Jupiter. Beyond the eye of

Zeus and even farther beyond the solar system. Fortia's heart raced just thinking about it. The universe held limitless mysteries and perils for those thirsting to comprehend it, and tested the wills of its explorers, forcing them to confront their mortality.

Fortia worried that the second generation's curiosity was being directed less toward space and more toward internal matters such as their relationship with the Monaurals.

The Rounds had overstayed their time on Jupiter-I.

Unlike Monaurals born on Earth and Mars, the Rounds had lived in proximity to Jupiter from the start. The law forbade them to travel to the planets.

Thus, the only home that existed for the Rounds from the very beginning was Saturn and beyond. That was where their curiosity should be directed. But because the construction of the supership was delayed, they had found a diversion in the Monaurals.

Something had to be done.

"I'm not surprised," said Album. "The Monaurals from Earth and Mars are too much of a temptation for the Rounds. As intelligent and inquisitive as the Rounds are, they can't help being fascinated by everything. It's a double-edged sword. We'll just have to make laws to restrain them. With laws of our own making."

"You want us to do something to restrict the Rounds?"

"They're only acting out because there's no penalty for doing so. All we have to do is increase our numbers and toss out the bad apples."

"And what becomes of these bad apples?"

"They can work in Monaural society," Album said. "After their sex is surgically fixed, of course."

Fortia pondered what Album was telling em. "The Monaurals control our procreation. We'll have to discuss it with Kline."

IV

1

ON THE DAY the first cargo vessels were scheduled to arrive, Shirosaki and Harding stationed eight members of the security teams at the entrance to the special district.

The remaining thirty-two guarded the docking bay. Two cargo ships were scheduled in from Asteroid City, and one unmanned vessel carrying lab specimens from Europa was also due.

The two vessels from Asteroid City arrived first.

The automated system transported the containers into the station's warehouse. The security teams inspected the cargo containers brought in on the lift one by one.

Next, the two fully armed squads boarded the vessels and searched inside and out. The members all wore full environmental suits to protect against biological or chemical weapons.

Shirosaki waited outside the warehouse along with the remaining members of the security teams.

Given the mundane nature of the operation, Harding had put Shirosaki in charge of the inspections. In the event of an emergency, however, Harding would assume operational command.

Having heard about the altercation in the mess, Shirosaki worried about Harding turning into a loose cannon in a combat situation.

Harding wasn't the type to lose control on a whim. In fact, despite his fierce temperament, he was probably actually a reasonable man. Which was why he would be harder to keep in check if he lost control. Shirosaki recognized how much harder it was to rein in someone acting on conviction than someone fueled by emotion.

As much as he understood the man's reticence, Shirosaki wished Harding would tell him what had gone on between his team and the Rounds. Harding and his team would return to Mars once this mission was over. But Shirosaki would be cooped up in this station for at least another year. He wanted as much information as humanly possible, especially about matters that had not been reported to Captain Hasukawa.

Harding silently looked on as his team continued the task at hand. He didn't so much as crack a joke with Shirosaki. Shirosaki entertained the idea of asking Harding point blank before he was set to leave the station, but the very thought made him uneasy.

The inspection turned up nothing from the two cargo vessels. The crew aboard were seasoned regulars who'd spent years shuttling between Asteroid City and Jupiter. Once the inspection was complete, the crewmembers made their way to the recreation facilities for a drink with some friends they'd made on the station. The security staff looked on in envy as the crew exited the docking bay.

A flashing light signaled the arrival of the unmanned vessel from Europa. This would be the last vessel. After this, the next shipment from Asteroid City would not arrive until next month. If everything on this incoming vessel checked out, the teams would be idle on this station for nearly thirty days.

Shirosaki stole a look at Harding's face. Harding was glaring in the direction of the vessel, his jaws clenched, as if he were willing the enemy onboard.

The automated system began to move. The security staff stood in front of the lift and waited.

The cargo was comprised of containers holding various microorganisms and other specimens drilled out of Europa's icy crust—not nearly big enough for anyone to stow away in. Having been repeatedly warned by Kline to handle the temperature-controlled specimens with care, the security team opened the containers and quickly sealed them back up again.

Suddenly, the lift stopped.

"The containers are stuck in the cargo hold," reported Arino, who'd been monitoring the activity from a computer terminal. "What should we do?"

"Something wrong with the lift?"

"I'm not sure. Maybe something got caught or one of the containers has jammed the door."

"It may be a trap. Let's send in some checkers."

Shirosaki sent in a dozen or so wireless checking devices by way of the automated system. The checkers fired their thrusters to move about the ship in zero gravity and checked for any monomolecular wire traps and explosives. The data were sent back and displayed in real time on the security team's data goggles.

Harding frowned at the temperature and humidity readings being sent back from inside the ship. "The humidity inside the cargo hold is at eighty percent. Why so high? Could it be a sensor malfunction?"

"All of the checkers are registering the same readings. Maybe the environmental controls are down. What do you want to do?" asked Shirosaki. "Send in an inspection team?"

"I'm not seeing any other abnormal readings. Let's get them in there."

"How many?"

"Eight."

Eight members from the team boarded the vessel with the checkers still in the cargo hold as a precaution.

There were roughly half of the containers remaining in the cargo hold. With one hand on their weapons, the security team members checked the lift and reported back to Shirosaki.

"Nothing blocking the path of the lift. And the cargo can get through the doors just fine. It may be a problem with the lift's controls—a bug or something."

"Check inside the containers."

"Roger that."

Though the individual pieces of cargo were small, the containers holding them were massive and could easily hide a number of people inside.

The members stood around one container in semispherical formation. They dug their feet against the floor, activating the adhesive suction on the soles of their shoes to fix them in place. Lowering their stances a bit, they steadied their guns loaded with alloy bullets. Standard-issue ammunition for space deployment had been developed to reduce the damage to the walls inside spacecraft and stations. Though not as dense as the ammunition used planetside, the bullets could pierce environmental suits at close range.

One man pressed a button, and the door of the container began to open.

The eyes of the security team members grew wide.

An enormous transparent mass covered by a thin membrane appeared from behind the door. The membrane suddenly burst as if someone had popped it with a needle. The checkers instantly began to analyze the chemical plume.

"Get back! Get clear of the gas!" Shirosaki and Harding yelled at the same time.

Kicking off the ground, the members scattered away from the containers. They grew ashen upon reading the numbers displayed on their data goggles.

"It's hydrogen sulfide. Two thousand ppm—that's enough to induce respiratory arrest."

"Take it easy," Harding said. "Your masks will protect you. The humidity is what we need to worry about. It's already exceeded ninety percent. If the sulfide mixes with the moisture in the air, it'll turn into sulfuric acid."

The rest of the containers slowly began to open at once, releasing the same transparent masses, which burst one after the next to disperse their toxic gas into the atmosphere.

A humidifier from somewhere inside the cargo hold appeared to be raising the humidity onboard.

Moisture began to coat the body armor of the security team and the outer shell of the checkers.

"A sulfuric acid mist is beginning to form," said Arino, reporting back the readings lighting up the computer terminal before him. "Something is emitting ultraviolet radiation to turn the sulfur dioxide into sulfur trioxide. The containers were filled with massive quantities of sulfur compounds."

"All right, get the hell out of there," Harding alerted the team. "Make sure you seal the door behind you. We have to keep this gas contained."

After the team was safely off the vessel, Miles turned to Shirosaki and Harding. "What now? If we don't do something, that ship's cargo hold will turn into a bottle bomb filled with sulfide. If there are any explosives aboard, the ship could blow and contaminate the docking bay."

"We either neutralize it or tow the entire vessel away from the station and abandon it somewhere near Jupiter," Shirosaki said.

"Sulfuric acid," said Harding with a disgusted look. "The bastards didn't have to look too hard for the stuff seeing how there's plenty of it on Europa and Io."

After making certain the evacuated team was all right, Shirosaki contacted Kline to recommend disengaging the cargo vessel from the dock.

Kline authorized the move almost immediately, adding that they would be able to control the ship by transmitting commands from the station's system. "We'll send the ship into Jupiter and let the internal atmospheric pressure implode it."

The control room operator sent the ship the requisite commands.

Slowly the ship lurched away from the docking bay. The bow turned away from the station.

"Why is the ship wobbling like that?" Miles asked, as he watched it pull away on a monitor. "Has the navigation program miscalculated its flight path?"

Suddenly, the ship's directional propulsion system seemed to falter. The ship listed to the side and crashed into the docking bay. A chill passed over the security team.

"What the hell happened?"

"I'm not sure, sir," responded the operator behind the controls.

"Any damage to the ship?"

"Negative, all green."

"The sulfide onboard?"

"I'm not reading any leaks."

"Any damage to the station?"

"Some exterior damage from the collision, but the environmental systems haven't been compromised."

"Smooth move, kid," said Harding, shooting a dirty look at the young operator on the monitor.

"The data I sent was correct, sir," the operator insisted. "Someone must have tampered with the ship's program."

"I don't want to hear it. Just get the damn thing pointed toward Jupiter and get it out of here!"

The operater transmitted the commands repeatedly to stop the ship's teetering. Every time the bow crashed against the inner walls of the docking bay shivers ran down Shirosaki's spine.

From the control room, Preda watched the ship stagger repeatedly like a drunkard. "I doubt anyone won the bet now," he mumbled to himself. "It's been an hour already."

Suddenly, everyone in the control room felt the ground beneath them shake and heard an explosion that sounded like a crack of thunder in the distance.

Preda and Kline looked at each other.

"What was that?"

A piercing siren rang throughout the station.

The threat was not in the docking bay. The explosion had come from somewhere inside the station.

2

TEI WAS ROUSTED awake from eir nap by the violent explosion that shook eir bed.

As ey leapt out of bed with a palpable disquiet, eir wearable bleeped. "Doctor, we need you in the lab right away. There's been an explosion."

"Did someone mishandle some volatile chemicals?"

"I don't know. But the damage is extensive. It's as if a bomb exploded."

"I'll be right there."

Tei darted down the corridor. Upon arriving outside the infirmary to retrieve eir medical pack, Tei was stunned.

The door of the infirmary was gone. The steel door lay in a twisted pile in the middle of the corridor. The smell of inert gas from the automatic extinguishing system filled the air, and the cabinets and medical equipment had been smashed to pieces. The infirmary had been reduced to rubble.

Had the earlier communication been some kind of mistake? It was the infirmary that had exploded, not the lab.

Tei found Dr. Wagi crouched over and attending to the wounds of the blood-soaked doctor who'd been on duty. "So the explosion was here," said Tei.

"And the lab. Everything inside the lab and the infirmary is useless. You'll have to get whatever supplies we need from the warehouse. I'll stay here. You get to the lab. The damage is worse over there."

Tei ran down the corridor.

Everyone had known the terrorists were targeting the station. How did they manage to plant the explosives? The security staff had been guarding the docking bay to intercept any intruders.

Suddenly, Tei was assailed by a feeling of unease.

Ey understood why they had bombed the lab, but why the infirmary? *Was it a preemptive strike to prevent our using the medical equipment and supplies? If so, why?*

Just as Wagi had warned, the damage to the lab was far worse than the infirmary. Several workers were scattered across the floor.

Tei slipped on a mask and goggles. Ey gave the injured a local anesthetic and began to treat their wounds.

"Were they after the equipment?" Tei asked the doctor nearby, as ey continued to treat the patient before em. "They must have known we would have backups of the data."

"Probably," he answered. "They really did a job on the hardware. It'll be months before we can resume our bioscientific experiments."

"Still, this isn't the way to put a stop to the experiments," Tei said. "We can easily resume our experiments with new equipment and continue to analyze our data by transferring the backup data elsewhere. If the terrorists were trying to paralyze us completely, they should have bombed the entire station."

"Maybe they were just trying to scare us."

"But that's ridiculous. None of the staff here would think of abandoning their research over a setback like this," Tei said.

"They're probably sending us a message that this could happen to our families. The sick bastards."

"How did they plant the explosives?"

"I don't know," said the doctor, shaking his head. "But this was done by someone who has access to the lab. Look around. Do you see how the room exploded from the interior out? Not from below or from the ceiling. The blast came from inside this room. Not to mention the way the research equipment was specifically targeted. Someone was able to bypass the docking bay and access this place without inviting suspicion."

"You don't think someone on the staff…?"

"As much as I hate to think about it, we can't rule out that possibility."

"Have you reported this to control?" Tei asked.

"Almost immediately. They're going to do a background check on all the staff. Hopefully it isn't too late."

3

THE MAINTENANCE SHAFTS were located in the outer portion of the station, or below the station from the point of view of its residents. The only route connecting the entire station, aside from using the high-velocity elevators, was a network of shafts crisscrossing the entire station like a grid.

Von Chaillot and her assistant Ted put on their data goggles and, after opening the the control center access hatch, slipped inside the maintenance shaft.

It was dark. Ted turned on a flashlight, and they took a moment to orient themselves to the surroundings.

The shaft was high enough for an adult to walk through without bumping his head. A taller man like Ted had to stoop a bit to make his way. Originally designed to accommodate maintenance machines and repair robots, the shafts were in no way comfortable for humans.

When they arrived at the rendezvous point, Ted sat down to rest. "Are you sure we can execute the job?" he asked Von. "The enemy is trained in counterterrorism. The longer this drags out, the greater will be our disadvantage."

"If you have doubts, you're welcome to leave. I won't stop you."

Pulling out a case she'd hidden in the shaft, Von opened it and checked its contents. The case was essentially a small armory of guns and ammunition. Von took one gun, put one bullet in the chamber, and stuck the gun in her waistband. She tossed another gun to Ted. Then she began to assemble a sniper rifle.

"I promised to get you and Wolfren out alive. It's better you worry about what happens after you get back to Earth. The Vessel of Life can't be trusted. You never know what more they'll want from you."

Ted dropped his head and sighed, draping his arms across his knees. "I still don't feel right about leaving you here."

"Don't worry yourself about it. That was always my intention."

Von opened another case, took out two bulletproof suits and protectors, and handed one of each to Ted. Turning his back to Von, Ted took off his jacket and slipped into the environmental suit. He activated the sensors on his glove and then went to work connecting his wearable and implant communicator. Once the data goggles were turned on, he was able to see in the dark.

Suddenly, they heard the whirr of a machine coming closer.

Ted shone the light in front of him. A maintenance machine appeared out of the darkness. Someone was hanging on to the back of the machine, like he was hitching a ride on the back of a trolley car.

Ted pointed the light and his gun at the approaching figure.

The man put on the brakes and stopped the maintenance machine. Shielding his eyes from the light, he asked, "Are you the Vessel of Life? I'm Barry Wolfren. Don't shoot."

"Prove it."

The man tossed his ID card and memory plate at Ted's feet. Picking them up, Ted checked the ID card first. A holographic image of the young man from the waist up materialized. Barry Wolfren. Maintenance engineer. History. Length of service. Everything checked out with the information he'd been given. Ted checked the contents of the memory plate next. It contained the data about the station he'd requested.

He lowered the light.

Wolfren breathed easier. "Your name?"

"David Lobe," answered Ted.

"Is that Karina Majella behind you?"

"Yes," replied Von, standing.

Von had changed into an elastic environmental suit and was wearing a bulky jacket over it. She now had the look of a seasoned soldier rather than a scientist.

"So," said Wolfren, marveling at the sight of her. "The rumors about Karina Majella were true. You *are* a woman."

Von didn't answer.

"You're lightly dressed. You going to be able to protect yourself against their task force?"

"This isn't a combat mission. I'll be fine."

"At least put on a flak jacket. You better not be wearing just lingerie underneath that suit."

"This is a ballistic enviro suit. They're very lightweight lately. Nothing for a child to worry about."

Wolfren shot her a crooked smile and waved them over. "Come with me."

There were two maintenance machines standing by behind the one Wolfren had ridden on.

"One for each of you," said Wolfren. "I'll be controlling them from my wearable, so you just need to hang on. They're automatically set to run. Just follow me."

"Is it faster than walking?"

"What do you think?"

Wolfren, Karina, and Lobe rode the maintenance machines down the shaft. Lobe was impressed by the smooth ride and relieved at having been spared the anxiety of walking the low-ceilinged shaft in a stoop.

As he stared at Karina's back, he reflected on how quickly two years had passed.

He remembered how vehemently Karina had fought for the time to prepare for this mission as if it had happened only yesterday.

When he and Eddie Morgan had gone to Cryse University two years ago, Karina had completely erased her past and had been living a life as a researcher. Lobe and Morgan had made contact with Karina, who'd come to the symposium to present a paper, and confronted her with the proposition.

Karina had changed her name to Von Chaillot and surgically altered her face. She'd completely left behind her teen years, when she'd been an Earthside terrorist.

Morgan had presented Karina with a job to sabotage Jupiter-I, citing the ease with which she could execute the mission using her present position. Kline and Von had been friends for ten years. With someone working on the inside, the leaders of the Vessel of Life had figured they would be able to execute their plan without being discovered.

Karina had flatly rejected the offer.

At first, the woman was nothing if not cynical, but Morgan had made a compelling argument. "We've taken something you treasure above everything else hostage. If you refuse the job, the hostage will die."

As enraged as Karina was, Morgan had succeeded in persuading her. Lobe remembered his own shock. He knew everyone had an Achilles' heel but didn't quite expect taking a hostage would prove so effective against Karina.

Morgan had assured her that not only would she be paid handsomely, she would also be remembered as a hero if she succeeded. Then he added, "The hostage will die even if you refuse the job via suicide. Simply put, you have no choice but to take it."

That had been the decisive turn of the screw.

Karina gave several conditions for her enlistment. First, she wouldn't be able to execute the mission on her own. She would need an assistant.

Morgan insisted that she would be able to carry out the mission on her own. For this kind of job, the fewer their numbers, the higher the likelihood they would succeed. Sending one terrorist was more effective than dispatching a squad, he had told her. In the event of an investigation, the Vessel of Life would be able to cut her loose and dissociate themselves from any wrongdoing. They had planned to make Karina a lizard's tail.

But Karina had argued just how unrealistic it would be to go at it alone.

That was when Morgan had pointed to Lobe and offered him

up as an assistant. She was free to do with him as she pleased.

Lobe had protested immediately. He was Morgan's bodyguard. If Karina turned violent in the negotiations, Lobe's duty was to protect Morgan. Short-term or otherwise, it was not a part of his job description to live on Europa. He pleaded with Morgan to reconsider.

But in the end, Lobe could not refuse an order.

Lobe's history had been falsified so he could accompany Von Chaillot as her lab assistant.

The second condition of Karina's enlistment was to wait two years before the plan would be set into motion. "I haven't done this in twenty years. My stamina and instincts aren't what they used to be. I'll only fail if I try something now. I'll also need weapons. I may know the station staff, but they're not going to allow me to walk in with explosives and ammunition. I'll need to transport everything piece by piece over many trips. And that's going to take some time."

Morgan had scowled at such a timeline, but knowing Jupiter-I could not be infiltrated otherwise and acting on the Vessel of Life's behalf, he had no choice but to relent.

The two had continued to volley their demands back and forth for some time until, finally, they had agreed upon several terms. In exchange for accepting Karina's conditions, Morgan had made her accept a couple of his own. One was for Karina to remain on the station until she had seen the mission through to completion. And the other was to get Wolfren, their informant, safely off the station.

Karina had agreed.

Karina had educated Lobe, who did not have a biology background, in how to play the part of a researcher. How to act and behave like a lab assistant. And to think and speak in the way scientists do. Every time Lobe wanted to throw up his hands, she had looked at him with those kind eyes. "I'm not saying you have to write a report. But you should at least be able to read the data and prepare specimens."

In the time he'd spent as her assistant, not once had Karina revealed to him her face as a terrorist. Had Lobe not witnessed the rage with which she had attacked Morgan at that first encounter, he would not have believed that this woman had perpetrated terrorist acts on Earth twenty years ago. Von Chaillot was an intelligent, decent, and quiet woman.

Was this woman really capable of carrying out a sabotage mission on Jupiter-I? Twenty years was an eternity. No doubt much had happened in that time. Perhaps the aggression in her had simply melted away.

But once the preparations began in earnest, Lobe had changed his estimation of her. Around the time she began to strategize a plan of attack, Lobe sensed a frightening change in her demeanor. That transformation was akin to a round rock being pounded by an even harder rock, its rounded edges being chipped away bit by bit until it was fashioned into a sharp point. By the time that rock had transformed into a steely weapon, Karina and Lobe had left for Jupiter-I.

And it was only moments ago when Lobe had seen the way Karina deftly handled her gun that he finally realized this was a woman to be reckoned with.

She was prepared to do it herself.

She would take on forty counterterrorist task force team members herself and carry out the mission to its successful and inevitable completion.

4

FORTIA SAT BEFORE the computer terminal and endured Dan Preda's barrage of instructions for several moments.

"There's been an incident in the docking bay. It's likely the terrorists are behind it. The infirmary and lab were hit as well. I have a feeling the terrorists may have infiltrated the station during the commotion. I want you to keep the access door to the special district secure. Even if someone on the staff requests access, I want you to check with control first."

"How many of them are there?"

"We don't know."

"Just what was the security staff doing?"

"Let's just say they dropped the ball."

"Utterly useless," said Fortia. "We would have fared better if we'd been the ones carrying the guns."

"What's done is done. Just stay alert."

Fortia ended the transmission and went into the next room.

Album was sleeping in the double bed with the covers pulled over eir head.

"Wake up," said Fortia, patting Album on the cheek several times. "Nap time is over. We have to issue an alert."

Album tossed languidly beneath the covers and opened eir eyes a sliver. "Do it without me. I'm feeling tired. I might be pregnant. What about you, Fortia?"

"I don't recall doing anything that'd get us pregnant, do you? Come on, hurry up and put some clothes on. The terrorists are somewhere on this station."

Album lowered the covers a bit and eyed em suspiciously. "Really?"

"Unless Preda's gone completely batty from the daily boredom, I think he's telling the truth."

"Do you think they're coming here?"

"That depends on our intrepid security team."

Album rolled out of bed and began to pick up the clothes strewn across the floor. "I swear these Monaurals are a pain in the ass. We're forced to live here because they want us out of plain sight and at arm's length. And still they barge into our territory."

"They can't help themselves. That's just their way."

"Fools. They come all the way out here and to do what? Murder people. If they have time enough for that, they should help maintain the station for a while."

While Album fixed the collar on eir tunic in front of the mirror, the intruder alarm sounded. Fortia knitted eir brows. Album quickly reached for the utility knife on the table.

The living room door blew open. A man and woman stormed in with their guns raised.

"Don't move," said the woman coolly. "Try anything funny and you're dead."

"Who are you?" asked Fortia bravely.

"We're with the Vessel of Life."

"I'm asking what your name is."

"Karina Majella. You must be Fortia."

"Yes."

"If you want to live, you'll round up all of your associates in the assembly hall. Every last one of them."

"And what if I refuse?" Fortia said.

"That boy growling next to you like a guard dog—I'll blow his pretty little head off."

Fortia looked Album in the eye and gestured for em to lower the knife.

"But why?" Album protested.

"I don't want any bloodshed here. We can at least talk in the assembly hall."

"She called me a *boy*. The bitch."

Karina snickered. "You move and I'll shoot you dead."

She produced some wrist ties from her pocket and tied Fortia's hands behind eir back. As she moved to restrain Album, ey twisted away and swung an elbow at Karina's face. Karina dodged the attack without any difficulty. Wringing the Round's arm up behind em, she threw em down on the floor, drew the gun from her waist, and pumped a bullet into Album's right leg in one fluid move.

Album screamed. Twisting eir face in agony, ey balled eir body on the carpet with both hands squeezing eir leg. Fortia let out a bestial cry. Ey charged head first at Karina, but Lobe hit em with the butt of his gun, and ey landed on eir back.

Fortia spat out blood at the floor where ey lay. "You murderer."

"I told you I'd shoot if you moved. You were given fair warning."

Fortia sidled up next to Album and, after exchanging several hushed words, looked up at the intruders. "Help em, please. If you don't do something ey'll bleed to death."

"Go right ahead. I'm sure you have some towels lying around."

"You think I can walk after what he's done to me?"

Karina went to the bed and shredded the sheets into thin strips with her knife. After instructing Lobe to keep Fortia back, Karina knelt down next to Album and wrapped the cloth strips tightly around the wound.

With the bandage acting as a tourniquet, the color began to return to eir face. The tension leaving eir body, Album lay on the floor and breathed easier.

"He'll live for now." Karina turned to Fortia and said, "But like you said, he'll only get worse. If you gather the rest of the Rounds, I'll make sure he gets the proper treatment."

"How do I know you'll keep your promise?"

"If you don't trust me—fine. We've got nothing to lose here."

"All right. Help me over to the terminal."

Lobe took Fortia to the computer terminal and tapped a few buttons on the panel. Once a channel was established, Fortia sat down in front of the terminal and calmly began to speak. "To the residents of the special district. I have an announcement to make."

All of the Rounds—in their living rooms, in the garden, and in their beds—waited for Fortia to speak.

It was rare that their leader would make a district-wide announcement outside of the assembly hall. The Rounds instantly recognized that something had happened.

"I'm sorry to interrupt you while you're all at work, but I'd like you to come to the assembly hall immediately. That means everyone—no exceptions." Then ey added, "On the orders of the terrorists standing next to me."

Lobe glared and tried to snatch Fortia away from the terminal.

But Fortia twisted free from his grasp and threw emself against the terminal. "Get out of here, all of you! Tell security the intruders are here in the special district!"

Karina kicked the chair out from under Fortia. The microphone picked up the sound of a thunderous crash and terrible cry.

Across the special district, Rounds who'd already been on the move stiffened and stood dead in their tracks.

Karina's voice echoed overhead. "Listen carefully. We have taken Fortia and Album hostage. Album's been shot and is severely injured. One false move out of any of you, and Album dies first. And if you still resist, we'll kill Fortia too."

Recovering eir feet, Fortia charged at Karina and staggered back to the terminal. "Don't listen to them!" ey shouted. "Forget about us and get yourselves to safety!"

Karina hit Fortia with the butt of her gun. Eir knees buckling, Fortia crumpled to the floor. Karina jabbed the Round in the ribs with a kick and turned to Lobe. "Start shooting with the sniper rifle when the Rounds get to the exit. Wait until they're all crowded around the door. Wolfren should have jammed the lock, so they won't be able to open the door immediately. That's when you shoot."

"Understood. All of the capsules?"

Karina nodded. "Do it." Then she took one look at the terminal and stared down at Fortia lying helplessly on the floor. "She pulled a fast one on you, Dave. The channel's been open this entire time."

"What?"

"She must have hit the switch with her shoulder when she threw herself against the terminal. The entire station must have heard. Along with Kline in the control room."

Switching off the transmission, she muttered, "You must think you're very clever, but not so. We've planned for every contingency."

After having heard Fortia's announcement, Tigris and Calendula gathered their children and rushed outside. Tigris insisted they go help Fortia, to which Calendula replied, "Ey told us to get to safety. Our priority is to follow the leader's orders."

"But—"

"I'm not about to let some opposition group from Earth hurt our family."

A mob was already pushing and shoving each other before the only door in and out of the special district. Unable to open the door from the control panel, some of the Rounds were trying to disengage the lock manually, but the door did not budge.

Tigris turned to Calendula. "I have to go back. The woman said they shot Album. Whoever these people are, they're armed. I have to help Fortia. You take care of the children."

"Right now we have to think of the others. It's the leader's duty to sacrifice for the sake of the many."

"How can you be so cold? Because you quarreled with Fortia about the Monaurals?" Tigris demanded. "Are you still bitter?"

"Stop it. That has nothing to do with it."

"They won't find me if I go alone. Go ahead without me."

"Listen to yourself. Are you out of your mind? How do you expect to rescue Fortia when you're not even armed?" Calendula said.

"I'll make due with what's around the house."

"These are professionals you're dealing with. What, are you going to fight them swinging a chair and desk?"

Suddenly, there was a tremendous noise as the top of the door was riddled with welts. What looked like shards of glass scattered in every direction at the same time, and something cool rained down over the Rounds' heads.

The Rounds let out cries and screams. Something ricocheted off a branch of a bush nearby and burst at Tigris's and Calendula's feet.

"It's coming from Fortia's unit."

"Bullets?"

"They look like capsules of some kind. There's something in them."

Fearing injury, the Rounds fled from the door at once. Being shot at was an entirely new experience for the Rounds. One of the Rounds, panic-stricken at the thought of being hit, began to run, pushing and shoving the others around em. Couples with children tried to get out of the way of the coming stampede. However, Calendula managed to calmly direct everyone from falling over each other, keeping the situation from devolving.

After several moments, the onslaught of capsules died down.

"Are they out of bullets?"

"I don't know."

"No one was hit. Were they just trying to scare us off?"

Tigris went to where one of the capsules fell. The ground was wet. The capsules were not metallic but appeared to be large liquid-filled spheroids. Just as Tigris moved closer for a smell, Calendula pulled em back.

"Don't! It could be toxic. You might be breathing in its vapors."

"It's all right. I don't smell a thing."

"Whoever they are, they were clearly aiming in our direction. Something's not right. The tingling sensation on my skin—don't you feel it? And my throat is sore."

Calendula contacted the control room via her wearable. "Maybe they'll be able to open the door from the outside. Quickly."

Because Fortia had had the presence of mind to switch to an all-station broadcast, Kline and Shirosaki had heard the last exchange.

The transmission from Calendula that followed alerted them to the situation inside the special district.

That was when the security units realized they had been completely duped. They also learned that because a possible toxic substance had been dispersed near the entrance, the Rounds were unable to open the door.

"What the hell happened?" Harding snarled. "SSD won't like this."

Once Harding, Arino, and Miles had arrived in the control room, Shirosaki said, "There were eight security staff stationed in front of that entrance, yet the intruders were able to enter the special district undetected. How can that be?"

"We're looking into it," Kline replied.

"Can you pull up the station schematic again?" Shirosaki asked Kline.

Kline tapped a button on the controls, and the same three-dimensional schematic of the station Shirosaki had studied at the meeting appeared.

"If they didn't go through the front door, they can only have used the maintenance shafts," said Harding. "But we already confirmed that the special district can't be accessed from the maintenance shafts."

"This data might have been falsified. Maybe there's an access point that's been erased from this schematic," Shirosaki said.

"You mean someone erased part of the existing shafts and access points from the schematic? We should check a hard copy."

"Whoever it is was able to overwrite the electronic data. They would have gotten to the paper data too." Shirosaki asked Kline, "Who on the staff would be able to tamper with the data like this?"

Kline grimaced. "One of the engineers on the maintenance staff."

"Anyone on that staff that hasn't reported back since the explosions in the infirmary and lab?"

"We confirmed the locations of all staff a moment ago. We didn't turn up anyone suspicious."

"There has to be a leak somewhere. Please check again. Are you still connected with Calendula?"

"Yes," Kline said.

"Good, keep em on the line. Have em report back everything that's going on inside the special district."

"Leave that to me," volunteered Miles. "Commander, you need to open a line of communication with the terrorists."

"I'd rather Shirosaki handle it," Harding said. "I don't have the patience for negotiating."

Shirosaki nodded. Going to one of the computer terminals, he opened a channel to the special district.

Shirosaki spoke calmly toward the blackened display.

"This is Commander Shirosaki of the Special Security Division. We have the access door of the special district completely surrounded. Throw down your weapons and we'll guarantee your lives. Respond."

A woman's voice issued forth from the terminal. "The Rounds certainly are a practical race—to abandon their leader so easily."

"First, tell us who you are."

"My name is Karina Majella. I'm certain you've heard of me."

Shirosaki couldn't hide his shock. Harding, Miles, and Arino were all struck dumb with astonishment.

Some of the station staff, sensing the ominous mood, looked at each other despite not recognizing the name.

"Karina Majella." Miles scowled. "What the hell is she doing here?"

Shirosaki leaned into the microphone. "Why are you here? For what purpose?"

"A little freelance work at the request of a group called the Vessel of Life. I'm not fond of putting on such a display, but this is what my employers wanted. Even this exchange we're having now is apparently necessary to announce the group's intentions. And to broadcast what's happening in real-time back to Mars."

The monitor in the control room switched on. A woman with a well-proportioned face of mixed Asian heritage blipped onscreen. She appeared to be in her late thirties. She was lightly dressed but armed. She smiled at Shirosaki.

Kline let out a cry that sounded like a shriek. Preda, standing next to her, swallowed hard.

"Calm down," warned Shirosaki under his breath. "We have no idea what she's planning. If we play this right, we might be able to end this right here."

But Kline pushed Shirosaki aside and slammed her hands down on the computer terminal. "What is the meaning of this? Answer me—Von Chaillot!"

Onscreen, an apologetic look came over Karina's face. "I appreciated our friendship over the years, Kline. Thanks to you, I feel like I know Jupiter-I like the back of my hand. Down to every detail. You taught me so many things. I'm grateful."

"You fooled me. Was that your plan from the start?"

"Believe me, I didn't want to do this if I could help it. But I didn't have a choice. You were a good friend, Kline. I won't ever forget that."

Kline's body trembled, but she could not speak.

"What's going on?" Shirosaki asked.

"That woman is a friend. Von Chaillot, a biologist researching Europa's ocean. We've been friends for ten years. She's been traveling back and forth between Europa and Jupiter-I to conduct her biological research. She wasn't playing the part of a researcher. She was an honest, hardworking scientist. She was going to take me in the research submarine to show me the ocean. She was a kind and intelligent woman. Why?"

"She's a sleeper," Harding said coolly. "Ten years is a long time to lie dormant, but a sure way to earn your trust."

"It's possible she came to Europa ten years ago as a researcher but was hired to sabotage the station only recently," Shirosaki interjected.

"How do you know that?"

"Karina isn't the type to sacrifice ten years of her life to lie low as a sleeper," explained Shirosaki. "Doesn't have the patience for it. Besides, she has no prior connection with the Vessel of Life. She said she was freelancing. From the sound of it, she may have taken the job for some reason we don't know about."

Ignoring Harding, who was looking none too satisfied, Shirosaki switched on the mic again. "You said you were freelancing—a hired gun. Then why don't we make a deal? I don't know what they're paying you, but maybe you'd like to hear some options in exchange for releasing the Rounds from the special district."

"Not likely. My orders are to kill every last one of them."

"Look, you don't have to answer right away. Let's you and I work this out."

"I'm afraid you don't have much time. I've disseminated a certain package in the special district. If you don't want the rest of the station to be contaminated, I suggest you stop the Rounds from trying to escape."

"What have you done?"

"That's for you to find out."

Had she released a chemical weapon? Some sort of lethal virus? Shirosaki turned down the audio feed and said to Kline, "We're going in."

"But, Commander—"

"Whatever's been disseminated, we'll eventually need to send a medical team inside. Or would you prefer to completely seal off the special district and allow the Rounds to die?"

"It's reckless to open the access door without knowing the kind of biological weapon we're dealing with," Preda cut in. "Rescuing the Rounds is critical, yes, but we also have to think of the staff."

"We can maintain the special district at negative pressure—manipulate the environmental controls so the special district is constantly drawing in air from the outside when we open the door. That way we can prevent the contaminant from spreading. The security teams are already in their environmental suits. As long as the suits don't tear, they won't be affected. I need you to lower the atmospheric pressure inside the special district. And do you have any UV irradiation units on the station?"

"Yes, we have several," replied Kline.

"Good, we'll use them for sanitation purposes. We also need antiseptics—sodium hypochlorite, isopropanol, phtharal—whatever you can get your hands on. A research station like this one should have plenty of what we need."

"You plan to go in without knowing how many terrorists you're up against?"

"We're trained in counterterrorism, Ms. Kline. Their numbers are irrelevant. There's no need for worry."

"That's right," Harding grunted. "Shirosaki, you keep negotiating with her. I'll command the rescue."

"Good. But don't kill her."

"Why not?"

"We need to know what exactly was spread in the special district. Karina is a biologist. If it's a virus of some kind, she could have valuable information about how to neutralize it."

"The captain's orders were to eliminate the terrorists."

"When we're through interrogating her, you're welcome to do what you want," Shirosaki said. "But keep her alive until we've had a chance to question Karina."

"I don't recall having to take orders from you, Shirosaki."

"Then I'm asking you as a fellow officer." Shirosaki bowed his head toward Harding. "There are babies in that community. I don't want them to die in vain."

Harding bit his lip and grumbled, "All right," before leaving the control room.

As soon as he was gone, Shirosaki instructed Arino. "Keep an eye on him. If you can, get to Karina before he does."

"Right."

After Arino rushed out of the room after Harding, Shirosaki raised the volume on the microphone and resumed negotiations. "All right, we'll hold off from opening the access door for now. But tell us at least what we're dealing with. Is it a biological weapon of some kind? Or chemical?"

"Now why would I tell you that?"

"Come on, Karina. What are the symptoms?"

"That's none of your concern."

"How long do the Rounds have if they're not treated?"

"I'm not sure."

"Then at least update us on Album's condition," Shirosaki said. "We can walk you through the steps to treat em."

"I've stopped the bleeding. He's alive for now."

"You're not a doctor, and ey needs to be properly treated."

Karina was nothing if not composed. Shirosaki wondered just where that self-assurance came from. Was she bluffing about having contaminated the Rounds? Or maybe she was telling the truth and intended to use the cure as a bargaining chip.

The cure. The data to create an antivirus. She might be planning to use that knowledge to demand something in return. Or maybe she had no interest in negotiating and had already secured an escape route off the station.

"I'm begging you. There are babies in the Round community. The babies and the young ones will be the first to go down if they're infected."

Karina's lip curled upward almost imperceptibly. She pointed the gun directly at the screen and said, "One thing you should know. Only I know the contents of the substance that was dispersed. If you kill me, you can kiss any hope of an antidote goodbye. Remember that."

There was a violent crack and then the monitor went black. The transmission abruptly ended.

"Just as I thought. She's planning to use whatever data she has to bargain her way off the station."

"But she shot out the screen."

"Probably to keep us from learning their numbers."

Miles, who'd been talking to Calendula on his wearable, turned around and reported, "There can't be too many of them, although it's hard to tell their exact numbers. Fortia and Album are the only hostages. The rest of the Rounds are concentrated around the access door. But no one appears to be watching over them. Calendula doesn't know what was disseminated, but so far no fatalities. Whatever this substance is, it hasn't taken effect yet."

"Then all we need to do is go in and secure the situation in

Fortia's residence."

"Yes, but the intruders are armed with a long-range sniper rifle. That's how they dispersed the contaminant."

"How far is Fortia's residence from the entrance?" Shirosaki asked Kline.

"About five hundred meters in a straight line."

"Someone is a good shot," muttered Miles.

"A straight line would take you there in six to seven minutes, but it actually takes about ten minutes on the winding path."

"How are the bioengineered plants arranged?"

Kline pulled up a schematic of the special district onto the big screen.

Shirosaki took a hard look at the layout, his mind working a mile a minute. They would be able to use the bushes as cover. The question was how they would access the special district.

They would be found out if they went through the front door. The access point the intruders had used would likely be blocked or booby-trapped by now. What other route could there be?

Shirosaki pointed to a spot on one wall of the space station that was in proximity to the special district. "What about this air lock?"

"We haven't had the occasion to use it since it was installed," Kline said.

"Was this air lock put here for the purpose of connecting the station with the supership—the one Fortia was talking about?"

"Yes, that's right. The air lock will be used to travel back and forth between the special district and the *Apertio*."

"Can it be opened?"

"Yes. It's locked, but we can deactivate the program from here."

"Then please do it. This is our way in. The task force will wear space suits and exit the station. They'll move along this inner wall here and enter the special district from this air lock. Since they won't be going out to the outer wall, their space suits should protect them from the cosmic radiation. Let's get to work."

Once they had procured the necessary supplies and completed preparations for the mission, Kline asked Shirosaki, "What kind of woman is Karina Majella?"

Shirosaki regarded Kline stone-faced. "I'd be revealing a part of your friend's past you may not want to hear."

"I want to know the truth."

"She's a notorious terrorist that various agencies have been hunting from Earth to Mars. She was active mainly in Asia, someone whose name I'd heard often up until twenty years ago. *Majella* isn't her actual name but something like a pseudonym, perhaps taken from the Latin word meaning 'greatness.' Rumor has it that she also carries around the medal of St. Gerard Majella."

"St. Gerard?"

"The patron saint of childbirth. This medal has an odd design. St. Gerard is depicted holding the crucifix with something like a skull or severed head sitting on top of the table next to him. As a non-Catholic, I find it a curious thing to have for a charm," Shirosaki said.

"Has Karina always been associated with the Vessel of Life?"

"Back when she lived on Earth, she belonged to an organization called Libra. In the early part of the twenty-first century, China established the free trade agreement with the Association of Southeast Asian Nations, giving birth to a massive market of 2.9 billion people. The agreement, along with the exploration of underground resources of the Russian Far East and the development of a logistics network for natural gas and oil resources, sparked a period of great economic activity in Asia. An Asian monetary unit and an unthinkable volume of products, electronic currency, and laws to regulate them were born.

"But economic development doesn't always work to eliminate inequality. This newfound prosperity gave rise to a whole new host of problems. When the economy is booming, the underworld grows more bloated and the powers that once acquired unimaginable wealth inevitably go to ruins. This is a fact of every society.

Societies are born to mutate. How much and in what direction you choose to correct that society determines its shape, however short-lived. Libra is an organization that chose to make those corrections through violent methods. They do not desire change through civic engagement or rely on the law enforcement agencies of the state, but resort to violence and strong-arm tactics to force reform. At first, vigilante groups from crime-ridden areas and well-meaning community groups gathered to protest against the government and transnational corporations, but in time, extremists transcending borders and race came together and called themselves Libra.

"Those seeking immediate and dramatic results became supporters of Libra's activities. The government authorities were none too pleased, of course, but they may have also benefited, in part, from having Libra as a common enemy against which they could rally their citizens and other countries to nurture a sense of solidarity. The terrorist organization has continued to thrive over fifty years after its formation.

"Karina joined Libra with her mother when she was nine. Her mother fell in love with a man belonging to the group and became involved in his activities. As Karina roamed the world, always a step ahead of the international police and government agencies pursuing them, she was trained in the ways of combat. After picking up a gun for the first time at the age of ten to provide cover fire for the members of the group, she began to actively engage in combat. By the time she was sixteen or seventeen, the word spread about Libra's frightfully accurate sharpshooter, and soon she was feared across Asia. That's the Karina I know."

"Have you ever confronted her?"

"No," Shirosaki said. "But there is one incident that's been talked about among the antiterror units. One task force—I don't know of what country—charged into the building where Karina was hiding. She and only three others wiped out the entire twenty-man team. The task force tried to conceal the incident, but they had been so completely obliterated that the scandal spread like wildfire."

"Maybe she was just lucky. She may not survive were it to happen again."

"You may be right. But that she had luck on her side even once is a part of her skill. It's because she survived that she's been able to torment as many people as she has and forced us here to Jupiter to confront her."

"Has she altered her face?"

"Yes. Not just once but many times. It's likely she's altered her bone structure on the molecular level. She clearly had Japanese features in the profile we received, but now she looks like she's of mixed heritage. She still looks Asian, of course, but she's also become a stunningly beautiful woman. I'm certain more than a few men have fallen prey to her feminine wiles."

Shirosaki saw the disgust on Kline's face and said no more.

"Why did she come to Europa as a researcher? Unlike the Vessel of Life, Libra doesn't actively oppose bioscientific research."

"She left Libra when she was nineteen."

"Why?"

"She wanted to leave earlier but waited until she had learned to survive on her own. She escaped in the midst of a fierce battle between military forces. Her whereabouts have been completely unknown these last twenty years. She must have gone to school in that time to become a scientist, which explains how you came to know Karina as a microbiologist on Europa. She's always been an intelligent woman; perhaps she'd had a childhood dream to go to school as normal people do and become a scientist. It's entirely possible she used her good looks as a weapon to survive on the run, to scrape together a living and save enough for college. While her methods were dubious at best, I believe Karina might have been maximizing the advantage accorded to her beauty. I suppose she was, to use an old phrase, exploiting her sexuality. Although, she must have gotten her hands dirty in other ways as well.

"Shall I go on?" Shirosaki asked.

"No, that's quite enough." Whatever Kline was feeling, she didn't let on. She thought long and hard with her arms crossed and finally said, "Whatever her motives, Karina is, at present, a threat that must be eliminated. You must apprehend her by any means necessary. Interrogate her in any way you see fit. Get her to talk about what exactly that substance is. The Rounds are my only concern now. Not Karina."

"I understand."

Kline sat at the computer terminal and reported back to Mars. There was a considerable time lag between interplanetary communications. Unable to hold a conversation in real time, the parties involved usually had to wait twenty to thirty minutes to receive a reply to a message they'd sent.

Kline viewed the response from Mars and sighed.

The news of the terrorist attack on Jupiter-I had reached Earth and Mars before Kline's message. The Vessel of Life had already released a message claiming responsibility for the attack.

"We, the Vessel of Life, firmly oppose the experiments taking place on Jupiter, which disregard bioethical principles and trample over the sanctity of human sexuality. The existence of a bigender subspecies is a desecration of our moral principles, serving only to spread values that it's permissible to sleep with anyone and to invite moral confusion. The Rounds will destroy the natural order of society, snuff out the richness of our cultures arising from sexual distinctions, and create a dull and homogenous society without individual difference. At present, the Rounds are legally prohibited from interplanetary travel, but they will eventually seize that right and invade our planets. Before that peril reaches our shores, we seek to destroy the research facilities on Jupiter. The existence of a bigender race signifies neither human progress nor evolution. The experiments on Jupiter-I are an inexcusable violation of human life."

For the love of God!

Kline nearly tore her hair out. Just what year did they think it was? She could hardly believe the stigma that continued to haunt sexual minorities in this way.

Did the Vessel of Life think the Rounds went around indiscriminately throwing themselves at every person they met? The Rounds chose their partners. They didn't sleep with anyone other than someone they had feelings for. They had individual tastes and criteria and exercised discretion regarding with whom to have relationships. In that regard, they were the same as ordinary humans. Did the Vessel supporters throw themselves at and grope whomever they laid eyes on? Or did they live every day in agony trying not to act on those impulses?

Eliminating gender differences would homogenize the culture? Kline thought. *What narrow-minded drivel! All we did was increase the number of humanity's possibilities by one. Not once have we demanded that everyone become like the Rounds.*

Why were these people incapable of accepting these newcomers to the human race? Why couldn't they recognize the Rounds as the living beings they were?

The Vessel of Life had also leaked images of the special district and the experiments being conducted in the lab. Karina had already admitted to transmitting the images to the Vessel of Life on Mars. It was probably after confirming Karina's progress with their plans that the Vessel of Life had announced their intentions.

The reply that came from the Martian government was twofold. Until the substance dispersed in the special district could be identified, the entire station was in lockdown. No one was to enter or leave the station. Any replacement equipment would be dispatched by unmanned vessels from Jupiter-II, Jupiter-III, and Asteroid City. The station's staff needed to ascertain what the substance was and keep in constant contact with the Martian government.

In other words, it was up to Jupiter-I to pull through the crisis on their own. Given the distance separating Mars and Jupiter, that was to be expected. Jupiter-I didn't have the luxury of waiting for help to arrive. They had yet to identify the dispersed substance or even begin to understand its ramifications. If anyone from the outside should come into contact with them, that person was susceptible to contamination or even infection.

The only recourse left to Kline and the station staff was to put in a request for the supplies, keep the lines of communication open, and see how the crisis played out.

5

AFTER WATCHING HARDING handpick the members of the rescue mission entirely from his own team, Arino voiced an objection.

"I have operational control here," Harding said contemptuously. "I need a team that's going to be familiar with and responsive to my commands."

"Then at least choose two or three from my unit to bring up the rear."

SSD had instructed Shirosaki and Harding to work together. If Shirosaki's team wasn't included in the mission, Harding would be the one who'd have to answer to Captain Hasukawa later.

Arino prayed that Harding still had enough sense to listen to reason.

Despite looking none too pleased, Harding relented.

Arino summoned Shiohara and Ogata and explained that Shirosaki needed information about the weapon dispersed in the special district.

"You've been inside the special district, so you should be able to move around faster than the others who'll be relying on maps. I want you to capture Karina Majella before Harding's team gets too reckless. I don't care if you have to injure her, but keep her alive. If you can, try to avoid an altercation with Harding's team. Karina will try to seize every opportunity if she senses dissension in our ranks."

"What do you think she's after? If her goal was to kill everyone on Jupiter-I, she would have blown up the entire station."

"No way she would have been able to smuggle in that many explosives alone. Tampering with the station's core power system wouldn't have been easy either. It would have been difficult to effectively use chemical weapons in a station of this size, especially since the partitions between each section would be automatically lowered at the first sign of trouble. But a biological weapon can easily be smuggled in in small quantities, multiply exponentially inside a host body, and infect others rapidly. That has to be what she's dispersed in the special district."

"Then maybe she's been vaccinated. If so, wouldn't it be possible to make an antivirus from her blood after we've captured her?" Ogata asked.

"I don't know if that's possible with the lab and infirmary in the shape they're in. But if we bring Karina in alive, she'll be of use to us."

The members of the rescue team stood in front of the air lock in the residential district and climbed into their hard space suits. They opened the hatch and stepped inside, carrying their hazmat suits and weapons in a sack. They waited several moments for decompression, and after the green light blinked on, opened the hatch on the other side.

The black void spread out before them.

One by one, the rescue members kicked away from the edge of the hatch door.

Shiohara and Ogata followed.

Holding their sacks close to them, they dove into the darkness with only the station's beacons to light their way. They immediately felt the burden of 0.3 Gs give way to utter weightlessness.

Their sacks felt like air in their grasps.

The silver exterior of the station's central axis gleamed before them. Twenty meters in diameter and eight hundred meters long, the axis housed the station's gravitational control and surveillance systems as well as a small laboratory and the relaxation room.

Using the gas jets on their space suits, the rescue team flew in the direction of the special district.

They made their way along the station's inner wall in a V formation, like migratory birds.

Upon arriving at the hatch outside the special district, the members of the team surrounded the door. They felt the gravity's pull return a bit when they pressed the adhesive backs of their shoes and gloves against the wall.

One of the men twisted open the hatch. Half of the rescue team went in first and commenced compression. Although the air blowing into the air lock came from the special district, the antimicrobial filter kept out any viruses that might have contaminated the exhaust.

When the air lock was sufficiently pressurized, the members took off their hard suits and changed into their hazmat suits. After slipping on their masks, they opened the hatch to the special district and stepped inside.

Once inside, they quickly moved about the garden in four-man units and hunkered behind the shadows of the bioengineered plants. They lay low until the air lock was decompressed again and the remaining half of the team entered and changed out of their hard suits.

The hatch opened and the remaining members joined the team taking cover in the brush.

They proceeded toward Fortia's residence, communicating occasionally over their implant devices.

The reserve units, standing by outside the special district, observed the image being sent back from the rescue team's data goggles.

Harding monitored the scene, while Arino kept a close eye on Harding.

According to Calendula, two Rounds had been taken hostage, one of whom was injured. Arino prayed they would stay put when the team charged in. As frantic as the Rounds probably were to find themselves in such a frightening situation, they were likely to be spared serious injury if they didn't get in the way.

The problem was with Karina. Harding had been intent on shooting her from the start. He might even order the team to aim for the head. Shiohara and Ogata would have to enter the residence another way and get to Karina first.

"Fortia's residence has a skylight on the roof," Shirosaki informed Arino through his implant. "Have Shiohara and Ogata go in through there. Look for an opportunity when the rescue team throws in the stun grenade."

The rescue team zigzagged behind one cover to the next and then surrounded Fortia's residence in groups of four.

Shiohara and Ogata climbed up to the roof and looked for the skylight. They found it exactly where Shirosaki had indicated.

"It'll be a crying shame if we swoop in and our own team mistakes us for the terrorists," muttered Ogata.

"Don't worry. We'll get workmen's comp for that."

After the breacher removed the keypad lock with a drill, the first four-man team slipped inside the house. They crept forward slowly, careful not to slip on the polished cedar floor. The living room was at the end of the hall. The men broke down into pairs and took turns providing cover while the other pair advanced until they reached the door.

They flanked the door with three men crouched down on one side and another man gripping a stun grenade on the other. One man confirmed the door did not have a lock and kicked it down.

From their vantage point on the roof, Shiohara and Ogata watched the stun grenade being tossed into the living room. An earsplitting bang filled the room. But thanks to the implants, capable of filtering out specific audio frequencies, Shiohara and Ogata weren't affected.

The two smashed through the skylight. They landed in a crouch and scanned around them amid the noise. The heat sensors on their data goggles could not pick up any sign of the terrorists. Someone lay motionless on the floor. Shiohara and Ogata scrambled next to the body and found Album.

At the same time, the four men outside the door burst into the room in staggered formation. They took one look at the women and cursed.

Once the noise died down, Album shouted, "What are you doing? What do you think you'll accomplish by throwing a stun grenade at me?"

"Where's Fortia? Where are the terrorists?"

"Dammit! My ears. My eyes." Album shook eir head violently. "They're gone. And took Fortia with them. They plan to use em as a shield if they're found. Go after them. Hurry!"

"Which way did they go? We've got security stationed at the door."

"How the hell should I know?"

"There has to be another route," said Ogata.

Using her implant, Shiohara reported back to Arino. "The terrorists will need a ship to get off this station. With the docking bay down, they'll try to get to one of the emergency shuttles. You'll have to put security on every one of the spacecraft, sir. And get a security system into the maintenance shafts. Karina's got to be somewhere in the shafts."

When the door to the special district opened, the air from the corridor was drawn into the negative-pressure environment. Hazmat-suited security entered the special district with the wind at their back. They gathered the fragments of the capsules scattered around the entrance and then went about the work of sterilizing the area. First they treated the area with UV irradiation units and sprayed the area with antiseptics.

Tei and the medical team also entered the special district, wearing their own protective gear. They gathered the Rounds and led them to the assembly hall for mass examinations. Many of the children presented with fevers. The adults, though only slightly feverish, complained of physical fatigue. Dr. Wagi told the others that these symptoms were likely the effects of the dispersed substance.

The youngest children were suffering from especially high fevers. Whereas the normal body temperature for Round infants was 37 degrees Celsius, all of the infants were running a fever of over 38 degrees. Since they were sweating profusely, the doctors prepared intravenous drips to keep them hydrated.

After hearing Dr. Wagi's report, Shirosaki asked, "Isn't there some way to find out if this is a virus?"

"Yes, with a simple electrophoresis test—if it's a virus we've already identified," Wagi replied. "But all of the equipment in the lab and infirmary was destroyed in the explosions. We can't even run a PCR test. But if it's a new virus we're dealing with, I doubt any tests would yield very useful information."

"Then what are our options?"

"We treat the symptoms. Administer antipyretics to treat fever and antiphlogistics for inflammations. I can't guarantee any results, but we try every antiviral drug we can think of—neuraminidase inhibitors, protease inhibitors, nucleoside analogues, and non-nucleoside analogues. We attack this thing with as many combinations of drugs we can find in our supply. If the equipment were still working, we could have tried autotransplantation of blood stem cells to boost immunological function."

"Will that be enough?"

"If it's not, the Rounds will die. The sooner you capture Karina, the better. She has the answers we're looking for. She must be planning to use that information as a bargaining chip if she's captured."

"Understood," said Shirosaki.

"In the meantime, I'll collect some blood samples from infected Rounds and send them to the lab on Europa. Since they're equipped for marine microbial research, they'll be able to analyze the samples for us. They're also the closest lab to Jupiter-I, so we can communicate with them in real time."

"Yes, that's good."

Wagi switched on his wearable and proposed the idea to Kline.

But Kline, in turn, informed the doctor of the Martian government's order to lock down the station and prohibit any contact with the outside.

"We're not asking to *move* the patients there," Wagi shouted. "We merely want to send the samples to the lab on Europa for analysis. If we simply listen to the Martian government, the Rounds will die. I recommend we send the samples to Europa."

"But if the staff and the facilities on Europa become contaminated, we'll be responsible for spreading the damage."

"Then we store the samples in hermetically sealed containers and hand them off to Europa's staff wearing protective gear," Dr. Wagi said. "Europa has hazmat suits and the staff is used to handling hazardous materials."

Kline bit her lip. There was no time to waste. But was involving the lab on Europa an acceptable risk? Even if the staff agreed to it, who would bear the responsibility if they were affected? This was a matter of life and death. If someone were to die, there was no taking responsibility for it.

There was also another concern to consider, and that was the risk of contaminating Europa's ocean.

"I'll discuss it with the director," Kline answered curtly. "Switch your wearable to the common circuit. I'll patch you in to the call."

Kline opened a channel to the research station on Europa.

The face of Paul Weil, the director of the research station, appeared onscreen. "Kline, I heard the news. Terrible what's happened."

"Then you understand I haven't much time." Kline proceeded to briefly explain how the equipment on Jupiter-I was destroyed and how there was no way for them to ascertain whether the weapon was chemical or biological. "Dr. Wagi, our chief of medicine, is requesting the use of the research facilities on Europa. But we're not about to put your staff at risk when we don't even know the nature of the agent we're dealing with."

"I would think not," replied Weil. "What do you have in mind?"

"What if your staff were to temporarily evacuate the research station?"

"Evacuate?"

"Yes, the entire staff would transfer to Jupiter-II near Ganymede by spacecraft. Then our bioscientists can go to Europa and analyze the substance themselves."

"While sparing my staff from contamination. I see."

"Once we know what this substance is we'll be able to sterilize your research facilities and make certain that your staff returns only after the risk of contamination has been eliminated."

"I guess we'll have to put a hold on our experiments."

"Yes, and I'm sorry about that. But I'm afraid I'm out of options," Kline said.

"I have no objection to what you're asking. We'll be able to analyze our data just as well on Jupiter-II or at Ganymede's research station. Since they're researching the organisms inhabiting the ocean beneath Ganymede's ice crust, their facilities are comparable to ours. We should be well-equipped at either lab. The problem is with the risk of contaminating Europa's ocean. Regardless of how carefully you transport the substance here, if it leaks, the damage would be irreversible."

"That's my concern as well. And there's no guarantee that we can contain it. After all, we have no idea what this thing is."

"But if I say no, your staff and the Rounds may die."

"Yes."

Weil exhaled deeply and shook his head. "I don't know. On the one hand, human life is precious, I realize. But on the other, so too are the organisms that humanity has discovered outside Earth. If they became extinct due to some foreign influence, the damage to Europa's ecosystem could not be undone."

"You're right. That's exactly what troubles me."

"I'd like some time to discuss it with the others. This isn't a decision I can make alone. I won't keep you waiting long."

"Please. And another thing. Would you check to see if Von Chaillot left behind any personal items there? You might be able to find something that might help us."

"Of course."

Kline ended the transmission, her face haggard as she slumped back in the chair.

Wagi chimed in on his wearable. "Thank you."

"You were awfully quiet."

"I didn't feel it was my place to speak. Your passion overwhelmed me."

"The lives of the staff and the Rounds or Europa's ecosystem. Which would you choose?"

"As a doctor, my job is to save human lives," Dr. Wagi said.

"Of course. I'm sorry for having even asked such an obvious question."

"I regret I've put you in an untenable situation."

6

KARINA AND LOBE moved down the maintenance shaft with Fortia, whose hands were still tied behind eir back. Having been knocked around mercilessly back at the residence, ey hobbled forward unsteadily but was in better shape than Album, who had been left behind.

Karina jabbed Fortia in the back with the barrel of the gun and prodded em to quicken eir pace.

Wolfren caught up to them several moments later. "It's done," he reported in virtual darkness. "It's coming along as scheduled."

"Good," replied Karina.

"Now to get out of here. Do you plan to take Fortia with us?"

Recognizing Wolfren's face, Fortia could not hide eir shock. "Tenebrae. So it was you that allowed these terrorists into the special district."

"My name isn't Tenebrae. It's Barry Wolfren. You know that better than anyone."

"How dare you betray us!"

"Consider it payback for not taking me seriously. I would never have done this if you and Kline had listened to what I had to say."

"You can bicker about it later," Karina interjected. "Dave, you and Wolfren get to a shuttlecraft. The rest is up to you."

"You sure you want to separate here?" asked Lobe. "I don't feel right leaving you. Have you secured a way out?"

"I'll be fine," Karina insisted. "Careful not to run into the security teams. They'll shoot you on sight."

"Then this is where we part ways."

At the intersection, Karina watched Lobe and Wolfren disappear down the long and narrow path, and then began to walk in the opposite direction. She walked behind Fortia, pointing the flashlight strapped to her waist ahead of them.

"How much farther do you think you'll get?" Fortia asked, gasping for air at the same time. "Splitting up won't make any difference. There are security forces all over this station. You won't escape."

"Shut up and walk. That's not for you to worry about."

"If you think I'm of any value to you as a hostage, you're wrong."

"Valuable enough to take the first bullet."

"They'll shoot you along with me," Fortia said.

"You may be right. Even the other Rounds abandoned you so they could escape. Is that the principle by which you Rounds operate—every Round for emself?"

"The Rounds exist as a collective entity. The lives of the many outweigh the life of an individual."

"That's a hell of a philosophy."

"That's the mindset necessary to survive in the frontier of space. To confront unexpected danger with the limited resources and people available to us, it's better the staff exists as a gigantic organism with one mind. Like a Portuguese Man o' War capable of surviving even if a part of it is cut off. I'm not afraid to die as long as the others are safe."

Karina laughed scornfully. "A convenient philosophy imposed upon you all by the station's staff, I'm sure. How can you obey without thinking about what you want? Don't you have a rebellious bone in your body? Why aren't you the one to determine your own worth?"

"Shut up. I don't need to hear this from you."

Karina wrapped an arm around Fortia's neck from behind and put em in a chokehold that nearly suspended em from the ground. Bringing her lips closer to Fortia's ear, she whispered, "Don't you have a will of your own? Is that your way? Does it make you proud to submit to your creators without so much as questioning the society into which you were born?"

"Better that than submit to the likes of you," Fortia managed to gasp.

Karina threw Fortia down on the ground and dropped a knee against Fortia's chest with the full weight of her body. Fortia's face twisted in pain. Karina grabbed em by the hair and brought her face closer to eirs until they were nose to nose. "Seeing people like you makes me want to tear you all to shreds. If I were a man, I would rape you right now."

"Too bad you're a Monaural woman. You don't have the necessary equipment."

"But I am capable of ruining you."

"Then do it."

Karina smashed the butt of her gun in the pit of Fortia's stomach. She watched Fortia writhe in pain and hit em again.

Fortia closed eir eyes, pale-faced, as Karina grabbed hold of eir tunic and ripped it down the middle with her knife.

The fabric fell away, revealing Fortia's modest breasts. Eir pink nipples resembled those of Monaural women. Karina pulled off Fortia's underwear, exposing eir pelvis. Outwardly, eir genital area looked much like a woman's. Although she had heard as much from

Kline, Karina could not hide her fascination with the real thing.

She slipped her fingers between Fortia's legs to discover that the Round copulatory organ was not external. The penis was stored in an urogenital slit. Like the male genitalia of many whales and dolphins, it became enlarged and protruded from the slit when blood rushed to it upon sexual arousal.

Karina also felt around for the female organ. *So the penis and vagina aren't arranged front to back but side by side. The penis on the right and vagina on the left.*

An effective formation. With the reproductive organs arranged in this way, the Rounds can engage in the act facing each other with one's penis inside the other's vagina and the other's penis inside one's vagina. Very convenient!

For a while, Karina studied Fortia with a biologist's eye. The urethral orifice was located toward the anterior and the anus located toward the posterior in relation to the reproductive organs. *They're arranged in a cross*, Karina mused, a smile escaping her lips. *No doubt, whoever was responsible for the Rounds' genetic design was precision-oriented.*

Fortia squirmed and opened eir eyes. Karina straddled em and pressed her lips against eirs. Gritting eir teeth, Fortia fought back. Curling her tongue like a feline, Karina slowly ran her tongue across Fortia's lips. Then, she put her hand inside Fortia, as one would do with an intimate partner. Fortia screamed as if ey'd been branded with a hot iron. Ey tried to push Karina away with all eir might.

Pulling away, Karina asked, "Why so scared?"

Fortia trembled feverishly and glared up at Karina, silent.

"You're a first-generation Round," Karina continued. "I can imagine the humiliating treatment you must have endured in the name of science. Being subjected to experiments like a lab animal. It must have wounded you deeply."

"You don't know what you're talking about."

"You and your partner must have been under constant observation too. How did it feel to engage in the act in front of a camera?"

Karina said. "To have your newborns taken from you for experiments before you'd had a chance to hold them?"

"As first-generation Rounds, that was our duty."

"What does that have to do with anything? You could have refused if you wanted to. Dr. Tei resisted and became an intermediary."

"I didn't have that choice when I was the doctor's age," Fortia said, looking away. "You Monaurals enjoy a broad habitat range from Earth to Jupiter. You're free to go wherever you please. Guaranteed the right of liberty, despite the disparity in your standard of living. We're promised no such thing. The only habitats promised to us are the station, the special district, and uncharted space. Even if we were opposed to this existence, we would still be denied acceptance into Monaural society. The Round experiments were approved under the condition that none of the data would leave the station. If we forsake the special district or our duty to explore space, the only life left to us would be to spend the rest of our days in service to the station staff. I'd rather put my hopes on traveling to the edge of space. I don't care if I have to be a Monaural lab experiment or a tool of space exploration. The excitement of seeing the undiscovered universe before anyone else is reason enough for living. And what about you? You came here on someone's orders yourself. Have you even once questioned the ideology and actions of the organization that you work for?"

"I'm here as a mercenary. The Vessel of Life's ideology is of no matter to me. Once I destroy the Rounds and the research facilities, my job is done."

"Then what's keeping you here when you can just kill me and escape?" Fortia said.

"The agent that's been dispersed in the special district takes some time to take effect. The agreement was that I leave after I've seen the Rounds manifest the symptoms of the agent." Karina let out a throaty laugh. "Now shall we go? Or would you rather I fondle you some more?"

Karina hacked into the security camera feed and observed the security units' movements from her data goggles. She and Fortia continued down the maze of shafts, maintaining a safe distance from security all the while. Escape would only become more difficult the longer she stayed here, but getting Lobe and Wolfren out alive first was part of the agreement with the Vessel of Life.

Karina could hear Lobe's signal from the implant in her ear. As long as the signal stayed constant, Lobe was on the move trying to secure an escape route. A change in pitch would signal an emergency. If the pinging in her ear stopped, that would tell her that Lobe had failed and died. A similar signal was also being sent from Karina to Lobe's implant. The moment one of them failed, the other was to move on to another course of action.

Karina glanced at her watch.

Lobe should be approaching the emergency shuttle by now.

Karina stopped Fortia and left em waiting inside the maintenance shaft as she opened the hatch above them and popped her head out into the corridor. Propping her elbows on the floor of the station corridor, she aimed her gun with both hands and waited for the security officers displayed on her goggles to come around the corner. There were eight of them lurking in the immediate vicinity.

The security team appeared from around the corner. Karina shot at their legs. Several of the men instantly went down where they stood. Some raised their guns, but Karina ducked back into the shaft before they could return fire and began to run with Fortia in tow.

Nobody appeared to be tailing them. The injured men were probably calling in reinforcements to send into the maintenance shafts, just as Karina wanted. It was a ploy to keep the security teams on her tail and to draw as many of the guards away from the emergency shuttle as possible. Then the rest would be up to Lobe. If he could take down the remaining men guarding the shuttle, he and Wolfren would be able to escape.

Before Karina and Fortia got too far, the lights inside the maintenance shaft flickered to life. Karina quickened her pace and forced Fortia to do the same. Running wasn't going to buy them much time. But it was better than doing nothing.

7

THE CONTROL CENTER was busy tracking Karina's present location based on the reports of the men she'd attacked. Harding and Arino had returned to the control room. Having allowed Karina to slip through his fingers in the special district, Harding was in a foul mood.

Shirosaki ordered tracking devices dropped inside the maintenance shafts from various access points. This would be the endgame. The terrorists had nowhere else to run.

The trackers were released inside the maintenance shafts and began to move at once toward a designated rendezvous point.

Miles stared intently at the monitor and, after a while, pointed. "Bingo. Found them."

"How many?

"The trackers are picking up only two. We're getting a visual lock on them now."

Shirosaki peered into the monitor. "Fortia and Karina. Any others?"

"No visual confirmation of anybody else."

"Not a lot of wiggle room down there. Maybe we can contain their movement with anesthetic gas. Ms. Kline, will using tear gas or an anesthetic agent pose a threat to Fortia?"

"Their components?"

"Halogen compounds and aerosolized synthetic narcotics."

Kline called up Dr. Wagi on the computer terminal and urged Shirosaki to consult the chief of medicine directly.

After Shirosaki informed the doctor of the main components

of the chemical agents, Wagi authorized their use.

"It won't do any good if Karina has a mask," said Miles.

"We have nothing to lose," Shirosaki answered. "Even knocking out Fortia would help us. Karina won't be able to easily drag around a hostage that's dead weight. We'll have an easier time of nabbing her with Fortia out of the picture."

"What if she kills em before making her getaway?"

"Karina won't do anything to waste bullets. Any movement in the shuttle bay?"

"Nothing suspicious yet," Miles said.

"Can we spare a couple of guards to help with chasing down Karina?"

"That might leave us shorthanded at the shuttle bay."

"Maybe they'll make their move if they see the guards moving out. We can try luring them into shuttle and apprehending them there."

"Do you want the men to use tranquilizer guns?"

"No. Live ammo," Shirosaki said.

Shirosaki glanced at Harding. Harding answered drily, "Be my guest."

After emerging from the maintenance shafts, Lobe and Wolfren arrived outside Shuttle Bay 2.

No doubt there were security forces standing by inside. Whoever shot first would be the ones left standing.

"Are you sure about this?" Wolfren asked, but Lobe didn't answer. Although they wore bulletproof suits, no amount of protection was going to save them in a close-range shootout, and a bullet to the head would surely kill them.

Lobe unstrapped the mask from his waist and tossed it to Wolfren. Wolfren scowled and put it on. After slipping on his own mask, Lobe threw a bottle filled with fentanyl against the boarding gate. Anesthetic gas billowed out of the bottle, filling the corridor. With their guns raised, they went inside the corridor only to find it empty. Arriving at the shuttle entrance,

Lobe tossed another bottle inside and waited a moment before boarding the craft. There was no one on board. An eerie silence pervaded the cockpit.

Wolfren lunged at the control panel and ran his fingers deftly across the buttons. The various levels on the controls jumped to life, signaling the start of the prelaunch sequence. Just as a look of relief twitched across Wolfren's face beneath the mask, the door blew open and an armed security squad, all masked, rushed inside.

Lobe squeezed the trigger on his submachine gun and sprayed the team with bullets. Wolfren instinctively threw himself on the floor. Protected by their environmental suits, the security squad continued their advance and returned fire. The bullets ricocheted off the walls of the cockpit.

Several bullets hit Lobe, sending him crashing against the controls on his back. The bullets penetrated clear through his bulletproof suit and buried themselves in the control panel. A hideous volume of blood splattered across the ceiling and spread over the controls, which now signaled all-green for launch. The rust-colored blood dripped below onto the mask covering Lobe's face and formed a small pool around his body.

A security officer stood over Lobe and drilled a lethal bullet into his head.

"Wait, don't shoot!" Wolfren shouted from the floor, his voice muffled by the mask. "I'm not a terrorist. I'm one of the station staff. This bastard forced me to bring him here. Help me, please."

"Get your hands behind your head," shouted the security officer.

Wolfren did as he was ordered. One of the men frisked him for weapons.

"Tell us your name."

"Barry Wolfren."

"Designation?"

"I'm an engineer with the maintenance department."

The security officer restrained Wolfren in handcuffs.

"Wait a minute." Wolfren squirmed on the floor. "I'm a victim here. Why am I being cuffed?"

"We'll let you go if you come up clean. Just stay put."

As Karina and Fortia continued their escape down the maintenance shaft, Lobe's signal went silent. Karina clicked her tongue.
So Lobe had failed. Just as well. No sense in both of them getting
caught and being used against each other in an interrogation.

And what about Wolfren? Was he dead too? Or did he manage
to beg for his life? Karina suspected it was the latter. Wolfren was
a wily one. He would find some way to survive.

A security tracker jumped out into Karina and Fortia's path.

Karina shot it down instantly.

Before they knew it, Karina and Fortia were surrounded by
countless tracking devices. Realizing shooting them all would be
a waste of ammunition, Karina drew Fortia closer to her. "Be very
still. Don't move." Pressing the gun against Fortia's temple, Karina
pressed her body closer to eirs.

A sanctimonious look came over Fortia's face. "There's no escaping now."

"Quiet."

Karina was still for a moment. After hearing a metallic ping
nearby, she immediately grabbed the mask strapped to her waist
and slipped it over her nose and mouth with one hand. Fortia
tried to wriggle free and suddenly realized ey could not move.

Fortia slumped limply to the floor, as if eir bones had turned liquid.

Karina forcibly pulled Fortia to eir feet. But Fortia, already
groggy from the gas, could barely hang on to Karina to keep emself upright.

Soon security guards appeared from out of the haze. They were
fully armed, faces covered by protective masks and data goggles.
They emerged from the gas cloud and flanked Karina and Fortia
from both sides.

Karina pressed her back against the wall, clutching Fortia in
one arm.

The security guards surrounded them in a hemispherical formation.

"Put down your weapon and let the hostage go," said one guard. "Do as we say, and no one gets hurt."

Karina said nothing and kept the barrel of the gun pointed at Fortia's head.

"I repeat. Let the hostage go."

Suddenly, Karina threw Fortia to the left. As Fortia staggered into the arms of the security guards, Karina pointed the gun in the opposite direction and shot at the guards on the right. One guard took a bullet in the forehead and toppled backward. One bullet pierced another guard's fiber-reinforced goggles. The blood gushed from between his eyes. Just as a guard pushed Fortia aside and aimed his gun at Karina's head, Shiohara restrained him from behind. The guard pulled the trigger and hit Karina in the left leg. Even as she crumpled to the ground, she whirled around and squeezed the trigger. The bullet ricocheted off the wall and hit Fortia in the back.

Another man jumped over the fallen guards and punched Karina to the ground just as she was staggering to her feet.

The security guards piled on top of Karina, disarmed her, and pushed her face down on the ground. Although she tried to resist, she let out a cry when a foot came down on her wounded leg. Karina gritted her teeth in agony and tried to keep the spasms from overtaking her entire body.

Shiohara applied pressure to Fortia's wound with both hands, shouting for someone to get her some bandages. Fortia was conscious, eir face twisted in considerable pain. "Your inefficiency astonishes me," ey said.

"Don't talk. Your wound isn't fatal, but you're still bleeding."

"How about 'don't worry' or 'you'll be just fine'?" Fortia said faintly.

"Please, you have to stop talking."

After restraining Karina's hands behind her head, the guards moved off. Karina lay on the floor, a moan escaping her clenched teeth.

"I don't believe it," muttered one of the guards. "She took out both men in two shots."

"Somebody get her some help!" shouted Shiohara. "Our orders are to bring her back alive. Where the hell are you aiming?"

8

AFTER WOLFREN WAS apprehended from the shuttle, he was taken into custody and held inside a room in the residential district.

When Arino entered, Wolfren looked in his direction but otherwise sat calmly in a chair showing no sign of resistance.

His hands, restrained by handcuffs, rested on his lap.

Arino stood over Wolfren and began, "Your name inside the special district was Tenebrae until five years ago you when renounced your standing as a Round. After having your bigender attributes surgically removed, you are now biologically male and identify as male. You have, at present, no partner. Am I right so far?"

Wolfren nodded.

"Why were you aiding the terrorists?"

"I wanted my freedom."

"Freedom—from what?"

"From this place." Wolfren smiled crookedly. "More than a few Rounds want to fix their sex. If you plead your case well enough to Fortia, ey'll put in a request to Kline for the surgery. To reconstruct a unisex body like a Monaural. A man or woman—whichever you choose. But becoming unisex doesn't give you the liberty to leave Jupiter-I. We aren't able to travel to the planets thanks to an agreement between the station and the Planetary Bioethics Association. Emigration to Mars or Earth is regarded as some kind of biohazard."

"You were born a Round—why would you want to fix your sex? There must be disadvantages to being unigender."

"Is that how you feel—that gender distinctions are an inconvenience? Do bigender Rounds really represent a human ideal? Are the Rounds wrong to want to become unigender? Are they wrong to want to freely choose their gender and sexuality?"

Arino couldn't offer a response.

Wolfren had a point. If Wolfren lived in a world where only Rounds existed, bigenderism would have been an unquestionable and inalienable concept. However, Jupiter-I was a research station inhabited by both Rounds and Monaurals, where the Rounds necessarily observed the lives of those possessing only one sex. That the knowledge of a unigender existence would have an effect on the Round psyche wasn't all that difficult to imagine.

Many of the Rounds grew fascinated with and yearned for a Monaural lifestyle, just as Arino felt his concept of gender and sexuality challenged by the Rounds' existence. The Rounds were not lab animals, after all, but intelligent beings, and it was only inevitable that curiosity would eventually get the better of them.

"I was born a Round but hated Round society," Wolfren continued. "The future of the Rounds is completely preordained and predictable. I have no interest in seeing the edge of the universe. I wanted to live on the planets. All I wanted was to be a man and test my limits in a society where no one knows anything about my lineage."

"Mars and Earth aren't nearly as great as you make them out to be. They're ugly and chaotic worlds."

"You lie. If that were true, why are all the staff so happy to go on leave to Mars? Why are they so overjoyed to end their time here and go back to Earth? If the edge of the universe was really all that wonderful, everyone would want to go there without having to create the Rounds to go on their behalf."

Arino could not speak.

"There are former Rounds among the station staff working as research assistants to Monaurals. I'm one of them, only as an engineer. But I wanted to leave this place—not because I was being treated unfairly at work or experiencing unbearable discrimination. But I always felt, however imperceptibly, that everyone reacted differently toward me. They all knew that…I used to be a bigender. In that sense, I would *always* be a bigender as long as I stayed here. I can never be solely male. And that's because your gender is determined by the perceptions of others. Whenever the Monaural staff went back to their homes on Earth and Mars, I was reminded that I'm not an average human. That I'm a Round even after the surgery. That I'm not a Monaural. I wanted to see Mars. Visit Earth. But interplanetary travel is forbidden. For as long as I live, I can never leave this station. That's why I hacked into the interplanetary network and searched, for years, for some way to get off the station. Then I found the Vessel of Life—an organization perpetrating acts of terrorism in the name of the sanctity of life. I thought they'd be useful. I agreed to help them in exchange for a counterfeit family register and interplanetary passport. And why not? It was obvious I wasn't going to get off the station through legal channels. Terrorists or not, I had to use whatever resources were available to me. They happened to be looking for someone on the inside to help them, so they were only too happy to oblige."

"Didn't you think about the genocide you'd be complicit in, all in exchange for your freedom?"

"Genocide? That would never happen. You have security all over this station. I didn't think for one second that the terrorists would succeed. But they would create an opportunity to escape. That was the window of opportunity I was looking for. Even if Karina had failed to infiltrate the station, I was going to use the commotion as a cover to get off the station. Whether the Rounds would be wiped out was a simple matter of chance. Besides, what allegiance could I feel for a community I was trying to leave behind?" Wolfren looked Arino dead in the eye. "You think I'm wrong? Is it so wrong for a Round like me to want his freedom?"

"It's the method I've got a problem with. You've put the entire station at risk."

"Really. So then I should have gone on enduring the life I'd been living? Lying to myself, killing a part of who I am?"

Arino couldn't answer.

But Wolfren wasn't expecting an answer. Arino's silence was answer enough.

"I always wondered if the Rounds were destined for space. Or if we're really just lab animals for the Monaurals, creatures to suck dry of all our acquired data so they could adapt their own bodies and venture beyond Jupiter themselves. If the Monaurals will always be the first to see the frontier, while we remain biological machines made for no other purpose than to output experimental data. Maybe you can ask Kline when you see her. What do the Monaurals really want with us? Are we just tools of space exploration to them? Or partners in a new age?"

"Just tell me one thing, Wolfren. What was the agent that was dispersed in the special district? Or maybe you know how to treat the symptoms. Anything you can tell me."

"That was something Karina smuggled in without my knowledge. I don't know anything about it."

Arino left Wolfren and headed for the control center where Shirosaki and Kline awaited his return.

After hearing the details of Wolfren's confession from Arino, Kline sighed. "Are you telling me *that* was the reason why he aided the terrorists?"

Kline's look of disappointment seemed to Arino a vivid reminder of Wolfren's desperation.

Her belittling reaction was precisely the cause of Wolfren's despair. Kline had failed to recognize it in all her associations with him and failed to recognize it still, even after she'd heard Wolfren confess as much.

"What will you do with Wolfren?" asked Arino.

"There's nothing we can do. We have no laws here to try him. Wolfren was born with the understanding that he would never leave this station. Neither the courts on Mars nor on Earth have the jurisdiction to try him," Kline said.

"I'm sure you're not thinking of taking matters into your own hands," Arino said, unable to completely hide his suspicion.

"The Rounds are human, no matter how they are formed. Even as a supervisor, I'm not empowered to take Wolfren's life."

"I see."

"The Rounds are our good partners and the hope of humanity. There's nothing about that statement anyone needs to be suspicious about. Tenebrae couldn't understand that. That's why he forsook his given name to become Barry Wolfren," Kline said. "A shame, really. We gave him a perfect body and home, yet he fled this paradise all on his own. Suck the Rounds dry of all their acquired data and toss them away? How can he be so delusional? He has no idea just how blessed his life has been."

The moment Arino heard that last statement, he felt an intense sympathy for Wolfren. He left Kline, however, without another word.

Kline received a message from Weil at the Europa Research Station.

"*The governments on Earth and Mars and the Planetary Bioethics Association have reached a decision, Kline. They're asking you to hold out a little longer. To try to ride out the storm yourselves as best you can until the situation reaches crisis point.*"

Kline listened to Weil's message calmly as if she'd expected this answer all along.

"*You have my word, Kline. I have no intention of turning my back on Jupiter-I. If the situation turns grim, you'll have the full support of Europa's research station. Hang tight, Kline. None of the staff have been affected thus far, am I right?*"

In the end, that was what it came down to. If the Rounds all died, the planetary authorities would just produce some more. But if the station staff were in peril, then they would intervene directly. That was the final answer from the outside.

"We'll have to find out the formulation of the chemical agent from Karina," Kline informed Shirosaki. "Apply a little pressure if necessary."

Karina was being held in a separate interrogation room. Her leg wound treated, she sat on a chair in the middle of the room with both hands cuffed behind her back.

Shirosaki and Harding entered the room with two security officers in tow, followed by Kline, then Tei.

After examining Karina, the doctor determined that the prisoner was well enough for questioning.

"You have something in there that could act like a truth serum?" Harding asked as Tei closed eir medical pack.

"We have nothing of the sort in this station," Tei replied, shaking eir head.

"Then I guess we'll have to *make* her talk."

"Please don't," said Tei, interposing emself between Harding and Karina. "Let me talk to her."

Karina looked up at the figure of Tei standing before her and smiled.

"You're Karina Majella," Tei said. "We've met once before. Kline brought you into the infirmary about five years ago with stomach pain. I remember giving you a prescription for painkillers."

"You remember well."

"Von Chaillot is not your real name?"

"I needed an alias to go to university. My given name is Karina, but I have no family name."

"Like the Rounds."

"Don't compare me to the Rounds," Karina said. "It's true some people on Earth do without last names as a matter of choice or culture, but many more don't have family names due to unfortunate circumstances of birth and upbringing."

Tei knitted eir brows. Karina lowered her gaze and let the tension out of her shoulders. "I remember you too, Doctor. You came across as a terribly attractive man and woman simultaneously. So much so that it's difficult to forget you. If you're not careful, a Monaural will have his or her way with you someday."

"I'll bear that in mind," Tei said perfunctorily. "You are now in custody. You've failed your mission. Tell us about the substance you dispersed in the special district—its name, composition, and cure. You'll only be helping yourself if you cooperate."

"Why do you give a damn what happens to me?"

"The Round children are running high fevers, especially the newborns and two- to three-year-old children. Until we find out what's making them sick, we can only treat their symptoms, and for how much longer, I don't know."

"As soon as I tell you, your friends are just going to kill me. In that case, I'd rather see you run yourselves ragged to find a cure before I die."

Tei put out eir arm to stop Harding's angry advance toward Karina. "You dispersed the agent even as you were inside the special district yourself," Tei continued. "Were you prepared to die with the Rounds, or did you and the others inoculate yourselves with a vaccine? There has to be a reason. Or is it a substance that only affects Rounds?"

Tei could hear Shirosaki and the others in the room gasp.

"Affect only Rounds? Is that possible?" asked Shirosaki.

"It's simple," Tei answered. "The Rounds have many synthetic genes that Monaurals don't. Unique among them is 'double-I'— the sex chromosome carrying the genetic information to create the hermaphroditic physiology. If you can create a substance that latches on to double-I as if it were a marker chromosome, it would be possible to create a biological weapon that only affects Rounds. If Karina didn't vaccinate herself beforehand, then that's the only plausible explanation for why she is unaffected. That's how she was able to disperse the agent. It would also explain why Barry Wolfren wasn't in the special district. He may look male physically, but he still carries the double-I sex chromosome. If he'd gone inside the special district, he would have been affected. That must be why he was working outside the special district, apart from Karina."

Harding pushed Tei aside and pulled Karina up by the collar. "Is what the doctor saying true?"

Karina looked Harding dead in the eye and sneered. Red-faced, Harding slapped her. Saying nothing, Karina looked away and spat blood on the floor, an imperceptible laugh escaping her twisted lips.

"Please stop," Tei cut in.

"Look, she's not going to talk unless you get rough with her." Harding glared at Tei as if he might knock em down next. "We don't have time to play games."

"What if she dies?"

"I won't let that happen. I won't kill her, but she'll damn well hope that she was dead."

"Stop him, Commander Shirosaki, please," Tei pleaded. Shirosaki could only shake his head. Tei could not hide eir disappointment. "Are you condoning this?"

"You forget that I'm a security officer."

"You disappoint me, Commander."

"Right now, our priority is to save the Rounds."

Taking Tei by the arm, Shirosaki wrangled both the doctor and Kline out to the corridor. "Don't come back until we're done here. This won't take long. She's isolated and with one of her accomplices dead…it's only a matter of time until she realizes it's over."

"I understand," said Kline. "You do what you have to do to get us the information that we need."

Bowing his head slightly, Shirosaki said, "Thank you," and returned inside.

Tei put eir hands on the door, but the lock had already been activated. Tei slammed eir fist against the door.

"He's right, Doctor. We should leave Karina to them and look after the Rounds."

"I don't believe you. Is this the way you Monaurals do things?"

"We're prepared to do anything to save the lives of the Rounds. That's our responsibility for having created you. Save your complaints until after we've saved the patients. You are a doctor, Lanterna."

Tei stepped away from the door and fixed a hard look on Kline. "I'll help them, yes. I don't want to see any more people die needlessly."

The children's fevers persisted. Although the doctors were able to keep the fever from exceeding 40 degrees Celsius, there was no telling how much longer the medication would remain effective.

Many of the patients, including the adult Rounds, were presenting with fevers and fatigue usually associated with a common cold. To Tei the symptoms seemed similar to those of acute hepatitis. With the proper equipment ey could run diagnostic analyses, but that option wasn't available.

The doctors, worrying about the possibility of Tei being infected, urged em to stay away from the makeshift treatment center, but Tei refused, insisting that eir suit would protect em.

Tei buried emself in caring for the patients in an effort to forget Shirosaki's sudden shift in attitude. The doctor had assumed Shirosaki was a peaceful man for a security officer. Ey had sensed something gentle and polite about him—that he was far more understanding than Harding.

But Tei had overestimated him terribly. Shirosaki was a man capable of divorcing his emotions from his duties; Tei was no match for his cool sobriety.

Even as Tei was often called on to treat eir patients as "subjects" of sorts, ey felt as if ey were made to realize eir own shortcomings in that regard.

Perhaps that was the difference between emself, who knew nothing of the world outside Jupiter-I, and Monaurals, who, for better or worse, weathered the storm of Mars' and Earth's complex societies.

If the Monaurals were fish swimming the open waters, the Rounds were plankton inside a droplet from a syringe—a simple life-form compared to Monaurals.

Tei could somewhat understand why Wolfren wanted to find a way off the station, even if it meant cooperating with the Vessel of Life. Enjoying relatively high standing as a doctor, Tei had not felt the kind of desperation Wolfren had. Though Tei was sensitive to the friction existing among the Rounds, ey had no cause to reject Round society as a whole.

As the doctor switched out an empty intravenous bag for a new one, ey received a call from Shirosaki on eir wearable. "We need you to check on Karina's condition."

Tei pursed eir lips. "You people beat and torture her and now you're demanding I treat her?"

"You must understand that if I wasn't present, Harding would have done a lot worse."

"Are you suggesting that you stayed behind so you could spare her?"

"That's right."

"That doesn't change the fact that you approved her torture."

"I felt that was the best course of action at the time, as hard as it may be for you to understand."

"There are other doctors. You can ask one of them."

"I trust you to give Karina the care she needs."

"You must believe me a fool."

"We can't allow the Rounds to die, you know that. You have to make Karina talk to you."

"How do you expect me to accomplish what you couldn't?"

"I'm not asking you to interrogate her. She might let down her guard and reveal something. Karina seems to feel some sort of connection to you."

"I wouldn't have a clue what to do," Tei said.

Tei fell silent for several moments, and after gathering the necessary first aid supplies onto a tray, left the special district.

Upon arriving at the residential district, Tei found a security guard stationed at the door to the room where Karina was being held. The guard prompted Tei to enter, saying, "I'll be right outside if you need anything."

"You're not going in with me?"

"Do you require my presence?"

Tei opened the door.

The woman, who'd been sitting on a chair when Tei had left her, now lay on her back, her clothes in terrible disarray.

She lay barefoot and nearly lifeless, with her hands tied behind her back. The toes of both feet were smeared with blood. Blood oozed out of the bullet wound on her left leg. Her eyes were shut, and only her chest heaved up and down.

Tei knelt down next to Karina, nearly sickened with anger, and opened eir medical pack.

Karina flinched as Tei began to wipe her face with a wet cloth. She was still conscious. *Not surprising*, Tei thought. *It was hard to imagine she could lose consciousness given the excruciating pain she must be in.*

Tei gingerly removed Karina's clothes to examine her. Her body was battered with bruises. She let out a cry and squirmed when Tei gently pressed down around her ribs. Perhaps they were cracked, or worse, broken. A simple MRI would give Tei an exact diagnosis, but it was Karina who had destroyed the medical equipment.

"Do you think you can answer a few questions?" Tei asked.

Karina nodded slowly.

"Any pain in your head or nausea?"

"No."

"Any pain when you breathe?"

"A little."

"Hold on, I'll get you a brace."

Standing up, Tei rushed to the door and stuck eir head out at the security officer standing guard. "I need you to go to the infirmary and ask for a rib brace."

"You're asking me?"

"Help me out, would you?"

"I can't leave this post. There's no telling what the prisoner might do if you two are left alone."

"Do you expect her to get up and flee after what you people did to her? She's been brutalized and all of her toes broken."

Without answering, the guard used his wearable to relay Tei's request. After several minutes, one of the station staff delivered a brace from the warehouse.

Tei swore and returned to the room with the brace.

Karina lay on the floor, laughing, the wet cloth on her forehead where Tei had left it. Her lips twitched into a twisted shape, not so much because of the pain but as if to ridicule Tei and the guards.

"What's so funny?"

"You're so serious, Doctor. The members of Shirosaki's team have been surprisingly kind. Shirosaki too. If he hadn't been around to intervene, Harding would have beaten me to death."

"How can you say that after you've been so badly beaten you can't move?"

"I can't move because they shocked me."

"What? I didn't notice any electrical burns."

"They put the electrodes where you can't see them. I have to admit, it packed quite a wallop."

Tei froze momentarily, ashamed of her failure to properly diagnose Karina.

As the doctor leaned over to treat Karina with a topical solution, ey kicked something with the tip of eir shoe. Ey picked up a pendant off the floor. It was a medallion of a man holding a crucifix and what appeared to be a skull on the table next to him.

"Is this yours?" Tei asked, dangling the pendant in front of Karina.

Karina nodded slightly.

"The chain is broken."

"Bastards ripped it off my neck. Must have thought there was something hidden inside, like a suicide pill or microchip. It's nothing. Just a lucky charm."

"What a peculiar design."

"A St. Gerard medal, given to me when I was on Earth."

"By whom?"

"Let's just say by fellow child soldiers. They're all dead now," Karina said.

Tei wiped the blood off the medal with the hem of eir white coat and tried to slip it in Karina's pocket.

Karina shook her head. "No."

"Why?"

"It's pointless for a dead woman to hold on to it, don't you think?"

"But it belongs to you."

"You take it, Doctor. St. Gerard is the patron saint of childbirth. Keep it as a lucky charm. Toss it after I'm gone if you don't want it."

After a moment's hesitation, Tei slipped the medal in eir coat pocket. Karina's eyes narrowed into a look of satisfaction.

"Interrogation will resume after I've treated you. Why don't you tell me about the agent you dispersed."

"What time is it?"

"Fourteen hundred. It's been almost a full day since you attacked the special district."

"Then you should be beginning to see the full effect of the agent."

"What do you mean?" Tei said.

"Exactly what I said. Go back to your patients, Doctor. You're no good to them here."

"Why do you hate the Rounds so much?" Tei asked, the tone of eir voice growing tense. "All we're doing is living here quietly on Jupiter without imposing any trouble on the people of Mars or Earth. Is that so wrong?"

"You don't understand. Your very existence is a threat to the people on the planets. How much do you think it costs to keep the special district and this station running in the first place?"

Karina asked. "The operating budget comes out of the pockets of the Monaurals. Kline seems to think the bigender subspecies was born out of cultural progress. But there are still people on Earth that die simply because they don't have enough to eat—never mind cultural progress. How do you suppose those people regard the Rounds?"

"And that's reason enough to annihilate us? You choose to kill us rather than to negotiate?"

"I've come here with a job to do, Doctor. Whether the Rounds die or live is none of my concern. Once I carry out my mission, I'm gone."

Tei's wearable bleeped. Tei moved away from Karina to the corner of the room and took the call. It was Wagi on the line. "There's been a change in some of the serious infant cases."

"Are they critical?"

"Five dead. Only a matter of the time with the other children."

"Cause of death?"

"Blood poisoning, meningitis, uremic shock—there's nothing we can do to save them. Has Karina revealed anything?"

"No."

"Get us the information we need!" Wagi shouted, uncharacteristically. "I don't want to see any more children die over here."

Tei ended the transmission and returned to Karina's side. "We've had five fatalities—all of them babies."

For an instant, Karina's eyes grew wide with shock. What Tei thought was a glimmer of compassion quickly dissipated and gave way to a stony look. "Oh. I guess they didn't last as long because of their underdeveloped immune systems."

"Tell me about the agent you dispersed. If you do, I might be able to talk the security unit into saving your life."

"That won't do me any good. If you and I reach some sort of agreement, they might spare my life. But that doesn't mean they'll let me go. They'll take me back to Earth to be tried, and while I may be spared the death penalty, I'll get life in prison for sure. If

I'm going to get locked up for the rest of my life anyway, I'd rather take my secret to the grave."

"Something else then. Isn't there something you'd like in exchange?"

"You can let me go without alerting security. I can manage on my own once you help me off the station."

"You know I can't do that."

"Then I guess I'm not talking."

Karina watched Tei bite eir lip with an amused look. "Well? If you get me to an escape shuttle, I'll hand over the data to you."

"When will I get that data—before or after you're on the shuttle?"

"Half before. I'll transmit the other half from the shuttle once I'm safely away from the station."

Tei shook eir head. "The decision isn't up to me."

"But you can save the Rounds."

"What guarantee do I have that you'll tell me the truth? If I help you escape and the data turns out to be fake, I'm left with nothing," Tei said.

"You don't trust me."

"How can I? I hardly know anything about you."

"You're welcome to your feelings. But even as you and I are having this conversation, the Rounds are dying one after the next, starting with the children."

For the first time, Tei felt something resembling hatred toward Karina. Fighting back the impulse to strike her, ey said, "You have nowhere to go. Kline will never forgive you if the Rounds perish. That goes for the police too. Do you really want to kill us at the expense of your own life? Is our existence such a hindrance to you? As vast as the universe is, why are the Monaurals incapable of accepting new life-forms?"

"Because Monaurals are petty people."

"But those same Monaurals were the ones to create us. It's their intellect I want to believe in."

"Including the Vessel of Life? They're a dirtier bunch than I am," Karina said. "I would have preferred to kill the whole lot of them before doing the Rounds."

"Then why didn't you refuse them?"

"I have my reasons."

"Why don't you tell me about them? I might be able to help in exchange for the data on the agent."

A hint of a smile came cross Karina's blood-caked lips. "Surely you must have a secret or two you don't want to talk about, Doctor. Regardless of how reprehensible my employers are, I've given them my word, and you're not going to get anything out of me."

"I've no secrets to hide."

"Oh really? Kline and I were for friends for ten years. Oftentimes, she came to me for advice. I acted as her psychological counselor. She used to talk about the special district. About you too."

"I don't know what you're talking about."

"I know why you became an intermediary," Karina said.

"You're lying. Kline would never tell anyone about my private life."

"Well, she told me plenty. Down to every last detail. Your sexual organs are configured differently from those of normal Rounds. You felt a deep sense of alienation about that. Kline came to me for advice about how best to console you."

"That's all in the past now," muttered Tei.

"Your name in the special district was Lanterna. Don't tell me it was another Round with the same name. Your penis and vagina are configured on the wrong side—the penis on the left and the vagina on the right. You're not able to engage in the act facing your partner because your configuration doesn't allow you to insert your penis and have your partner's penis be inserted into you at the same time. You have never felt the sensation of simultaneous ejaculation and insemination. You, Doctor, are a special case who can only do one or the other. At present, there are no other Rounds in the special district with your abnormality. You're a misfit of Round society." Then Karina said, in a contemptuously gentle tone, "You're deformed, isn't that right?"

"You're wrong," Tei answered with as much conviction as ey could muster. "It happens every once in a while. It's a simple genetic aberration—not an abnormality."

"Then why didn't you choose surgery? It's a simple reconstructive procedure, yet you chose not to go under the knife. I don't understand it."

"Because people like me are necessary," Tei said. "If there is no one with such differences, nothing to regard as a mark of one's individuality, Round society will become homogenized and eventually stagnate."

"So what you're telling me is that Round society will eventually develop a binary system like the gender distinctions separating Monaurals," Karina said. "If a Round majority and minority were born of physiological differences, you're going to have the same disagreements that exist among Monaurals, regardless of your elimination of gender distinctions. In time, these differences will be the standard by which you discriminate against others."

"If we don't dwell on the numbers, that these differences exist at all will be rendered meaningless."

"I wonder," Karina mused. "Do you really believe you can achieve in three generations what we could not in thousands of years, and overcome such a deeply entrenched way of thinking?"

Saying nothing, Tei gathered eir medical supplies onto the tray and stood up.

"Leaving so soon?" Karina asked in a mocking tone.

"Have you any compassion—any concern for others?"

"Do you have any knowledge of my activities on Earth?"

"Yes, I do. But surely you feel something. You're human after all."

"If I haven't forsaken my humanity, that is," Karina said.

"I won't pretend to know the hell you suffered in the past, but that doesn't acquit you of your actions now. Many of the things people believe they cannot do are merely things they don't out of inconvenience."

"You're a blunt one for a counselor."

"I don't recall taking you on as a client," Tei said.

Karina let out a laugh that sounded like a purr. "Since you patched me up, I'll tell you one thing. The so-called 'package' I dispersed isn't a virus or chemical weapon. It's a parasitic machine."

"A what?"

Karina said it slowly. "Par. Ah. Sit. Ic. Mash. Een." Then she raised an arm and traced a pair of characters in the air with a finger. "There's some *kanji* for you too. Understand now, maybe?"

"Parasitic?" Tei's face froze. "A parasite?"

Karina slowly lowered her finger. "That's all I can tell you. The rest is up to what you have to offer. Go talk to Kline if you aren't able to negotiate with me on your own. She loves you like you were her own children; she won't turn her back on the special district. You talk to her without involving special security, and I'm sure she'll think of something."

Tei watched Karina's eyes slowly close and a satisfied smile come across her face.

When Tei stepped out into the corridor, with the tension leaving eir body, ey was assaulted by a feeling of vertigo.

These Monaurals were underhanded to be sure.

Tei felt powerless against the likes of Karina.

The doctor called Shirosaki on eir wearable and arranged to meet him in eir room to avoid any surveillance.

When Shirosaki arrived, Tei reported every detail of eir conversation with Karina. "I played right into her hands."

"You did well to learn as much as you did. Karina didn't talk at all to Harding or me."

"Not at all?"

"Not one word. She may feel some sort of affinity with you."

"What affinity could she possibly feel with me?"

"I can't answer that," Shirosaki said. "But you mentioned that you'd met her before. Five years ago, was it?"

"Strictly as a doctor. I don't recall talking about anything of note or counseling her in any way."

"What was she like back then?"

"She was a typical scientist. A kind, cheerful, charming woman without a single hint of a violent nature. She was a true friend to Kline, someone with whom Kline seemed to open up. So when I first heard that Von Chaillot was Karina Majella, I didn't make the connection. I still can't believe that Karina is her true identity. Even now I feel as though she remains Von Chaillot and not the woman before us. She seems to harbor some kind of enmity toward the Vessel of Life, which may indicate some extenuating circumstances we don't know about."

"Exactly what I was thinking."

"You too?"

"It's been twenty years since she quit the terrorism business. I suspect she had a special reason for taking on this job," Shirosaki said.

"When I told Karina about the children that had died, she seemed to waver for a moment. So I thought I could appeal to her compassion—but no." Tei took out the medal from eir coat pocket. "She gave me this. I don't know why."

"I would say it's a sign that she trusts you."

"Even if that were true, just what am I supposed to trust about her?" asked Tei, staring at the medal in her hand. "Somewhere deep inside Karina, something has stopped working—completely broken down."

"You don't have to trust her, Doctor. As long as she puts her trust in you, we're at an advantage. As a counselor, I'm sure you're prone to empathizing with whomever you're talking to. But you can't let her get to you. Whatever her reasons, Karina has killed hundreds of people in the past."

"I had hoped to at least get her to tell me how the agent works."

The phrase *parasitic machine* didn't turn up in any of the databases. Based on the name, which Karina had likely come up with on her own, Shirosaki and Tei surmised they were dealing with a molec machine that functioned like a parasite. Whether it was a completely man-made creation or a parasite that had been modified on a nanomolecular level, however, they couldn't say.

"Karina will likely reveal what she knows piecemeal until she can find a way off this station. She doesn't want to be tried on Earth and even said she'd rather die here than face life imprisonment," Tei pointed out. "What is she thinking, Commander? How can she be so careless with her life?"

"Something called human folly. A part of Monaural nature that may be foreign to you." Tei lowered eir gaze. Seeing the tears welling up around the corners of eir eyes, Shirosaki added, "You should try and get some rest, Doctor. You've been working around the clock."

"There isn't time for that," said Tei, looking up. "I've been so consumed by the Rounds that I'd forgotten. You should get some rest yourself, Commander. You haven't slept since the incident in the docking bay."

"I'll be fine—I've been trained for this sort of thing."

"I've no problem working a twenty-four-hour shift."

Shirosaki rested his hands on Tei's shoulders, pushed em toward the bed, and sat em down. "Sleep, Doctor. It won't do for you to collapse in front of your patients."

"I can't sleep now. I'm worried about the special district."

"I'll get you a sedative."

"No, wait. I have to ask."

"What is it?"

"Why are the Monaurals so bothered by our existence? And so extreme in the way they express their love and hatred for us?" Tei asked. "What is it about us that upsets you?"

"If you have time to dwell on such silly things, you really ought to get some sleep."

"Silly?"

"What is the point in trying to characterize Monaurals on the strength of only a few examples? Regardless of their hate or love for you, they're all acting upon their personal feelings, and those emotions are subject to change at any given moment. Someone that loves you today may very well hate you tomorrow. In a few years, that same person may even lose interest in the Rounds altogether. Our intense reaction isn't directed at the fact of your being Rounds—it's your humanity that inspires so many different feelings in us. In the end, the conflict between Rounds and Monaurals represents nothing more than one kind of human relationship. Why do you insist on stereotyping us? We are, like you, a diverse subspecies. There are people who are fascinated by the Rounds and people who aren't. Many people never act upon that interest. Some may seek friendship and nothing more. While some people invest their heart and soul, others couldn't give a damn about a relationship with the Rounds. You mustn't try to pigeonhole us. We don't want a conflict any more than the Rounds."

"What about you, Commander? Don't you give a damn?"

"If I'm honest, I don't. But should the day come when Monaurals and Rounds have to work side by side, I wouldn't be opposed to it."

"That's unfair," Tei said.

"What is?" Shirosaki said.

"The day you're referring to won't arrive of its own accord. Such a world will only come to fruition by those willing to build a relationship and see it fail again and again, by those risking hurt to learn the truth about each other. But you say you're happy to wait for others to lay the groundwork for you. To come as you please after the groundwork has been laid and the foundation built without getting dirty yourself."

"It's one way to live, wouldn't you say?"

"Yes, but it's an awfully lonely way," Tei said.

"You may be right about that. But I doubt my thinking will change. Neither should you try to change it for me."

Tei said nothing for a moment as ey lay down on the bed. "I think I'll rest now. Don't worry about that sedative. Just close the door behind you."

Shirosaki muttered, "Of course," and moved away from the bed.

"One last question," said Tei. "If a Round were to confess eir love for you now, would you accept em or reject em?"

"It's a moot question unless you specify to whom you're referring. I'm not seeking a relationship with just anybody, and that goes for Round or Monaural."

"That's reasonable. But that person would be terribly sad to hear it."

"Who is this Round you're speaking of? Did ey ask you to intervene on eir behalf?"

Tei looked Shirosaki in the eye. "No," ey answered. "It was a hypothetical question. Forget it."

Tei closed eir eyes and said nothing more.

Shirosaki watched over Tei for a good several seconds before leaving the room without making a sound.

V

1

SHIROSAKI WALKED DOWN the station corridor and made a mental list of the various matters he would have to detail in his report: the number of security staff casualties, the number of Round casualties, the current situation of the Rounds, the damage incurred inside the station.

His head was spinning. He had allowed three terrorists to inflict unimaginable damage on the station. What could he possibly say to explain the situation to the top brass? When he thought about the harsh censure he was sure to receive, the energy in his body left him.

Karina had yet to come clean about everything. The composition of and antidote for the dispersed agent were still unknown. At this rate, the Round fatalities were bound to increase.

Karina had demanded her freedom in exchange for the data. But she must have known the SSD would never agree to such an arrangement. Was she trying to strike some sort of deal? Or planning to negotiate directly with Kline and the superintendents of the special district?

Would Kline allow Karina to escape without his knowledge in exchange for the data? Regardless of the initial shock of having been betrayed, she and Karina had shared a ten-year friendship. There was no telling whether Kline still felt any attachment to

Karina, and it was entirely possible she might resort to extreme measures to save Jupiter-I and the special district.

Shirosaki quickened his pace.

When he arrived at the control room, Kline was talking with five members of the station staff. Although like Shirosaki, Kline had not had a moment's respite since the onset of the attack, she was barking out orders without any hint of fatigue.

Kline caught a glimpse of Shirosaki out of the corner of her eye and gestured with a finger for him to wait. "The engineers are working on repairing the diagnostic equipment in the lab and infirmary," she told Shirosaki, after dismissing the staff from the room. "They'll have to procure the necessary replacement parts out of the warehouse and from what astrometrics equipment they can afford to shut down."

"Will they be able to make the repairs with what's available?"

"Some things yes and some things no. But once we get the virus detection system and diagnostic equipment up and running again, we'll be in much better shape. The station staff have pledged to do whatever is in their power to aid the special district. They've already started work on what they can." Then Kline asked, "Any headway with Karina?"

Shirosaki proceeded to give Kline a succinct account of what Tei had told him. Kline could only tilt her head quizzically when Shirosaki asked about whether she'd heard of a parasitic machine. "It may be a type of molecular machine that Karina created herself," said Kline. "Or a parasite from Earth, or Europa's ocean, that's been genetically altered."

"If we're dealing with an organism from Europa, what are our chances of finding a cure?"

"I doubt it'll be as easy as prescribing a vermicide. It probably multiplies exponentially, making it hard to eradicate. And what about how it spreads? According to Calendula, the terrorists fired capsules into an area where the Rounds had gathered and achieved nearly 100 percent morbidity without hitting any of the Rounds directly."

"Maybe the parasite burrows under the skin like scabies," said Shirosaki. "With that disease, a mite about 0.4 mm in length burrows a tunnel beneath the skin and lays eggs inside the host. If left untreated, a person can host as many as two million mites inside the body. The mature parasites then spread, falling away with the dead skin cells."

"Norwegian scabies. I'm getting itchy just thinking about it."

"Karina said she'll only talk on one condition."

"Something we can live with?" Kline asked.

"Hardly. She demanded that we let her go—she wants to avoid trial."

"But she might be able to plea bargain down to life imprisonment."

"Apparently she'd rather take her secret to the grave than accept a life behind bars."

Kline sighed.

"She may try to negotiate with you directly," Shirosaki pressed. "But you mustn't listen to her."

"You think I'll betray you in exchange for the Rounds' lives."

"Forgive me, but it's my job to suspect everything."

"I understand, and you're right to suspect me. Even though I've tried to remain emotionally detached for the sake of the station, I'm not certain I've entirely succeeded." For the first time, Kline revealed a look of dismay. As supervisor of Jupiter-I, she was bearing both a public and private burden that would make anyone buckle. "Don't worry, Commander," she said. "I would rather see the special district perish than let Karina go in order to save the Rounds. She's lied to us once already. We can't trust her to tell us the truth. Karina must be planning to buy her freedom by giving us fake information. We can't fall for her tricks."

Shirosaki realized that Kline had already made up her mind to sacrifice the special district. Was it because the help from Europa had been delayed? Even so, the decision could not have been an easy one. No doubt she had drawn the line in the sand and bet her fate through sheer will.

"Have any of Karina's personal effects turned up on Europa?" Shirosaki asked.

"Nothing yet. But knowing Karina as I do, she wouldn't have left behind anything that would put her at a disadvantage."

"I'm convinced Karina has the data we need," said Shirosaki. "She wouldn't be as calm otherwise. But since we don't know how Karina's going to play her hand, I don't want to rule out the possibility of a deal."

"I understand. Getting that information out of her is your job, I know. But please don't make any deals that give her the advantage. We're prepared for the worst-case scenario."

Shirosaki hesitated for a moment, and then asked, "Does that include the Rounds?"

Kline didn't answer. "I realize this is a dangerous risk, Commander Shirosaki. But if we stand our ground, Karina will have to flinch first. If she realizes she isn't holding all the cards, she'll panic and lower her demands. That could turn the tide in our favor. Please tell Karina," Kline went on, "that I have no intention of giving in to her demands. And that no amount of bargaining is going to break me."

"I'll pass it on. And of course I'll continue to keep an eye on Karina as I discuss a new plan of attack with Harding."

Shirosaki exited the control room and called Harding on his implant. Harding complained, "Later. I'm on break. I'm sure you've heard of it."

"How much later?"

"Give me half an hour."

"That long? The situation inside the special district is deteriorating, you know that."

"The Rounds can all go to hell."

"We're here with a job to do, Harding. What do you plan on telling Hasukawa if the special district is annihilated?"

"That it was an act of God."

"The younger Rounds are already dying—doesn't that mean anything to you?"

"They're not my family or compatriots. I don't give a damn what happens to them."

"Thirty minutes. Not a minute more."

"Yeah, and call Miles and Arino while you're at it. When the time comes, I'll get to work."

"All right."

"Why don't you get some rest yourself?" Harding said without a hint of ridicule. "Best you give yourself a break so you can stay quick on your feet, or Karina will play you."

After thanking him for the warning, Shirosaki ended the transmission and headed for the room where Karina was being held.

"Would you like to go in, sir?" the guard on duty asked. Shirosaki refused and activated the intercom by the door instead.

Shirosaki stood at the window looking into the room and observed Karina's reaction as he told her Kline's message.

Karina listened quietly, but once Shirosaki was through, she said hoarsely, "The fool. That woman is ready to turn her back on the special district because of her damn pride. Some supervisor she turned out to be. And the doctor? Ey ran straight to you after I'd told her to talk to Kline."

"Who's the fool here? You won't get anywhere by holding out any longer. It's best you give up while you still have some lives to bargain with."

"At this rate, the special district will surely perish," Karina said. "The entire world, not just the Rounds, will blame you and hold you responsible."

"Better that than bend to your demands," Shirosaki said. "I'll be back. In the meantime, I suggest you think about it."

"Wait," Karina called out.

"You ready to talk?"

"No—what about you? Would you be willing to make a deal?"

Karina's tone didn't reveal a hint of panic. Either she was still sure of her position or she was determined to hide any vulnerability to the end.

Shirosaki was just as hungry for information as the others. In fact, he might have been even more desperate for it, since he was helpless to offer medical care to the Rounds in the way Tei and Kline could.

Should he play along or rebuff her to see what she did next?

"If the special district perishes, you'll be held responsible," Karina continued. "Don't you want to absolve yourself even a little?"

"I have no opinion on the matter. I am nothing more than an arm of a very large system."

"Forget the system. I'm asking about your pride and principles as a man."

"You think appealing to my emotions will get you anywhere?"

"That isn't my intention. I just thought you might like to talk. You just seem to be a more decent sort than Harding."

"I'll be back in half an hour," replied Shirosaki. "We can talk then."

Tigris and Calendula trembled as they gazed at a dead child, the offspring of two of their friends.

The tiny body, wrapped in soft cloth, lay lifeless in the cradle. It was hard to believe ey had been suffering and crying only moments before.

The soul had slipped away, leaving only the empty shell. But even the shell, ravaged by disease, was already starting to turn cold. All it would do now was decompose.

Choked sobs echoed throughout the assembly hall. Parents of the dead children held each other and let out mournful wails.

Tigris and Calendula wanted to shield their ears, afraid that they might go mad, that they were witnessing tragedy that would befall them soon enough. There was no telling when their own children would suffer the same fate. Or perhaps they were next.

None of the Rounds were in the state of mind to console the parents of the children that had died. Fortia had been shot and was in serious condition, and Album had been ordered to rest. Although the elder members assembled an emergency council, they proved mostly impotent and acted primarily as liaisons between the special district and the station staff. Afflicted with fever themselves, the elders took as much medication to reduce their fever as they could stomach. Having heard of the infants' deaths, they were shaken by the fear that they were next.

Despite some variance, every one of the Rounds had been infected. Even to the untrained eye, it was painfully clear that the Rounds with weaker immune systems were suffering the most. To the Rounds, born and raised inside the hygienic confines of the space station without ever having caught so much as a cold, the suffering of even a two-degree spike in body temperature was unbearable.

When Wagi requested that the children's bodies be frozen instead of being given a space burial, the Rounds were struck dumb with horror. The doctor reasoned that the bodies might help them find a cure, but none of the Rounds were satisfied with the explanation.

"Do you mean to cut these children to pieces?" Calendula shouted, making no attempt to hide eir hostility. "They died in such pain and you want to use them still?"

"Please, I'm begging you as a doctor," pleaded Wagi, bowing his head.

"No," said one couple. "We refuse. If you must, you can use my body when I'm gone."

"You may still survive. I'm speaking of those who have already passed."

"Please don't touch the children. Surely you understand if you have children of your own."

One after the next, the Rounds began to voice their opposition. "Leave them be."

"We've been nothing but cooperative with you in the past."

"Let them be, just this once. Please."

Wagi listened silently and finally spoke, his lips quivering. "Even so, as a doctor I implore you to reconsider. For the sake of those still hanging on, you must understand."

"What was the security team doing?" Calendula spat. "So many of them and still they allowed the terrorists to attack us. Not only that, they allowed some mysterious substance to be dispersed in the special district. What good are they to us now? We would have been better off fighting the terrorists ourselves. We should have killed them the moment they came into the special district."

"There's no sense in talking about what's done."

Calendula slapped Wagi across the face, staggering the doctor.

"The incompetence of you Monaurals!" Calendula glowered. "Now I understand why Fortia wanted nothing to do with you."

Wagi did not raise any objection. Saying nothing more about collecting the bodies, he turned and walked away to administer to the other patients.

"I want the terrorists dead." Calendula seethed. "I'm going to form a party. I'm going to break out of the special district and kill the terrorists."

"Just what good do you think that's going to do?" Tigris asked.

"At least it'll give me some peace of mind."

"We can have more children—as many as we can stand. We're still young, Calendula. We can always have more."

"We can't replace the children we lost by having more babies. You can't bring back the children that died. Don't you know that?" Calendula demanded.

"Calm down. I can barely keep from going crazy myself. Don't do anything to make things worse than they already are."

"Aren't you bitter? Are you going to sit there and do nothing?"

"Of course I'm bitter. And sad. But don't do anything stupid," Tigris said.

"Stupid, is it? How about giving the others something to feel good about?"

Tigris grabbed Calendula's hand as ey stirred to leave. "Wait, where are you going?"

"I'm going to find some recruits, starting with the parents."

Kline and Preda were engaged in a long discussion in the control room when Wagi walked in and sank down on the sofa. The look on Wagi's face had turned completely desolate over the past day. Kline asked if he wanted something to drink; Wagi asked for coffee with a nip of brandy.

"Dammit, if our hands aren't tied," Wagi groaned, holding his head in his hands. "It's unbearable enough for the Rounds to see their own die in front of them, but to have to see their children die first…"

"How are the adults faring?" asked Kline.

"Every one of them is infected, of course, but none of them critically. They're better off than the children."

"Could it be the effect of the treatments?"

"Hard to say. Their temperatures have leveled off, so I suspect this period of remission will continue. What bothers me is the next stage Karina was hinting at—some other impairment following the fever, I suppose." Wagi turned to Preda and asked, "Anything useful from Wolfren?"

"Arino's been interrogating him, but Wolfren hasn't said anything about the contaminant."

"Why not put Harding on his case?"

"He was there during the interrogations. I hear Harding gave him a good licking, but nothing. Then Wolfren suffered asphyxiation."

"What the hell did Harding do to him? We get nothing if he dies."

"It wasn't Harding's fault," Preda said. "Wolfren ingested some poison he had hidden on him."

"He tried to kill himself?"

"He self-induced a coma so he couldn't talk. Some kind of drug that disrupts the blood-brain barrier and cranial nerves.

We injected a molecular machine into the vein to dissolve the drug's effects. If it works, we might be able to wake him, but that might take some time."

Wagi cursed.

"According to Dr. Tei, Karina is stalling for time," Preda continued, "until the contaminant achieves its full effect, thereby giving her the advantage. She probably planned to elude the security teams a bit longer but was unexpectedly captured because the teams moved so quickly."

"So does that mean there's a cure for this thing even after the symptoms progress?"

"Apparently, Karina was shaken when the doctor told her about the infant deaths. Could it be their deaths were an unintended consequence?"

"We can't be sure unless we ask Karina."

Kline set down a coffee pack in front of Wagi. Wagi thanked her and took a sip. "Anyone among the station staff presenting with any symptoms?" Kline asked.

"No one thus far. How are you feeling?" Wagi asked of Kline and Preda.

"We're fine," Kline answered.

"Either the contaminant has been contained or it's ineffectual against us. It's hard to say," said Wagi, shaking his head. "Dammit, if we only had the diagnostic equipment."

"What if the Rounds should all die?" muttered Preda. After a pregnant pause, he continued, "Who would be held responsible?"

Kline scowled. "Stop it."

"I'm just asking. The security teams were deployed at their stations, and all security systems were operational—nothing we need to be held accountable for. If it came to a question of who's responsible, I suppose the commanders in charge of security—"

"Commander Shirosaki has done a commendable job," Kline interjected. "Harding too."

"If someone goes down, I'd rather have Harding take the

fall over Shirosaki."

Kline glowered at Preda. "You don't mean to make Harding the scapegoat."

"The commander of the stationed team has operational command. Shirosaki's team merely joined the security detail already in place."

"You know Harding won't take it sitting down. He may even talk to the higher-ups about the incident."

"No, he won't. He'd only be disgracing himself."

"He may try to take us all down with him."

"I wonder," Preda said, dubious.

"Stop looking for a way out," said Kline with a severe look. "We've all been through so much together on this station. We need to stand firm."

Preda pursed his lips. "Perhaps this was a mistake—to bioengineer a bigender subspecies in this way. We needn't have done it just because we have the technology. The conservative majority on the planets have to be cheering in the streets about now. About how the overzealous scientists had it coming to them."

"The desire to innovate is an essential part of human nature. Suppressing that desire is far more sinful than gender experiments," Kline said.

"I know that. The experiments here had the approval of the Planetary Bioethics Association. I understand it was a path we had to go down once, but knowing when we've strayed down the wrong path and knowing when to turn back is the better part of wisdom."

"If you want to turn back now, you go right ahead. I'm not leaving this place."

Kline felt responsible for not having recognized Von Chaillot's true nature. Neither had she been able to anticipate Wolfren's betrayal. Those two failures might very well lead to her dismissal. She didn't want to imagine having to leave Jupiter-I or having to end her twenty-year career in this way.

"Well, I never said I was abandoning you," Preda equivocated. He flashed a cynical smile. "You've enjoyed a very long tenure here. I just don't want to see you have to step down dishonorably. If we act now, we can still pin this on Harding."

"If someone has to take the fall, then we all do. It's the only way I can live with myself."

"Speak for yourself."

"Look, there's no sense in arguing over responsibility while the crisis continues. I don't believe our experiments here are wrong, and I have no intention of ending them because we've failed. Think of how tragic that would be for all the Rounds born here. Think of the children that died in vain. As much as for myself as for the Rounds, I refuse to believe these experiments on Jupiter were meaningless."

"Excuse me, I'm sorry to interrupt," said Wagi. "What should we do with the bodies of the children? The Rounds refused my request to cryopreserve them so we might be able to find a cure. I'd like your opinion on the matter."

"Let's respect the Rounds' wishes," Kline responded instantly. "We don't rule over the Rounds. Although I realize that isn't the answer you wanted to hear."

"Completely understandable," said Wagi. "We should be able to extrapolate some data from the blood samples we collected from the children. Although I would have liked to record the general condition of the bodies." Wagi swept one hand through his disheveled hair and slowly got up from the sofa. "Well, it's time this quack went back to the special district to be the Rounds' whipping boy."

2

Just as Harding was putting on his hazmat suit, he had received a call from Shirosaki on his implant.

"We need to talk," said Shirosaki.

"Later. I'm on break. I'm sure you've heard of it," Harding answered, pulling up the padded gloves around his wrists.

"How much later?"

"Give me half an hour."

Harding ended the transmission and headed for the special district. After ordering the security guard to open the access door, Harding drew the hood of the hazmat suit over his head.

When the door slid open, the air blew inward toward the negative-pressure environment of the special district.

Harding stepped inside. This was his first visit in quite some time. How many months had passed since he'd stopped coming here?

Walking down the familiar path he'd used many times before, Harding made his way toward the assembly hall.

He peered inside to see the medical staff, dressed in the same protective gear Harding wore, busy unloading various supplies. How much of Jupiter-I's store of intravenous fluids, fever reducers, anti-inflammatories, and antiviral drugs had been depleted? Would they be able to hold out until the cargo vessel brought in new supplies?

The cots filling the hall looked to be reserved for the most serious cases. Harding could not help but grimace. The patients lying on the cots were all children, ranging in age from toddler to adolescent. Feverish and dehydrated, they were hooked up to fluid pumps and receiving oxygen through masks.

The adult Rounds looking after them looked more stricken than the children—not because they felt sick, but because they felt guilty for being better off than the children. Some of them wept for want of taking the children's place and were being consoled by the medical staff.

Harding looked for Veritas and eir child. He spotted em with the child—the infant lying on a cot in the back of the assembly hall—and weaved his way past the others toward them.

Noticing someone approaching, Veritas looked up at the familiar face shrouded beneath the hood of the environmental suit and immediately became flushed with anger. "What are you doing here? You and I can't see each other anymore."

"I wanted to see if you were all right. The medical reports don't tell me anything."

"You've been shunned by the Round community. Whatever your reasons, you can't come here."

"If you don't like that I'm here, fine. Hit me—kill me. Round up a lynch mob if you want, I don't care."

"Why now?"

"I was worried about how you were doing," Harding said.

"How do you think I'm doing? I've been taking fever reducers and antiviral medicine."

"I know that. I just wanted to know how sick you were." Then he looked down at the tiny figure lying in bed. "How is ey?"

"Eir condition isn't as bad as the others. Ey must get eir toughness from eir other parent. Eir fever was high for a while, but it began to go down about an hour ago. The doctor says it's a sign that whatever this thing is will go into remission."

"Good. Glad to hear it."

"Ey's not your child. I wish you wouldn't talk as if you know em. Gives me the creeps."

Harding stared gravely at the child.

"Now if you're done here, I'd like you to leave," Veritas said, raising eir voice irritably. "Everyone here is on edge after the infant deaths. If they find you, a lynching isn't out of the question."

"I'd like to stay a little longer."

"Why?" Veritas said.

"I just need a minute. Being in the residential district is making me crazy. When I see Karina, I want to break her neck."

"Why don't you? You *should* kill her. Nothing would make us happier."

"We can't. Karina is holding the information about the agent that's infected all of you and is using it as a bargaining chip. Until we find out what she's hiding, my hands are tied."

"Why don't you make her talk? That's what you're good at."

"She refuses to talk," said Harding, shaking his head. "She's been playing for time, and putting her body through a whole lot of hurt at the same time."

"Still, you can't just show up here. While you may be looking for a place to unwind, your presence here is distressing."

"I won't stay long. I just want to take a walk in the bioengineered forest. I won't get in anyone's way. No one will recognize me in this suit."

"Five minutes—not a minute longer."

"Hey, I'll decide how long my walk will be."

Harding reached out to the child on the bed only to have Veritas slap his hand away. Harding looked at em grimly but then quietly left the hall.

Harding made his way to the forest and began to thrash his way through the brush in search of a place to meditate.

When he had first stepped foot inside the special district, Harding felt a deep attraction to the forest. The sight of bulbous red fruit peering out from beneath the leaves had been enough to tickle his appetite. Although that feeling waned somewhat after learning they were bioengineered, what only existed as images in the residential district was real in the special district. Even as he knew they were inedible, the crimson fruit was beautiful nevertheless. In the same way, even though Harding knew the Rounds were bioengineered, they appeared unmistakably, naturally human.

The forest was unnaturally quiet. Though it was usually a place where children played in the day and lovers confessed their devotion to one another at night, none of the Rounds were in any shape to do either at the moment. They were all receiving treatment in the assembly hall or resting in their homes.

Unlike the forests of the planets, this one had no birds or insects flying about, nor even a breeze to rustle the treetops. Without the

Rounds, the place had descended into a kind of dead stillness.

Harding continued to walk the forest, smelling what might have been the subtle stench of death. He imagined the mysterious particles of the dispersed contaminant penetrating the tiny seams in his protective suit, and suddenly started to sweat.

Harding believed Shirosaki to be a cunning man, but not in a way that made Shirosaki untrustworthy. Shirosaki's every move thus far had been precise and expedient. Had Shirosaki been under his command, Harding would have grown to rely on him in much the same way he did Miles.

But at present, Shirosaki was acting commander of the relief team. Whenever he anticipated a tactical conflict with Harding, he had proposed a number of countermeasures with the exacting clarity of a team leader. Shirosaki had deftly guided this operation to his will while respecting the chain of command and without arguing against Harding in front of the others. That was what bothered Harding. He wanted Shirosaki to either obey or resist. "Keep Karina alive." "Get her to talk." Neither option had been part of Harding's plans. Yet before Harding realized it, Shirosaki had managed to convince Harding and to prioritize the Rounds' rescue before anything else. *That son of a bitch.*

The Rounds are a strange and godless people, Harding thought. *Despite living entirely apart from the planets and without sexual distinctions, they're too much like us. Even as they're given the privilege of a special community, they're curious to know us, and we can't seem to refuse them. We are just as much drawn to them as we are threatened by their foreignness.*

And why is that? Because they're human, or because they have ceased to be? Why do we just sit and observe them quietly cultivating a new culture inside the confines of their presdestined world, just to fall prey to the illusion that we might somehow become a part of that world?

The memories came back to Harding in vivid detail. A flood of regret came raging back along with them.

Why had he felt so strongly, both hate and otherwise, for someone who might as well have been, chromosomally speaking, a different species altogether? Was it simply a part of human nature to become fixated on anything and everything?

We get Karina to tell us the cure in order to save the Rounds. But if we accept that they'll die regardless, we can end this right now by killing Karina and Wolfren. Then I can write up the report and go back to Mars.

The dispersed agent has yet to affect anyone other than the Rounds. None of the doctors treating them have been infected either. If this agent works only against the Round physiology like Dr. Tei says, then as long as we're prepared to turn our back on the Rounds, there isn't much else we can do.

Cut loose the special district. Give up on the Rounds. The children and Veritas.

Harding bit his lip. *The only reason I go along with Shirosaki's plans is because every time he mentions the special district, Veritas is on my mind. I could very easily forget about em, seeing as I'm never going to see em again, but I can't. That was why Shirosaki can push my buttons.*

Of course, Shirosaki knows nothing about Veritas and me. He was simply acting out of an unwavering sense of humanitarianism and sober integrity. Or maybe he instinctually knew what to say to keep me from killing Karina.

Harding felt a shiver run down his spine. He hated the idea of Shirosaki taking advantage of him in that way, no matter how sensible that decision was.

Shirosaki's methods were indeed fair. But for that reason, there was also something fragile about them. Harding couldn't quite put his finger on it. There was always the possibility that jealousy was clouding his judgment. Even so, his years of experience commanding the antiterror unit was trying to tell him something— that this would not end quietly. That they were better off killing Karina while they still had the chance. Against Karina Majella, there was no telling what would happen.

As he continued to look for a quiet place to rest, Harding came upon a Round sitting at the base of a bush. Cradling eir knees in both arms, the Round was slumped underneath the leafy cover of the bush. Ey made no effort to move, even as Harding approached.

"What's the matter with you? Are you feeling sick?"

The Round raised eir head languidly. Eir face appeared flushed compared to Veritas, perhaps from fever, and worn down by fatigue. Ey saw the man, whose face was half-concealed behind the hood of the protective suit, and assumed he was part of the station staff.

"Can you stand up?" Harding asked. "Can I get you to a doctor?"

"No, I've been getting my injections," said the Round, shaking eir head.

"You should be home resting. You don't look so good."

"I can't. When I think about the children, I can't sleep."

Harding looked back at the path from which he had come and understood instantly. No doubt this Round had been in the assembly hall looking after the children and had wandered here for a moment's reprieve. No wonder. Unless you were a doctor, anyone would be hard pressed to stay for hours on end in such grim surroundings.

"I am an education supervisor in the special district, charged with teaching and disciplining the children," said the Round. "The children dying in the assembly hall are my students." With a pained look on eir face, ey continued, "Several days ago, I caught some of the children playing rough in the zero-G area and scolded them harshly. Even asked the top supervisor to reprimand them for causing injury to an adult. I threatened the children with punishment if they refused to listen. The children nodded, of course, but deep down they didn't understand. And who can blame them? They're two—they don't want to listen to anything grown-ups have to say. They were back to bouncing around the relaxation room the very next day. Now, those children have been infected by whatever the terrorists have dispersed, suffering from a fever that has no cure. When I rushed to their bedside, they asked if they were being punished. If God were mad at them for not listening to me. I asked them where they had heard such a thing, and the children answered from the second generation.

"Some of the adult Rounds had told them that Monaurals believe in a god that watches over the conduct of all living beings. And that this god judges people and punishes unrepentant sinners with unbearable suffering in order to reform them. I took the children in my arms and told them not to believe any of it. That there is no such god. That all they had to worry about was living, and think and act in any way they pleased and be willing to bear the responsibility of those choices. They need not be tied down by the outdated religions and belief systems of the Monaurals. We are a new type of human. The universe we believe in has no need for a god." The Round let out a deep sigh and glanced furtively at Harding. "Probably not what you wanted to hear."

"It's all right."

"It's a denial of your faith."

"Forget it," Harding said. "That debate's been raging on Earth for centuries. Sorry we let you down."

"It isn't your fault. I'm told we had a traitor."

"Word travels fast."

"As an education supervisor, I have some advantage of receiving information relatively quickly. Tenebrae and I are from the same generation. As a kid, ey wasn't like the way ey is now. When Tenebrae entered adolescence, eir thinking gradually began to change. I don't know why. Tenebrae didn't seem to know emself. In an effort to stay true to those feelings welling up from within, ey said ey had no choice but to leave the special district. And become just a man."

"There are misfits in every seemingly ideal society."

"I tried to get Tenebrae to stay but was powerless to do anything. That failure has brought so much misfortune upon the special district."

"You're an educator. Now is not the time to be thinking about Tenebrae. You should be near the kids, trying to cheer them. You should pull yourself together and go back to them. Your presence has to be more effective than any medicine the kids are getting right now," said Harding.

"I wonder."

"All I can do is eliminate the terrorists. The rest is in your hands." Harding stood up and said, "We'll do everything humanly possible. I hope you'll do the same."

"My name is Mare. What's yours?"

"The name's not important—I'm part of the security staff."

Harding left Mare and the bioengineered forest, feeling a greater burden than when he came.

3

FORTIA AWAKENED FROM a long slumber and was instantly assaulted by the aches and pains in eir joints and back.

Ey scanned the interior and recognized that ey was in eir own residence.

The skylight had been shattered and the floors were black with grime and dust.

It was obvious much had gone on during eir short absence.

Album, who'd been sitting by eir bedside operating eir wearable, leaned forward and asked, "How are you feeling?"

"Thirsty."

"You're being hydrated intravenously, so try not drink."

"Please, I'm parched."

"Just a little, all right?"

Album stood up to get Fortia some water. "Wait!" Fortia said hastily, seeing the leg brace covering Album's right leg. "Forget it. Stay here."

"Why?"

"I'm sorry—I'd forgotten you'd been shot."

"It's okay," Album said. "The brace electronically facilitates ambulatory function, so I can walk without any pain."

"Never mind."

"Really, it's no bother."

Album returned from the kitchen with a water bottle and inserted a straw in Fortia's mouth. Fortia sipped the water a little at a time, and when ey had had enough, asked Album to set the bottle next to the bed. "So what's happened?"

"The security forces captured Karina."

"That much I remember."

"I have some sad news. Five of the third-generation children have died."

"What?" Fortia said.

"Because of the agent Karina dispersed. The medical team did what they could without the usual equipment on hand, but the immunologically weaker infants were the first to succumb to the disease."

"Isn't there a way to treat it?"

"Maybe if we can identify what this thing is. But Karina refuses to talk. It's hard to tell whether she's withholding the information as a bargaining chip or she really doesn't know."

Fortia recalled the hours ey'd passed inside the maintenance shafts with Karina. The very thought sent a chill up eir spine. Karina's bony fingers inside em. Her lukewarm tongue sliding across Fortia's lips. The pain of her nails digging into eir penis. Fortia nearly screamed, reliving every one of those sensations. Karina had fondled Fortia's body with gentle malice. Fortia had tried desperately to keep from crying, knowing that would only excite Karina, but in the end, Fortia could not stop the tears from coming.

Fortia recognized the reason for Karina's actions. To Karina, the leader of the special district represented all of the Rounds, a sacrificial lamb to be hacked to pieces at the hands of the Monaurals. Fortia had been victim of a hideous examination inside the dark shaft to be made an offering to the Monaurals living on the planets.

"Karina's hatred for the Rounds is real," muttered Fortia. "She'll never reveal the information, even if she knew."

"At this point all the Rounds are at risk. You and I may be contaminated already."

"What can be done?"

"Commander Shirosaki asked if you remember talking about anything while you were alone with her. He wanted you to tell him anything, no matter how small. It may give them something to go on."

"We argued about a lot of things, I remember that."

"Anything about the agent she dispersed?"

"Something about needing time for it to take full effect. And oh—she said she couldn't escape until she confirmed the full manifestation of the symptoms. That was the agreement."

"So does that mean she's bound by some sort of prior arrangement?" Album asked. "Something that's keeping her from leaving right away even if she wanted to?"

"I think so."

"All right. I'll pass it on to Commander Shirosaki. Maybe it'll be useful."

Album's wearable bleeped. The face of Tigris appeared on the tiny portable screen.

"We have a situation. Calendula and some others are trying to break out of the special district."

"What are you talking about?" asked Album.

"They're looking to lash out for the children's deaths. They're prepared to kill Karina themselves."

Fortia gestured for Album to angle the display in eir direction. Tigris could not hide eir shock. "Fortia, all you all right?"

"I'm not in any shape to move, but my mind is clear enough to assume charge."

"I'm so glad."

"Tigris, you have to stop Calendula. I'm giving you full authority to find them and talk them out of this lunacy."

"I'm just an ordinary Round. None of them will listen to what I have to say."

"The duty usually falls to the subleader to take over when the leader is indisposed, but Album here is also injured. Ey won't be much good against an angry mob. You are Calendula's partner, Tigris. You'll have to convince em."

"My relationship with em may only serve to inflame the situation."

"You don't have to go alone. Find some others who can back you. I'll put out an announcement myself. I'm giving you a direct order, Tigris. You have no choice."

Despite looking like ey might break down in tears, Tigris nodded eir assent and ended the transmission.

Falling back exhausted in bed, Fortia instructed Album to relay this development to Shirosaki.

As Tigris went around to the less-affected Rounds, some of them began to fall in line behind em. Thanks to the announcement Fortia transmitted over their wearables, Tigris was able to gather a sizeable party without much trouble.

The group stood in front of the access door and waited for Calendula to arrive.

Calendula soon appeared leading a party that easily outnumbered Tigris's. Ey took one look at Tigris and the rest standing shoulder-to-shoulder in front of the access door and snickered.

After announcing that ey had come on Fortia's behalf, Tigris repeated what ey'd already told Calendula many times before:

"You can't leave the special district, you know that. That goes for all of you. I understand you're angry, but I suggest you all go home and think about what you're trying to do here."

"We're going to fight the enemy," said Calendula.

"The security teams are handling it."

"They beat us because we let them. They play us for fools because we rely on others to protect us. If we show them we can fight back with weapons, the Monaurals will think twice about sending terrorists here."

"We're already a threat to the Monaurals as it is. Do it and you could be dragging us into war. Is that what you want?"

"Tell me, Tigris. Are we so horrible that we don't deserve to exist in this world? So objectionable to warrant death?" Calendula asked. "Is it so wrong for one human to be biologically male and female at the same time, to be psychologically bigender?"

"Of course not. But that has nothing to do with this."

"But it does, Tigris. It's exactly the reason we're going to kill Karina Majella—to send the Monaurals a message that we have the might and will to fight back."

Suddenly the door slid open and in came a doctor wearing protective gear.

Calendula and eir group rushed forward at once. Tigris and the others held their ground and pushed back. Caught in the middle of what quickly escalated into a generalized melee, the doctor was pulled into the fray. The doctor, slowed down by his cumbersome environmental suit, cried out as he was knocked around between the two opposing groups.

The security guards standing outside the door burst in, yelling and waving their batons to quell the clash. Assuming all of the Rounds were threatening to break out of the special district, however, the guards pushed back against Tigris's supporters, only exacerbating the chaos.

Tigris grabbed Calendula's arm but was blindsided by an elbow. As ey covered her nose, Calendula bolted out into the corridor. Calendula ran, picking eir way through the mass of Rounds and security guards at the entrance, toward the residential district.

Tigris called out Calendula's name, but ey did not look back.

Tigris could only watch helplessly as Calendula's figure quickly receded down the corridor.

4

KARINA LAY ON her back on the floor and worked her fingers along the chain of the handcuffs. Clamping the chain link between the thumb and middle finger of both hands, she began to pull.

The steel cuffs couldn't normally be snapped by human hands. However, both Karina's arms were artificial, having just the necessary strength to break the chain link.

Karina had been injured countless times working for Libra. Every time a limb had been damaged beyond healing, she had replaced them with artificial limbs. As a result, the skeletal structures of both arms were made not of bone but of metal alloy. The skin and muscle were also made of synthetic materials.

Since the synthetic tissue covering the alloy limbs contained both nerves and blood vessels, Karina bled and felt pain when cut. Which was why no one ever suspected her of being a cybernetic organism, why Karina was able to pull the wool over the security staff's eyes.

Karina operated the panel hidden in the roof of her mouth with the tip of her tongue. In the event of undue stress on her skin and muscle, Karina was able to shut down her neural pathways with a flick of her tongue. The effects, however, were only temporary and the pain would return in time.

After temporarily shutting down nerve function in her fingers, Karina broke the chain link in two with her fingers.

Sitting up on the floor, Karina breathed a sigh of relief.

She examined her fingers. Though rivulets of blood were beginning to form around the deep cuts, Karina felt no pain. The molecular machine inside her body would heal the cuts completely soon enough.

Although Dr. Tei's treatment had been superficial, ey had stopped the bleeding and bandaged up Karina's leg wound. Karina's ribs had also been bound with a brace. Since Karina had shut down much of the neural function in her body, the pain from her various injuries had disappeared. She also changed the neural settings on the interface in the roof of her mouth to minimize the sensitivity to sudden pain stimulus such as a gunshot wound. While this would do nothing to regenerate cell damage, by manipulating the nociceptors that transmit pain impulses to the brain, Karina would be able to keep on running despite the physical damage she incurred.

Karina slowly flexed her muscles. Her body, now completely rid of any pain, felt entirely artificial. She had gritted her teeth through the pain of the interrogation to keep her pain-inhibition abilities secret. Every time they had beaten and brutalized her, she had cried out in pain, but it was an act to lull the torturers into complacency.

Harding had appeared pleased with himself while Shirosaki had tried to restrain him and had benevolently sent the doctor in to care for her wounds. Karina was convinced she had not let on about her special abilities.

Karina remembered the faces of the security team and gnashed her teeth. *If I run into any of them during my escape, they'll pay for what they did. I'll kill every one of the bastards who laughed at my torture.*

Karina removed her left leg from her body suit. Pressing her nails against the inner thigh, she carefully began to peel back the epidermis. She pulled the skin back without any loss of blood, as there were no blood vessels running through the permeable dermal layer. It peeled away like a sticker, revealing a deep fissure resembling an old wound underneath. Karina stuck her thumb and forefinger inside the fissure that ran down the length of her thigh. Fumbling inside the synthetic muscle sac, slowly she pulled out a slender bundle slightly smaller than the size of her arm.

Protected by synthetic tissue, the bundle had remained dry and free of blood and other bodily fluids. Karina massaged the opening in her left thigh with both hands, and the fissure melded shut into its original form. She covered the fissure back up, and after pressing down on the skin layers for several seconds, slipped her left leg back into her body suit.

Then she retrieved the shoes that had been tossed about by her torturers. Since the neural inhibitor was set to maximum, she was able to slip them on without any pain, despite her broken toes. She should be able to run without much trouble.

She unraveled the bundle that she'd removed from her body.

There was a long, silver cylinder inside.

They're desperate for the data on the parasitic machine, so they can't kill me. That's my advantage.

Karina had known from the start that Kline would reject her demands. It was a move worthy of a station superintendent. In fact, Karina wanted to salute her bold decision. *Though if Kline had agreed to the deal, the outcome would be so much easier for everyone involved.*

What about Shirosaki? Is he thinking about what I told him? Or did the offer of a trade only arouse suspicion? Whatever, at this point he's the only one who might be open to making a deal. I'll have to use that to my advantage.

Karina smiled.

The security division must be convinced that I'm only after a deal. I told them as much from the start. Tei and Shirosaki must have sensed it in our conversations. But my aim isn't to escape with my life, it's to protect Europa.

I'm fighting for Europa. I'm prepared to die to save her.

5

SHIROSAKI, ARINO, HARDING, and Miles gathered in the meeting room to discuss options.

Unbeknownst to Tei, the room where Karina was being held had been bugged so the security team could listen in on Tei and Karina's conversation. Shirosaki had listened to Tei's report after having heard the entire exchange between Tei and Karina.

As a result, the four men had overheard something they had never intended to hear—the secret of Tei's physiology. None of the men had said a word about it afterward, recognizing that silence was the bare minimum of courtesy that they could extend to Tei.

"Captain Hasukawa's orders were to eliminate the terrorists," said Shirosaki. "But we've also been ordered to protect the special district. And to protect the Round inhabitants, we need to get whatever information Karina's holding about the dispersed substance. Until we do, we can't kill her."

"I still say we beat it out of her," said Harding. "All the doctor's talking didn't get anything useful out of her."

"Well, we learned something. Karina seems to be more forth-coming with the doctor. It was the doctor who got us the description of the agent."

"All we have is that. We got nothing unless we learn how the damn thing works."

"Karina seems to bear some sort of grudge against the Vessel of Life. If we play this right, we can get her to make a deal."

"We're wasting our time. Let me get another crack at her," Harding said.

"Karina won't talk as long as we continue these coercion tactics. If she were going to submit to violence, she would have done so already. She has no allies here, no one to save her. That she refuses to talk is a strong indication that she believes she's holding a powerful bargaining chip. I have to believe the information she has is real."

"Then what are you suggesting we do?"

"All we're doing is going around in circles," cut in Miles. "I'm for resuming the interrogation. Torture aside, we won't get any-where in this meeting room. Let me try talking to her. You can talk me through it with the implant."

"You're just going to go in there?" Harding asked.

"Maybe the talk with the doctor got her thinking. Maybe talk-ing to someone else could yield something more. I'll start there."

Miles took two of his men with him to Karina's cell.

Karina lay on her back on the floor. One of the guards made a straight line to where Karina lay and kicked her in the side. "Wake up. Naptime's over."

The woman's hands were cuffed behind her back. But Miles stopped dead in his tracks, sensing something was amiss.

Her shoes.

He realized Karina was wearing shoes. *When did she put them on? Did the doctor put them on for her? For what purpose?*

In that instant, Karina sprang to her feet and pointed a silver cylinder at Miles.

Something shot out of the cylinder and plunged into his carotid artery. Miles instinctively pressed a hand up against his neck, but it was too late to stop the bleeding.

A hot spray spurted forth from between his fingers. Miles recognized in an instant that his molec machine would not be able to repair the wound. He reached for the gun in his holster but fell to his knees before he could find the grip. He put out his hands to stop his fall, but his blood-soaked hands slipped across the floor.

Miles fell sideways in a pool of his own blood. *Jesus. So this is where I die. Without having even drawn my gun.*

As Miles panted for air in a sea of red, the two security guards were struck down in the same way. With one swing of Karina's arm, the slender spear that had brought down Miles arced like a snapping whip and pierced one guard's windpipe and medulla and the other through the side of the throat.

Karina bent down and stripped the bodies of weapons. She holstered one gun on either side of her waist and held another in her left hand.

She strode over to the door and kicked it down.

The guard outside the door reflexively pointed his gun at Karina before he had time to grasp what was happening. But Karina's spear had already found its target, plunging into the guard's eye. The monomolecular carbon tip pierced the skull and brain and emerged through the back of his head.

Pressing a button on the cylinder, Karina retracted the spear back into the tube. The guard's body twitched uncontrollably as he slumped to the floor.

The speargun required neither gunpowder nor batteries, so it was capable of taking down the enemy without a sound. Since it was propelled by an elastic sling and reeled back into the barrel, there was no worry about running out of ammunition. Although the speargun necessitated shooting at closer range than a gun, it could be just as lethal as a bullet. Karina's spear was made of monomolecular carbon, capable of piercing flesh and bone and also effective against ballistic suits.

Karina took off the guard's soft vest and put it on over her body suit. Though not as protective as a reinforced ballistic vest, it would keep her alive as long as she didn't take a bullet at close range.

Karina also seized the guard's data goggles and submachine gun. Taking the side arm out of his holster, she removed the clip and shoved it in her pocket.

Karina started to run in the direction of the escape shuttle.

Miles's implant had gone dead soon after he had entered Karina's cell. Assaulted by a feeling of dread, Shirosaki, Harding, and Arino ran immediately for the room.

Harding felt his knees go weak, aghast at the brutality wrought inside the room.

The security guards were already dead.

Harding lifted Miles off the floor and drew the man's colorless face closer to his chest. Harding shook with grief as he tried to keep from crying out.

Arino averted his eyes and let out a gasp.

Shirosaki bit his lip. Desperately fighting back the chaotic feelings roiling in his soul, he evaluated and reevaluated his actions thus far. Where did he go wrong? Where had he strayed? What was the next course of action? Shirosaki was working his brain a mile a minute to devise a counterstrategy. It was all that kept him from going to pieces like Harding.

At that moment, the three men received a transmission over their implants from a security team member in the special district. The officer gave a brief account of the brawl between the security guards and Rounds and warned that Calendula had escaped the special district.

Coming to his senses, Shirosaki clicked his tongue. "Dammit, we don't have time for this!"

"Should we go after em, sir?"

"We don't have the manpower to spare. Karina's escaped. Our priority is to go after her first."

"What if we run into Calendula?"

"Do what you need to disable em. We can't have the Rounds getting in our way."

Harding lay Miles back down on the floor and stood up slowly. "I'm going to kill Karina Majella," he said, turning to Shirosaki. "You got any complaints?"

Shirosaki did not answer.

Harding grabbed him by the collar. "Say something," he said, his teeth clenched.

"I have to agree with him, Commander," said Arino. "Keeping Karina alive is a mistake. Even the Rounds have risen up against her. It's clear everyone's reached their boiling point."

"Then what about the data on the parasitic machine?" asked Shirosaki. "Without it, the special district will be wiped out."

"Karina's been playing us because she thinks we can't touch her," Harding said. "She's got to be stopped. The fact that she escaped can only mean she doesn't have anything on the parasitic machine."

"We don't know that."

"I'm tired of these guessing games. Even if she gives us the information we need, it's still not going to bring Miles back. Or the Round children. Don't you see? Karina's got you completely wrapped around her finger."

Suddenly, the lights went out. This was no burned-out light panel, but rather a power outage that appeared to be affecting much of the station.

With Harding still clutching him by the collar, Shirosaki reached down and contacted Kline on his wearable. "What's going on? Has something happened?"

"The system shut down the power generator. We're trying to locate the cause now."

"How long before you can get it working again?"

"That depends on the damage. Stand by."

Harding, realizing the gravity of the situation, finally loosened his grip on Shirosaki.

The three men waited in the dark for Kline's response.

After what seemed like an eternity, Kline responded, "It's no good. There's a problem with the mainframe."

"Was it sabotaged? Blown up like the medical labs?"

"No, this time it's fungi and bacteria."

"Fungi?"

"A fungus called *Cladosporium resinae* and the bacterium *Desulfovibrio*, both of which corrode metal and circuit boards. They were found growing all over the circuit boards in the server room."

"But the mainframe should be made of bacteria-resistant materials. How did the stuff work its way into the circuitry?"

"The antibacterial coating must have been peeled off somehow. The server room is usually kept in dry environment conditions, but the air-conditioning settings were tampered with so the humidity and temperature have been rising steadily. What is considered a comfortable humidity and temperature for humans is also an ideal breeding ground for fungi and bacteria. At 20 degrees Celsius, they'll multiply at an alarming rate and will grow only more rapidly as the humidity rises."

"That takes some planning. Someone must have planted this surprise in advance."

"Barry Wolfren," Kline said. "He must have sabotaged the mainframe well before he was captured. Then all he had to do was hack into the air conditioning system at the right time."

Shirosaki recalled belatedly that Karina's area of expertise was microbiology. No doubt she had genetically manipulated the fungi and bacteria so they could not be easily exterminated.

"Check the other facilities immediately. If Wolfren got to the electrical systems, there's a good chance he tampered with the rest. If the station's life support goes down, especially the atmospheric controls, none of us will survive."

"The station's Environmental Control and Life Support System can't be so easily tampered with. We'll check, of course, but I don't think we have anything to worry about. First, we'll lower the temperature and humidity in the station. That should stop the fungus and bacteria from spreading. We'll be able to restore electricity quickly by replacing the damaged parts."

"Understood," Shirosaki said and ended the transmission.

"Why the electrical systems?" asked Arino.

"I don't know. With the power generator down, the high-velocity elevators will be inoperable, and the various security locks will be harder to disengage. I don't see how Karina stands to gain an advantage."

"The surveillance cameras," said Harding. "With the electrical systems down, we won't be able to get a visual lock on the terrorists' location with the surveillance cameras. And the emergency partitions won't come down to hinder their escape."

"Where do you think Karina is headed?"

"Either the cargo vessels from Asteroid City or the escape shuttles," Harding answered.

"Shuttle number two's cockpit console was destroyed in the shootout with Lobe. That leaves five. We'll have to dispatch security teams to each of the shuttles."

"How many to a team?"

"Excepting the casualties, I'd say about five or six to a team. Not exactly a sure bet against Karina."

"Five or six men is plenty if they shoot on sight," Harding said. "Listen to me, Shirosaki. We'll be split into teams to guard the shuttles. We don't actually know where Karina's headed. If she shows up where you are, you apprehend her however you please. But if she finds me, I'm going to kill her. Any complaints?"

Shirosaki pulled his lips taut and nodded slowly. "All right. But if I find out Karina's gone to you, I'm going to do everything in my power to stop you."

"Fine," Harding said. "By the time you get to me, Karina will already be dead."

6

THE PLAN HAD been for Wolfren to remain in a coma for three days. At least, that had been his intention when he crushed the capsule embedded in the base of his tongue.

He had been wafting along in a dark but pleasant and dreamless slumber, when he abruptly found himself back in reality.

Wolfren squinted at the light from above and felt an uncomfortable bed beneath him. A dull pain shot through his shoulder and the base of his neck. He remembered Harding kicking him to the floor, chair and all, during the interrogation and suddenly flushed with anger.

"Looks like it worked."

Wolfren saw Tei and Arino standing next to the bed and swore. "What did you do?"

"We injected you with a drug-resolving molec machine and pumped you full of every psychotropic drug we could think of," answered Arino. "We guessed at the chemical substance or 'key' plugging up the brain cell receptors and simply pulled the key from the keyhole."

"You son of a bitch."

"You didn't think you were going to get off so easy, did you?"

"How many times do I have to tell you? I don't know anything about the dispersed substance," Wolfren said.

"Then maybe you can tell me where you dispersed the mold."

Wolfren fell silent.

Arino grabbed Wolfren by the arm and shook him.

"Let go of me," said Wolfren through clenched teeth, flailing in pain.

"The station's surveillance system is down," Arino said. "Replacing the circuit boards only partially restored the electrical systems. Many of the station's corridors are still dark, and we can't get a visual read on Karina's location." Arino tightened his grip around Wolfren's arm. "You know which circuits are rigged."

"What makes you think there aren't others on this station working with me?" Wolfren forced a laugh through the pain. "Like I said, I'm not the only one who questions Round society."

"No, it had to be you that sabotaged the system. And then you induced yourself into a coma to avoid further interrogation."

Clamping a hand over Wolfren's forehead, Arino slammed Wolfren's head down against the bed and twisted the arm in his grip. Wolfren cried out. Tei looked away but made no effort to stop Arino.

"Listen to me very carefully," Arino said, his voice full of menace. "I don't want to see people die. I want to get Karina without any more casualties. And in order for that to happen, we need to get the surveillance system working again. I'm looking at the bastard that can tell me how."

"I've got my life riding on this plan," Wolfren said in a rasp. "Someone like you who's just here to earn a paycheck has no idea what that means."

"Earn a paycheck? Our job is to protect the people that require our help, Round or Monaural. If *you* were somewhere and needed saving, we would dive into harm's way without a second thought. Only those with the unconditional desire to do good are assigned to this job. What do you think you know, anyway? You don't know the first thing about surviving on the planets or about the hardships of living in our society."

"Shut up, you pig."

"Start talking or I'll break your arm."

"Then do it," Wolfren said.

"Tenebrae," Tei interjected. "You didn't really want to aid Karina. If there were another way, you would never have gotten involved with the Vessel of Life. If you had another choice, you would have preferred it to resorting to terrorism, isn't that right?"

"I argued with Fortia and Kline time and again," answered Wolfren. "The Planetary Bioethics Association had engaged in serious deliberations before establishing the special district. I pleaded with them to take up a similar discussion about creating laws to address the misfits of Round society, and to change the laws that restrict people's lifestyle choices. You want to know what they said? That would go against the principles of why the special district was established in the first place. Its creation was approved on the condition that the Rounds would never leave the Jovian system, so they refuse to compromise those principles. What choice did I have? If they won't listen to reason, then the only alternative is force."

"The Vessel of Life is using you, Tenebrae. They oppose the existence of the Rounds. Don't you see that their motives don't conform with your own?"

"Of course I know. But they were a hell of a lot more accommodating than Kline or Fortia."

"You prefer to deal with terrorists who will tell you anything you want to hear over your friends on Jupiter-I?" Tei said.

"Friends? I don't have any friends here, and I certainly don't trust the terrorists or Jupiter-I. I'm alone here and everywhere else. That suits me just fine."

Arino loosened his grip. The tension leaving his body, Wolfren lay limply on the bed, gasping for air.

"People can't choose where they are born," muttered Arino. "So I can appreciate your wanting to leave of your own volition. But you can't win your freedom at the expense of the lives of others."

"That was the only choice I had. If you can't understand that, then go ahead and kill me, like you did Lobe in the shuttle," said Wolfren, closing his eyes. "To hell with this damn place. Destroying Jupiter-I would put an end to this senseless killing once and for all."

Arino drew his gun and pointed it at Wolfren. Tei instantly put eir hand on Arino's arm. "No, you mustn't."

"Stay out of the way, Doctor."

"What good will come from killing him?"

"This is what he wants."

"Please," Tei said. "Wolfren is a friend and colleague. There is no justice to be won by killing someone who wants to die. No atonement."

"My orders are to eliminate the terrorists. We kept him alive this long because he may be holding some information we need. But the original order stands if he refuses to cooperate."

Arino nudged Wolfren's head with the barrel of the gun. Wolfren scowled.

"I'll ask you one last time. Tell me how to restore the station's electrical systems."

"So this is the Monaural way," Wolfren said with a sneer. "You seek a resolution through guns and violence. Whenever anyone proposes a different idea, you people pretend to listen, going through the motions of a discussion, but in the end, you crush the new and revolutionary by brandishing morality and common sense as weapons. Looking at you, I know I'm justified in my actions." Leaning away from the gun, Wolfren cast a pitying look up at Arino. "Shoot me if you want. If that's what you believe to be right."

Arino twisted his flushed face into an anguished look. The barrel of the gun shook imperceptibly as he pulled the trigger.

A shot rang out. The bullet shot a clean hole, not through Wolfren, but through the mattress. Wincing from the crack of the gun in his ear, Wolfren glared up at Arino.

Arino lowered his gun. "I'll fix this on my own," he told Tei, who was nearly in tears. "I'll leave him in your hands, Doctor. Don't let him escape."

"Are you sure?" asked Tei.

"I'm wasting my time. I can't stay here while the others are running into danger without me. Better to fight along with them." A sad smile came across Arino's face. "Looks like I'm not very good at these psychological head games. I have neither the talent for persuasion nor Harding's fervor for violence."

"Please be careful, and look after yourself."

"Thank you. If we come out of this on the other side, maybe you'll take me to the special district again."

"Of course," answered Tei. "Tigris and Calendula would like that."

After returning the gun to his holster, Arino exited the room without looking back.

Wolfren lay perfectly still and stared up at the ceiling with a look of silent conviction.

7

AS SHAKEN AS Calendula was over the darkness that had descended upon the corridors, ey had no choice but to push forward.

No doubt the security team was on eir tail.

Calendula resolved to find Karina before they caught up to em.

But first, ey had to get eir hands on a weapon. Ey should be able to find something in the warehouse in the residential district. Although the warehouse was typically kept under lock and key, this was a crisis situation. Calendula was counting on the door being unlocked in order to facilitate mobilizing supplies. At least that was the way it had been during a fire many years ago.

Calendula hadn't a clue where Karina was being held but figured Tei would have some information.

Calendula turned the corner of the corridor and stumbled on a mass blocking eir path. Falling to the ground, ey recognized instantly upon impact that it was a human body. As Calendula searched the body, ey felt something warm coating eir hands.

Ey brought a hand closer to eir nose and nearly cried out.

The security team member was already cold. His ballistic suit had been stripped from his body. The ground around him was sticky with blood.

Calendula gagged as ey backed away on eir hands and knees.

Then ey had a flash of inspiration.

Ey reversed eir retreat and crept toward the guard. Ey patted down his entire body and found what ey was looking for
in his boot.

A backup pistol.

Calendula removed the gun from the ankle holster. Though
ey'd never handled a weapon before, ey pointed the barrel toward
the ground and tried pulling the trigger.

The trigger did not budge. The revolver did not discharge.
Calendula fumbled with the gun for a moment, wondering if
there might be a safety somewhere, but found nothing.

Calendula pulled the trigger again, squeezing the grip with
both hands this time.

There was a muffled bang as the revolver recoiled in eir hands
and drilled a hole in the ground. The safety, a lever located on the
grip itself, was automatically disengaged when ey squeezed the
grip and pulled the trigger at the same time.

Calendula removed the data goggles from the guard. Slipping
them on enabled em to see in the dark corridor. Calendula stood
up with the gun cocked in eir hand.

Now to kill Karina Majella.

Calendula's wearable bleeped. Ey pressed a button and Tigris's
voice blared out of the speaker. "Where are you, Calendula?"

"I couldn't tell you. With the lights down, I'm not sure where
I am."

"Then retrace your steps back here. Karina's escaped. There's no
telling where she might be lurking."

"Escaped? Perfect."

"Calendula?"

"I didn't know how I was going to find out where they were
keeping her. But if she's escaped, there's only one place she can be
headed. The emergency escape shuttles."

"What are you thinking? Don't be stupid."

"I'll be fine, I'm armed."

"What?"

"I found a gun on one of the guards Karina took out. She must have taken his primary weapon but overlooked his backup."

"You don't know the first thing about handling a gun. You'll only be a danger to yourself. Get back here right now," Tigris pleaded.

"I didn't have any trouble shooting it. I also found some data goggles to help me see in the dark."

"Stop what you're doing, Calendula. I can't bear to see you die."

"I'm sorry, but there's no turning back now," Calendula said. "I feel as if something inside me has been shattered. At the same time, my mind is clear."

"That's the fever talking. You've been infected. You're sick. Right now you're not thinking straight. Come home so you can have your medicine and rest, Calendula. I promise I won't leave your side."

"How are the children?"

"Fighting the fever like the others, but they're tough. They'll stay strong until they enter remission."

"Look after them for me, Tigris."

"Please don't go. I'm begging you."

Calendula ended the transmission. Then ey ran down the corridor with the gun in eir hand.

Using his implant, Shirosaki split up the members of his security unit into teams and dispatched them to guard the escape shuttles. Then he proceeded to put on his ballistic suit. With their depleted numbers, he would have to engage in combat himself. Even if Karina did not surface near his position, he would have to get between Karina and Harding to keep him from killing her.

Harding was intent on killing Karina. Miles's death had put him over the edge.

Shirosaki was painfully aware of Harding's need for revenge. But at the same time, he desperately wanted the data Karina was holding—coveted it, in fact. Even learning how the parasitic machine worked would help the medical team save the Rounds.

Shirosaki called Kline from his implant. "I'm headed for

shuttle number three now. How much power has been restored to the station?"

"We managed to get some of the high-velocity elevators working."

"Any near my current location?"

"There is one working elevator in your vicinity."

"Any concern about it malfunctioning?"

"No, it's been cleared with maintenance." After a pause, Kline informed Shirosaki of another piece of bad news. "Dr. Tei is down with the fever."

"The doctor's been infected?"

"It appears so."

"The doctor was wearing eir protective suit when ey was examining the Rounds. How in the world was ey infected?"

"The doctor thinks it was Karina."

"I don't understand."

"None of the station staff or Karina have manifested symptoms, so the doctor assumed that Monaurals can't be infected. But maybe they can be carriers of the disease," Kline explained. "If what the doctor is saying is true, it's possible everyone who's been in contact with Karina, including the people who interrogated her, may have been infected. We may be looking at a good number of security personnel, including you."

Shirosaki quickly did the math in his head. The security team members who had cornered Karina in the maintenance shaft, Harding and the two guards present during the interrogation, and himself. "So the reason Karina has been running around the station is—"

"She may be a carrier and is trying to spread the agent throughout the station."

Unbelievable, Shirosaki thought. *To think that Karina would use her own body to spread a potentially lethal contagion.*

But if she would resort to such methods, she must be familiar with the nature of the dispersed substance. Even she isn't so suicidal as to poison her own body without knowing how to neutralize its effects afterward.

"What is the doctor's condition?" Shirosaki asked.

"Despite running a very high fever, ey seems conscious and alert. Ey asked me to pass a message on to you."

"What is it?"

"Ey was sorry for having accused you earlier. Ey knows you're here fighting as much as the Rounds. Ey also said, please don't die. Ey asked me to tell you that ey didn't want you to throw away your life needlessly."

"Please tell the doctor that ey needn't worry. I'm not so easily angered. Once we've dealt with Karina, I'll look in on the doctor. Tell em ey can count on it."

"I'll do that," said Kline. "Be careful, Commander."

"You too, Ms. Kline."

8

KARINA WAS ABLE to visualize her exact location as she continued moving toward the shuttle. She had been coming to Jupiter-I as a scientist for ten years, and in the last two years especially, Karina had walked every inch of the station and committed it to memory.

From the location of the room where she'd been kept to the closest high-velocity elevator that would take her to the shuttle, as well as the alternative routes to get to her destination—all flashed across Karina's mind without having to rely on a map.

Karina took a mental tally of how many security personnel she had disposed of.

The two in the maintenance shafts, four during the escape from the room, the three that had pursued her afterward. The four she'd shot when she'd been on the run with Fortia. That made thirteen. Since there were forty members on the security force, that made twenty-seven left standing.

The cockpit of the shuttle that Lobe attempted to board had been destroyed in the gunfight. Aside from the shuttles dedicated to the special district, there were only three operable shuttles remaining. And the two cargo vessels from Asteroid City. With the exception of the passenger vessel the relief team had come in on, the security force would have to split up to guard all five of the remaining space-craft, making out to roughly five members per vessel. Even if the station staff were sent to aid in the defense, there was little help that a bunch of gun-toting amateurs would be able to offer.

Five more. Five more kills and she would be able to board a vessel.

Having seized not just the ballistic vests but the firearms and ammunition of the guards she'd killed, Karina was amply armed.

Although a bullet at close range would likely break her ribs or certainly injure her anywhere else, thanks to her vest neither would prove fatal. She would be able to go on fighting as long as the neural inhibitor was working. She would be able to withstand a hit or two.

And as long as they wanted the data, they couldn't kill her. But there was nothing stopping Karina from killing them.

Harding was the one she had to worry about. The bastard was out for blood. She could see it in his eyes. Harding was using the job as an excuse to come after her with everything he had.

As prepared as she'd been, Karina could not help but smile bit-terly at how she'd been doing nothing but killing since she'd ar-rived. When she left Libra, she had sworn to never pick up a gun again. How had her life come to this?

After Karina had learned to fire a gun at age nine and been party to countless acts of terrorism by the end of her teens, her last kill on Earth had been her own mother.

When a Libra sleeper cell took an all-out attack by antiterror forces, Karina and her mother had run into each other during their ragged escape.

Her mother had been trying to catch up to the others fleeing the compound.

Karina had been in the midst of fleeing Libra.

"Help me get back with the others," her mother had begged. Karina had cried, "No more," and pointed her gun. Her mother's face grew red with rage and terror, and she opened her mouth like a snake threatening to swallow her prey whole and shouted hysterically. "You're going to shoot me? Your own mother? Who do you think raised you? Put food in your mouth?"

"I've had enough," cried Karina. "You—a mother? Don't make me laugh. You fell in with a good-for-nothing man and dragged me along for your selfish desires. I couldn't go to school. I have been on the run my entire life because of you. I've wanted to kill you for a very long time. Since I was a kid, I knew I had to kill you to get out of this life."

"You'll go to hell for this," her mother said. "God will never forgive what you're about to do. Never." She pointed to the sky and, like a ruined woman, let out a shriek with her very last breath. "Look up at the sky! The eye of God."

Karina pulled the trigger. It took all of two bullets to fell her mother, who'd been worn down by years of fugitive life. She had gone quietly. Like a toy whose batteries had run down, she fell to the ground never to be revived again.

In that moment, Karina felt as if a wall had come crumbling down around her. Karina had heard the angels trumpeting the end of her imprisonment and saw Jacob's ladder descend from the heavens where her mother had pointed. And while she had obviously not seen angels dancing atop its rungs, she had clearly heard a benediction rain down from the gray sky above.

She had sobbed and basked in how suddenly vast her world had become. How this beautiful world belonged to her. She was free to live as she pleased without anything to tie her down, without having to live on the run.

Karina left her mother's body where it fell and ran.

Run. Forget. She was done with this life. She would go back to the life before Libra. She was ready for any hardship, prepared to work her fingers to the bone. Karina resolved to save some money and live on her own. As long as she didn't have to kill, she would find some reason to live, no matter how mundane it was.

For several years afterward, Karina experienced a different kind of adversity. Living a normal life had turned out to be a greater challenge than a life of killing.

Nevertheless, Karina endured. She had toiled and saved through less than commendable methods, and although she had no one to celebrate her admission to university with, she was happy.

Finally, a life I can call my own.

Before Karina knew it, twenty years had passed. Having abandoned Earth, she had moved to Europa, one of Jupiter's satellites, spending her days researching the marine organisms inhabiting the ocean. As tedious as the job was, she had grown to appreciate its simple rewards. Above all, she had grown to love Europa's microorganisms. There was something tender and precious about the way they persevered in Europa's harsh environment without complaint.

Karina had reached an age where she could look at herself in the mirror and count the number of years she had left.

There was also a hint of her mother creeping into her aging countenance.

So you've chased me down here, Karina sneered. But that threat was no longer something she had to worry about.

In killing her, Karina had deprived her mother of the opportunity to speak for her sins and deprived herself of the chance to hear an apology.

There would be no apology from her mother, ever. Nor any admission of guilt. She had died believing she was right, and it was Karina who'd killed off the opportunity to make her repent and squandered her only chance to witness her mother's remorse.

But whether such an opportunity would have ever arrived was never clear.

One day, several years after Karina had started working at the research station on Europa, the director of the station received a package of frozen fruit from Earth.

After opening the package for all of the researchers to see, Director Weil had boasted that while research supplies and provisions were brought in from Mars, these had been sent to him from a friend on Earth.

"They're frozen but naturally grown," Weil had said. "These fruit weren't grown in any greenhouse but in a tropical region on Earth. They smell and taste like the sun."

Weil had shared the fruit with everyone in the station.

Karina took the mango in her hand; a distant memory came rushing back to her.

Mangoes.

The Summer Dome.

The Summer Dome was a conservatory housing tropical plants and animals where Karina liked to go when she was seven and still living in Japan.

She had looked forward to seeing how various tropical fruits had grown with every visit and delighted in observing the green, unripened fruit gradually turn color. Mangoes, papayas, passion fruit. Although she had tasted them as juices or sherbet, she had never eaten the actual fruit.

I wonder what they taste like, she had mused as a curious seven-year-old. *Are they more delicious when picked off the branch? Or maybe they're surprisingly bitter. No, they have to be delicious, considering how much care is given to growing them.*

One day, giving in to temptation, Karina had climbed up onto the stone wall and reached for one of the fruit. After struggling on her tiptoes, she picked a mango off a branch and was caressing it tenderly in her arms when someone called out to her.

"Do you like mangoes?"

Karina nearly jumped out of her shoes and shot her eyes in every direction.

She found a boy several years older than she looking up at her from a distance. The moment their eyes met, she felt a shiver run down her spine. Her body went stiff, overcome by shame at having been seen. It was enough to make her want to cry.

The boy bounded closer and scrambled up the stone wall to where she stood. Though he didn't speak his name, he appeared innocent enough. Standing on his toes, he began to pick the mangoes that had been out of Karina's reach and tossed them in her arms until she told him to stop.

The conservatory, though open to the public, wasn't an orchard where picking fruit was allowed. But like Karina, the boy appeared to be itching to get his hands on them.

Perhaps he was glad to have found a co-conspirator.

Struggling with the mangoes in her arms, Karina found herself laughing. When she looked at him, the boy smiled bashfully for the first time.

By then they had become fast friends.

Karina and the boy went around the conservatory picking fruit from one tree after the next. Every time they happened upon a rare fruit, they twisted it off the tree without any reservation, not for the purpose of eating it but just to revel in the act when no adults were looking. It was their delinquency that thrilled them. They were enthralled by what was forbidden. The two might have romped around together for about an hour. As night began to descend over the conservatory, the boy simply said, "I'll see you around," and left.

But Karina never saw the boy again. Any chance of returning to the Summer Dome had been lost forever when she began her fugitive life with her mother.

Such was the memory that had flitted across Karina's mind as she sat in her room in Europa's research station and stared at the half-frozen mango on the plate.

That's right. There was some part of the past worth holding on to. Some good memories.

Karina cut the dewy mango lengthwise first and then into

smaller slices. She popped one of the slices in her mouth and felt a freezing pain pulsate in her brain. She grinned at the absurdity of eating something so cold on a frozen rock like Europa. The mango neither tasted nor smelled like the sun as Weil had touted, but the juicy flesh was delicious.

More than the novelty of receiving such an expensive package, the mango had made her acutely aware of the distance between Europa and Earth.

Karina wondered if that boy had waited for her at the Summer Dome. Did he go back to the stone wall where they met and wait for her, until he gave up and eventually forgot that their day in the trees had ever happened?

If the boy were still alive, he would be middle-aged by now. Karina doubted he'd be very happy to see her, especially given the woman she was. A killer of dozens of innocent victims.

Karina heard the echo of footsteps trotting toward her and hugged her body close to the wall.

The memories of the Summer Dome quickly faded as she sharpened her senses to confront the reality at hand. She held her breath and waited in the darkness for the enemy to come to her.

The footsteps stopped. Having sensed Karina's presence, the enemy appeared to be creeping closer without making a sound. He was a trained professional. It had to be a security team member. In which case, the enemy would be wearing data goggles, as Karina was, to see in the dark.

Karina jumped out and sighted the enemy through her data goggles.

Harding.

Karina reflexively squeezed the trigger on the submachine gun. Harding shot back. She immediately felt the shock of several bullets across her chest and torso. Despite the ballistic suit protecting her, the pain would have been excruciating were it not for the neural inhibitor. At close range, Harding also had to have taken some hard shots.

Karina endured the blunt impact of several more bullets as she continued to fire down the corridor. A strange numbness came over her. The submachine gun felt like a lead weight in her arms, until she could no longer hold up the barrel to aim for Harding's head. Despite being able to suppress the pain sensors, she was still expending an enormous amount of energy.

Suddenly, she began to fade as if she were about to fall into a deep sleep.

Karina swore and willed herself forward. She was almost to the shuttle. She wasn't about to die here.

9

SINCE HARDING HAD not counted on running into Karina en route to the shuttle, he felt his blood turn hot at the sight of her in the dark corridor. *Just my luck. I'll end this right here.*

He set aim on Karina's head but missed wide of the mark upon taking a spray of bullets from Karina's submachine gun. Although wearing a ballistic suit, he lacked Karina's pain-suppression capability, and the impact of the bullets nearly put him on his knees. He fell back against the wall. Despite the dull pain in his bones and muscles clouding his mind, he kept himself from falling unconscious through sheer will.

When she ran out of bullets, Karina threw down the gun and fired her speargun. The tip traced a straight line for Harding's chest. Harding twisted his body, and the spear stuck his side. As the tip tore through the reinforced fiber of his suit and pierced clean through his back, Harding raised his gun and fired at Karina.

Karina instantly let go of the speargun and dropped and rolled across the floor. Drawing a pistol as she took to her feet, Karina set her aim, but before she could shoot a bullet hit her left shoulder from the blind side.

Harding glanced in the direction from where the bullet had come and saw Calendula. The Round was holding a gun in eir outstretched arms, wild-eyed and trembling.

Damn it! Harding panicked.

"Stay back!" Harding yelled, but it was useless. Calendula fired one shot after the next in an attempt to finish the job, but none of the shots found their target. Choosing escape over killing Harding or Calendula, Karina spun back out of sight.

"She got away because of you!" Harding shouted at Calendula, who ran to his side.

"You would have been dead if I hadn't shot her."

Harding grabbed Calendula by the arm.

"Let go of me!" Calendula said, struggling to get free. "Karina is getting away."

"Your going after her is suicide. Stay out of the way, do you hear me?"

"I'll be fine. Next time, I'll shoot her in the head."

Harding rammed Calendula in the stomach with the butt of his gun. The shock of the impact ran up his arm to his injured side, nearly rendering him unconscious. But it worked on the ill Round.

After laying the Round on the floor, Harding contacted the control center on his implant. "I've apprehended the Round that broke out of the special district. Have somebody pick em up."

"Is Calendula all right?" asked Kline. "What is eir condition?"

"Out like a light, but otherwise uninjured."

"Good."

"Good, you say? I lost Karina because of em."

"You found Karina?"

"And exchanged fire. I had her in my sights, but this one got in the way. Karina got away."

"What about you? Are you all right?"

Harding cupped a hand around the spear stuck in his side and answered, "I'm fine."

"From your present location, the closest shuttle is number three," said Kline. "Karina is probably headed there."

"Who's been dispatched?"

"Security personnel from Shirosaki's team are on their way there now."

"Tell me which elevator will take me there."

"You'll find one just up ahead."

"Good, I'm heading there now."

Harding wasn't about to let Shirosaki get there ahead of him. *Karina is mine.* After ending the transmission, Harding tended to the spear stuck in his side. He felt around his back and realized the tip of the spear was barbed.

Pulling the spear out would seriously aggravate the wound. But there was no conceivable way he would be able to run or negotiate tight spaces with it sticking out of his side. Harding braced himself, gripping the end of the shaft with both hands, and pulled out the spear in one motion.

He clenched his teeth as a flash of pain more violent than when the spear had entered shot through his entire body. The molecular machine inside his body would temporarily repair the wound. He was still able to run. Karina wasn't getting away from him so easily.

Harding squeezed a hand against the wound and staggered forward.

Karina had to have been injured in the exchange. In fact, Harding had put a considerable hurt on Karina during the interrogation. Though she might have been using something to dull the pain now, she would be the one to tire out first when its effects started to fade. He would put a bullet in her head when she could run no longer. Getting the information about the plague afflicting the Rounds was no longer a concern to him. Harding was going to end her himself, no matter what the cost. Then he would write up a report detailing a successful mission and go on home to Mars.

Back to Mars. The brother-in-arms with whom he'd made that promise was gone. No matter how Harding might call out to him, Miles would never answer again. He and the Round children were with God now. Harding had made an irredeemable mistake. He had failed as a commander.

No, Harding had lost his fitness to lead long ago. Which was why he burned to lay his life on the line this one last time.

Harding slowly limped toward the shuttle, leaving a slick blood trail behind him.

It was only malice that kept Harding upright.

Karina arrived about the same time the Shirosaki team members were gathering outside shuttle number three. She made a break for the gate, spraying a barrage of bullets at the enemy, and disappeared down the corridor leading to the shuttle. The five security team members chased Karina into the corridor.

Karina continued to shoot as the enemy funneled into the corridor after her. As soon as one gun ran out of bullets, she threw it down and drew another one, gradually inching her way toward the shuttle.

She felt her body going numb, unresponsive. Unable to take down the advancing forces with carefully aimed shots, she continued to pepper the enemy with bullets, until finally she slipped into the shuttle's cockpit and locked the door behind her.

Although the navigational system was locked, Wolfren had told her the security code beforehand. Karina punched in the fifty-digit code and the navigational program came online.

Karina remained standing as she worked her fingers over the control panel. After setting a course for Asteroid City and firing up the main engines, Karina set the controls on autopilot. The mooring lock was disengaged and the shuttlecraft began to pull away from the bay.

Karina breathed a sigh of relief. Some rest, at last. She fell back into the helmsman's chair with the gun still gripped limply in her hand.

Suddenly, she heard a voice from behind. "Drop your weapon and get your hands above your head."

Karina made no attempt to move. "Well, this is a surprise," she said without looking back.

"I came a little late, so I was able to sneak aboard without any-one noticing. You put a world of hurt on my men," Shirosaki said, his gun pointed at the back of Karina's head. "Why did you run? I was prepared to listen to a deal."

"What deal could I have made from my cell? I had to secure an escape route first. Once this shuttle is safely away from the station, I'll listen to what you have to say."

"It's time you started talking to me. Tell me about the parasitic machine."

"If you kill me now, you'll never find out."

"Do you hate the Rounds that much?"

"I'm not motivated by such trifling emotions. I'm merely here on a job."

"That isn't what Fortia would have me believe."

"Well, maybe jealousy has something to do with it," Karina said with a cynical laugh. "The Rounds live a carefree life, protected by a security detail, without any knowledge about Earth or Mars. They're afforded every comfort. I'm not the only one that feels this way. Apart from the conservative majority and the Vessel of Life, there have to be more than a few among those who usually turn a blind eye that hate the Rounds."

"Their silence merely signals their acceptance."

"Are you speaking of the silent majority? Just because they say nothing doesn't mean they accept the Rounds. What proof do you have that they don't despise the Rounds? If they knew the astronomical operating costs of the special district and the names of the officials skimming off the top, the silent majority would be sure to rethink how they regard the Rounds. They'll demand that money go into welfare programs, not toward creating bigenders."

"That isn't what this is about," Shirosaki said.

"The ordinary masses think on the same plane. The police are nothing more than an arm of the state—the ruling class. You have no idea what the masses are feeling."

"You're not suggesting the ruled masses are always right."

"That's a difficult question to answer. There are idiots all around us."

"The conservative majority is driven by instinctual hate, by the knee-jerk fear of anyone unlike themselves. They want to crush whatever they view as worthless before it acquires any sort of newfound value. There is nothing rational or sensible about them," Shirosaki said. "They're consumed by twisted prejudice, pure and simple. They're afraid of the minority overtaking them someday to become the majority. But if that's how the tide shifts, so be it. Eventually, there will be another shift and another, like a seesaw."

"How very radical of you," said Karina. "Have you been poisoned by Kline's ideas too?"

Suddenly, Shirosaki felt himself being jerked back as the shuttle thrusted forward. Without skipping a beat, Karina launched out of the chair, twirled around easily in the reduced-gravity environment, and pointed her gun at Shirosaki.

Shirosaki dodged the first shot and fired back. They exchanged fire at close range, the bullets shredding the fiber of their ballistic suits. Shirosaki winced as one bullet grazed his cheek and ear.

Karina's gun clicked empty. Karina threw the gun down and lunged at Shirosaki. He swept aside her punch and swung with his gun. Karina evaded the attack and unleashed a kick. Shirosaki wrung his body away hard.

The shuttlecraft cleared the station and the autopilot program began to take a flight angle toward Asteroid City.

Karina grabbed Shirosaki's gun arm. Overpowered by Karina's strong grip, Shirosaki reflexively pulled the trigger. Several shots hit the control panel, and Karina's face grew ashen. The shuttlecraft accelerated before the navigational system had fixed course and began to veer from the flight plan.

Karina pummeled Shirosaki in the face, wrested away his gun, and leapt at the controls. The shuttlecraft decelerated per Karina's command and switched to inertial guidance mode, rendering the inside of the vessel a zero-gravity environment. The reverse thrusters and directional controls were not responding.

Unable to repair the damage, Karina turned to Shirosaki and said, "Look at what you've done. We've gone off course."

In zero-gravity conditions, Karina was easily able to yank Shirosaki toward her and shove him in front of the controls. "Get the shuttle to stop."

Shirosaki quickly scanned the gauges and said slowly, "Give me the data on the parasitic machine first."

Karina turned her back on the cockpit entrance and aimed the gun at the back of Shirosaki's head. "If you want to live, you'll do as I say."

"In exchange for the data." Turning around, Shirosaki confronted Karina with a look of calm. "Your move, Karina. If you kill me now, you won't stop this shuttle. Turnabout is fair play."

The two looked each other in the eye for several moments until Karina bit her lip and silently pulled the trigger.

Shirosaki stood motionless. *Click.*

When Karina realized she was out of bullets, an enervated look came over her face.

Shirosaki looked at her with sad eyes. "You lose, Karina Majella."

Just then, he heard a quick, sharp noise, like a harsh whisper. Karina froze.

Shirosaki's eyes grew wide at the reddish-black stain spreading around the spear sticking out of Karina's chest. She swept a hand across the wound and gazed at the blood glistening on her palm. Her body quivered, not out of shock but from the spasms foretelling her death.

Suddenly Karina twisted her face and thrashed violently, like a harpooned fish, her usual look of scorn a distant memory. What stood before Shirosaki now was an animal struggling desperately to pull the spear out of its chest.

Unbeknownst to Shirosaki, the effects of the neural inhibitor had worn off, and Karina was instantly assaulted by excruciating

pain. The collective pain from the shocks and beating of the interrogation, her broken toes, the gunshot wound in her leg, and the
speargun piercing through her back and lung had bombarded her
brain at once, signaling her end. Karina cried out from the pain
tearing through her body. No longer in any condition to devise a
counterattack, Karina could only writhe in agony.

Karina's impaler flung her against the wall by the spear. Harding walked stiff-leggedly into the cockpit, his boots magnetized.
Harding trained his gun at Karina, making certain Shirosaki
would not get caught in the crossfire, and drilled two bullets into
the back of her neck.

Crimson blood spurted out of her throat and mouth, the drop-
lets spraying the air like beads from a broken necklace.

Shirosaki swallowed and stared at Karina's profile.

Karina continued to twist and turn, drenched in her own blood,
frantically resisting the moment her light would be snuffed out,
her soul plucked from her body. With one hand clutching her
chest, she reached out with the other at something imaginary.
Watching as she cradled something in her arms, Shirosaki was hit
with a pang of nostalgia but didn't know why.

Karina stopped in mid-motion with a look of agony frozen
on her face. The light in her eyes had gone out. Her body floated
inside the vessel, a lifeless mass.

Harding approached and after putting his fingers against her
neck to confirm Karina's death, he muttered, "Good riddance."

"Thanks."

"I didn't do it to save you. I was only thinking of killing her."

Shirosaki checked over the navigational system and a cold
sweat began to form on his brow.

"Don't tell me we lost control of the shuttle," said Harding.

"The system's been shot out. The shuttle is headed for Jupiter."

"Are you telling me we're flying into Jupiter?"

"No, we'll probably crash into Io first," Shirosaki said.

"The thought of diving headfirst into a sea of magma doesn't exactly turn me on. Can you fix it?"

"Negative. We don't have the necessary equipment, not the least which I don't have that kind of engineering knowledge."

"So we're just going to go down with Karina in a ball of flames?"

"There's another way—we get the station to send another shuttle after us. We might be saved if we can rendezvous with the shuttle."

Shirosaki moved out of the cockpit to check the shuttle door to see if it could be opened manually. But when he got there, he discovered the manual controls had been damaged in the shootout with Karina. Shirosaki couldn't get the door to budge.

Giving up, Shirosaki checked the air lock used to exit the spacecraft for extravehicular activity. With the green lamp on, the air lock appeared to be operational. But the hatch could not be used to dock with another shuttle. Shirosaki and Harding would have to exit the spacecraft wearing space suits and spacewalk to the shuttle themselves.

Shirosaki returned to the cockpit and explained the escape plan to Harding.

Harding looked pale, having lost a lot of blood. Though the bleeding had stopped, he appeared stricken and spent, not to mention irritable.

"Exit the shuttle?" Harding snapped. "The radiation in the Jovian atmosphere will fry our cells beyond repair."

"Not immediately. The hard-shell suit should protect us a little, and the molec machines in our bodies should repair some of the damage."

"If you want to go, you go on ahead. I'm too banged up to get into a suit. Forget about me and get the hell out of here."

"Don't talk like that," said Shirosaki. "We're not done here."

Shirosaki dragged down two space suits from the rack.

"You're wasting your time," said Harding.

"If we do nothing, we'll fly straight into Io. You and I will hold out somehow until the rescue shuttle gets here. That's the choice we've got. You have a family too. Don't you want to get back to them on Mars, or would you rather die here with Karina? You can't let her have the last laugh for taking you down with her."

Harding made no effort to move.

"Get up," barked Shirosaki. "Think about getting back to your family."

Shirosaki forced Harding's body into a suit. Harding twisted his face in pain but did not put up a fight. Thanks to the zero-gravity environment aboard the shuttlecraft, Shirosaki found it surprisingly easy to strap Harding into the hard-shell suit. After confirming Harding's suit was leakproof, Shirosaki climbed into one of his own. Holding Harding under his arm, Shirosaki kicked off the floor and floated toward the exit.

Harding kicked Karina's lifeless body with his good leg as they floated past. Karina and the blood globules surrounding her drifted slowly toward the control panel.

Shirosaki moved along the wall to reach the air lock and operated the touch panel to deactivate the lock. He entered the chamber with Harding and closed the hatch behind them. The decompression sequence initiated automatically. After confirming that the pressure inside the air lock had reached zero, Shirosaki opened the outer hatch.

Without any scenic markers in the star-filled darkness as frames of reference to determine their inertial velocity, the shuttle appeared to be at a complete stop.

Shirosaki thrust himself into the void.

Suddenly his left periphery took on a colorful hue. He twisted his body in that direction, and a majestic vision of Jupiter filled his view. So enormous was the planet before him that it barely looked spherical but like a flat wasteland, etched with intricate striations that stretched as far as the eye could see.

Shirosaki burned the gas jets on his suit in the direction of Jupiter, slowing their velocity.

The two men silently watched the hulking white shuttle pass their flanks.

"You still with me?" Shirosaki asked Harding, after activating the rescue beacon.

"Yeah, I'm here," mumbled Harding.

"Look," Shirosaki said. "Io."

A small shadow floated before them with Jupiter's striations in the background. The radius of Io was approximately three hundred kilometers larger than that of Europa. In contrast to Europa, a moon covered in ice, Io was a fiery moon rife with volcanic activity. The active volcanoes, whose names were derived from the fire gods of many Earth cultures, erupted, spewed molten lava across the rocky terrain, and at times spit plumes reaching a height of over a hundred kilometers. Up close, Io was a blazing yellow moon dotted with black and auburn spots.

Shirosaki and Harding stared at the gaseous plumes climbing into space. The shuttlecraft flew a straight path toward Io. Shirosaki imagined the moment the shuttle would crash into Io's surface. The metal coffin containing Karina's body would break in two, completely engulfed by the molten waves, and be incinerated. Or perhaps the shuttle would plummet straight into the gaping mouth of a volcano, and Karina would disappear into the volcanic ocean along with the vessel. It was a fitting end for a woman who'd chosen to live violently and known only killing. She had been like a flame. Having burned herself and others to ruin her entire life, Karina had only found meaning in turning everything to ash. Shirosaki had no ruler by which to measure the value of such a way of life.

"Feels a little like offering up a sacrificial lamb," muttered Harding. "Like making a sacrifice to the gods with Io as the altar. Makes me want to sing a mass for the dead." Harding hoarsely recited one verse from Mozart's *Requiem*: "'When the damned are confounded and consigned to keen flames, call me with the blessed.'"

Saying nothing, Shirosaki floated in space, holding Harding in his arms.

"Will you listen to my confession, Shirosaki?" Harding asked.

"I'm not a priest. I have no interest in hearing penance."

"Not that. It's about Veritas."

"Veritas?"

"A Round in the special district. Ey was...a friend."

"A friend? But you hate the Rounds."

"It was because we were friends that I grew to hate em. I thought I understood, but then I wasn't so sure and I got scared. I had to push em away."

"Why don't you tell me about it when we're back at the station?" said Shirosaki, sensing a lengthy confession. "Right now, you should conserve your energy."

"I may not last until the shuttle gets here. Let me get this off my chest."

Shirosaki did not answer.

Taking Shirosaki's silence as a sign of consent, Harding began to talk in a deep murmur.

"When my team began our year-long detail on Jupiter-I, the special district wasn't as restricted as it is now. It was common to see the Rounds roaming the residential district, and the staff were fine with it. When we first arrived here, we often mistook the Rounds for staff, since they wear the same uniforms, and we could only recognize the Rounds as either male or female," Harding said. "We chatted with them when we saw them in the mess and relaxation room and visited the special district. Even enjoyed a game of zero-gravity squash in the zero-G zone from time to time.

"And you saw that bioengineered forest," said Harding. "To those of us raised on planets, the special district was like a lush greenhouse. It was a place I used to go to relax.

"Veritas was an astrophysicist, whose job was planetary observation, and was researching Jupiter. Ey had that slender look of a woman, but once we got to talking, ey seemed like a stand-up guy to me, so we hit it off right away. We shared the same generational sensibilities that made you forget ey was a Round, probably because ey had spent so much time working with the staff outside the special district, like Dr. Tei. Veritas had an impartial way of looking at things that was like a breath of fresh air to me. Who knows what Veritas saw in me?" he said. "Although, ey said ey didn't know any security-types like me in the special district. Many of the Rounds act on their curiosity, I suppose. They're a subspecies driven by space exploration, so if that need isn't being met, they have a tendency of satisfying their inquisitiveness through those around them. Just as we were trying to figure them out, the Rounds were trying to do the same just as intensely.

"As time passed, my relationship with Veritas began to change. It's hard to say how it started. But we liked each other from the start, so we were suddenly drawn to each other. I realized that I was feeling something more than male camaraderie. Not in a homosexual way. I was attracted to the female part of Veritas. Humans are nothing more than animals. Once I became aware of the female half of em, I got a little skittish. And to make matters worse, half of Veritas is biologically female. Maybe it's because I could recognize the male half of em, too, that eir female half seemed all the more radiant.

"Pitiful, right?" Harding said. "A man in his forties with a wife and kids. But I couldn't help myself. I couldn't get Veritas out of my head. I tried to resist, but it didn't work. One day, I finally crossed the line."

Harding paused for a moment. Shirosaki could hear Harding breathing heavily over the transmitter inside the suit. "You should stop talking."

"No, let me do this. This is where the story gets good," Harding said. "I figured, we're both adults responsible for our own actions. Maybe if I sleep with em once, I'll stop fantasizing about it and be able to put it out of my mind. Veritas consented right away. Since the Round male sexual organs are hidden from view, I was able to get inside Veritas without feeling too weird about it. Eir male organ began to react too, of course, but by then, I was engaged in the act and frankly, I did everything not to notice that part of em. Out of sight, out of mind. I chose not to see what I'd rather not. I made love to Veritas as if ey were a woman, and Veritas let me. It was a convenient trick, but we were both satisfied at the time.

"Under normal circumstances, we would have been fine. All we did was satisfy our sexual needs. It was there and then gone. A one-night stand between two consenting adults, but we didn't stop there. At first, I was the one to make love to em, but soon, that wasn't enough for Veritas. It was inevitable, considering the Rounds are absolute hermaphrodites. They achieve a psychological balance by simultaneously loving as a man and being loved as a woman. Their mentality is fundamentally different from ours. Sure, Veritas knew that I was a Monaural from the start. Ey must've known what ey was getting into, but the body reacts independently from what the brain might be thinking. This arrangement couldn't last.

"As cold as this may sound, I was content to go on satisfying my sexual needs as a man. But Veritas didn't know how to relieve eir own needs as a man. What, you think ey should have got off with another Round?" asked Harding. "At first, that's exactly what ey did, but Veritas soon discovered it wasn't going to work. That eir lust wasn't going to disappear until ey'd satisfied those feelings with me. Because that's essentially what love is—the burning desire to consummate a relationship with a specific partner. Which is why Veritas couldn't stand not being able to love me as a man."

Shirosaki's eyes grew wide. "Wa—wait," he stuttered. "You're not saying Veritas—"

"Ey came to me wanting to love me as a man. What ey was demanding was that I engage in a homosexual relationship. Now I'm perfectly aware that as a social norm, we're not supposed to discriminate against queers. At the same time, I have both a reason and the right to refuse that kind of proposition.

"I only wanted Veritas's female half. So I did everything to deny eir male half any sexual pleasure. I suppose that kind of sadism got me off even more. And I have to admit, the fact that I was flouting a taboo had something to do with it. It was a dirty way to treat Veritas, I know. But I kept telling myself that I wasn't a Round. I told em that I could never be the woman in this relationship. I'm not a woman, but a Monaural man. I couldn't do what ey asked, I told Veritas. I just couldn't give over my body in that way.

"Veritas didn't back down after one or two rejections. Ey started chasing me around the station, not like a jilted woman but like a dog in rut. That was when I realized just how serious this situation had become. Seeing no easy way out, all I could do was run. It was around this time that the members of my security team got wind of the mess that I was in—suddenly I was some kind of laughingstock. They were outraged, of course, but their reaction was more resigned than critical, probably because they recognized it was a trap any warm-blooded man would have fallen for. So it was Veritas they made a target of their mockery."

"So what happened?" asked Shirosaki.

"I was painted into a corner, damn it," answered Harding. "I punched Veritas in front of the men. Called em a pervert and told em to never come near me again. It wasn't that I hated em, but I thought Veritas might give up with a strong enough push. The team looked at us and laughed—I mean, bent over with tears in their eyes. We were quite a freak show. But they were looking for a diversion from their duties on the station, so I guess our affair seemed like a farce to them.

"No one laughed out of malice, really. In a way, they had borne witness to what was essentially human nature. They had seen an incident that could very easily have happened to them, and their reaction was to laugh, that's all.

"But a Round like Veritas couldn't understand that or what was so wrong about eir behavior. Couldn't understand why I hit em or why the team was laughing at us. I found out later that even the Rounds had turned a cold shoulder to Veritas. But ey had insisted that ey had done nothing wrong. Ey believed that I would come around eventually if we talked about it. But my team and I had crushed eir resolve by laughing at em.

"That night, after realizing there was no place for em inside the station, Veritas tried to kill emself. Ey slit eir throat with a knife, but I guess the cut wasn't deep enough. One of the Rounds found em soaked in eir own blood.

"It was shocking the way the entire station swept the incident under the rug. Kline shrugged it off as a cultural collision that was bound to happen eventually. Preda used Wagi's medical diagnosis and advice to craft a report that would nip the incident in the bud. He treated Veritas's attempted suicide as an accident to avoid an investigation by the Planetary Bioethics Association.

"The Rounds also kept quiet, feeling they were responsible for Veritas too.

"To prevent another incident, the supervisors restricted access and contact with the special district. Everyone did their damnedest to keep from pointing fingers, recognizing that if a heated debate broke out, it would tear this tiny station apart. Yeah, everyone was real adult about it. Not a single punk screaming justice among them. Neither was there a clear villain to condemn. It all went down pretty quietly, really.

"Veritas and I were made to swear before Kline to never see each other again. Wagi ordered me to counseling, but I ignored it. I wasn't sick, for crying out loud, just stupid at love. I didn't much like the idea of seeing Dr. Tei either. Seeing the doctor only reminded me of Veritas.

"The moment I was denied access to the special district and Veritas, for some reason, I began to feel bitter.

"Don't ask me why," said Harding. "I didn't even know what I was angry about. Before I knew it, I was the only one obsessing over an incident that was supposed to have been settled.

"Did I really hate the Rounds or love them? Was I angry at Veritas or at myself? Or maybe I was just spooked that my relationship with Veritas made me realize that I might have been bisexual all along and was desperately trying to deny it."

Shirosaki remained silent.

"Well, are you going to say something?" Harding asked.

"I'm not a Catholic, so this confession of sins is lost on me. You start taking count, there's no end to it. That goes for this assignment. Just look at the body count we racked up on Jupiter-I over this mission. That's a heck of a lot more sinful if you ask me."

Harding let out a deep sigh.

With Harding in his arms, Shirosaki burned the gas jets to reposition themselves.

When they turned around, they saw the rescue shuttle, piloted by Arino, approaching.

VI

AFTER SHIROSAKI AND Harding were picked up and flown back to the station, they were immediately examined by the medical team. Their wounds were treated and the two received a booster injection of molecs to repair the tissue damage.

Harding lay unconscious in the bed next to Shirosaki. "How is he doing?" Shirosaki asked Wagi.

"Not good," answered the doctor. "On top of being badly injured, he's suffering from severe radiation exposure."

"I see."

"That goes for you too," said Wagi disapprovingly. "You shaved ten to twenty years off your life."

After a while, Tei entered the sickroom. Ey looked gaunt, but ey seemed less feverish and steadier on eir feet.

Tei whispered something in Dr. Wagi's ear. After Wagi nodded and excused himself from the room, Tei came around to Shirosaki's bedside.

"How are you feeling?" Shirosaki asked.

"Strange—to have a patient asking after me," answered Tei with a wan smile. "I thought you should know there was some critical information found on Karina's personal computer at Europa's research station."

"Really?" said Shirosaki, raising a brow. "The data on the parasitic machine?"

"No, the names of the Vessel of Life's main players behind this plot and a detailed record of their plans—more like Karina's last will and testament. Just as Karina had said, she was reluctant to go along with the plan. She'd lost interest in terrorism after leaving Libra. Apparently she'd studied biology because she genuinely wanted to research the marine life on Europa. When she met Kline ten years ago, she had been completely clean, which was probably why Kline had trusted her. Karina took on the plan two years ago. By then she was a trusted presence here, so she was able to get past all the security checks. That was probably the reason why the Vessel of Life recruited her. They had anticipated the difficulty of infiltrating Jupiter-I otherwise."

"Why did she do it?"

"It appears she was being threatened," Tei said. "Someone with knowledge of her past had made contact with Karina to enlist her services. At first, Karina refused. Even when they threatened to out her as a terrorist, she didn't bend at first. Perhaps because she'd braced for that possibility all along, that tactic proved ineffective. It was upon learning that Europa's marine organisms had been taken hostage that Karina had buckled."

"Wait, what hostages on Europa?"

"The Vessel of Life threatened to poison and wipe out the biotic community in Europa's ocean if she didn't cooperate. Even if she were to resist by committing suicide, Europa's marine life would die. In short, however she tried to resist, unless Karina agreed to infiltrate and sabotage Jupiter-I, Europa's biotic community would be destroyed."

"And that was more than Karina could bear."

"Karina thought nothing about the lives of other humans, much less her own. But she seemed to have regarded Europa's organisms with the utmost respect, perhaps because in their presence she could forget her own past. To Karina, those tiny lives were as sacred as the gods themselves, and we far paled by comparison."

"That sounds exactly the way Karina might see things," said

Shirosaki, flashing a bitter smile.

"There's more. Apparently the Vessel of Life had handed her a package—a virus with a 99 percent morbidity rate, capable of infecting and killing indiscriminately, Round or Monaural. When Karina learned the nature of this virus, she had mocked her employers. What was the point of using such a weapon? It would shut down Jupiter-I only temporarily, and the researchers and Rounds would eventually return. That wasn't the way to achieve absolute success. Then she offered to create a bioweapon herself. And in two years, Karina had created the parasitic machine, designed after a species of crustacean parasite discovered in Europa's ocean. A parasite about two millimeters in length that reproduces inside its crab host. Karina's creation undergoes multiple metamorphoses from larva to adult and acts upon its Round host differently at each stage."

"A genetically modified organism?"

"Without a thorough examination, it's hard to say whether it's organic or artificial. All we know is that it does unthinkable damage to the human host."

"How does it work?"

"Karina didn't leave us any details, but Dr. Wagi discussed it with Director Weil at Europa's research station and came up with several theories. After Dr. Wagi did some research on the data on the crustacean parasite on which the parasitic machine is based, and the various parasites on Earth, we came up with a theory. First, the deaths of the Round infants had us fooled; the parasitic machine isn't lethal. In fact, it had been made to infect the Rounds without killing them. The Round infants died because of their underdeveloped immune systems. The parasitic machine isn't meant to kill the Rounds. It is meant to fix their sex."

Shirosaki swallowed hard.

"The parasitic machine invades the Round host and attacks the sex hormone system. In a short period, it renders one set of reproductive organs—male or female—useless. Surgically transplanting synthetic organs wouldn't do any good. Once the parasitic machine inhabits the Round host, it changes forms repeatedly and reproduces within the host until it dies, the way parasites do. And continually attacks the reproductive organs of one sex."

"So when a Round is infected…"

"Eir biological sex is forcibly fixed as either male or female."

"Which does it shut down?"

"That varies with the individual," Tei said.

"Then how does it differentiate which sexual organs to attack?"

"Only one parasitic machine inhabits the host at any given time. The infected Round's sex is fixed according to the sexual organs the parasitic machine chooses to attack. The substance dispersed inside the special district was comprised not of eggs but first-stage larvae. About one micron in length, the larvae have four dorsal wings."

"Wings?"

"They fly. With the molecular motors attached to their wings. Actually, the wings move like the fins of the crustacean parasites after which the parasitic machine was designed. They've been engineered to glide on the airstream of the air conditioning system and the 0.38 G atmosphere of the special district. It's thought the capsules contained hundreds of thousands of these first-stage larvae. The capsules were shot at the Rounds and burst, dispersing a fine mist containing the larvae."

Shirosaki shivered at the thought of hordes of microscopic insects taking flight and latching onto the bodies of the Rounds.

"The first-stage larvae invade the respiratory organs and penetrate the host through the skin too," Tei continued. "When they enter the blood vessels and detect the double-I chromosomes unique to Rounds, the parasites shed their wings and enter the second stage of metamorphosis by feeding on the host's blood. At the same time, they produce toxins to prevent other parasites from growing, probably so the host's body doesn't weaken from over-infestation. It's likely the toxins caused the fever the Rounds have been experiencing since onset. It takes about a day for the second-stage larvae to die, leaving just one parasite to enter the third stage of metamorphosis. Once the liver neutralizes the toxins in the body, the fever goes down and the infected Round enters remission."

"So the reason why Karina was running around with Fortia as her hostage and refused to talk—"

"She was stalling until this third stage. As the surviving third-stage larva continues to travel inside the body, it eventually finds either the male or female reproductive organ. Which one is completely left up to chance. It burrows inside the tissue and matures, never to leave the organ again. The parasite takes root inside the tissue, essentially becoming a part of the body and shutting down the organ's functions. And that's how the Round host's sex becomes fixed—male if the mature parasite inhabits the female reproductive organ and female if the parasite inhabits the male reproductive organ. Parasites lay one egg after the next through self-fertilization. But since the parasite secretes an incubation-inhibiting substance, the eggs do not hatch immediately. They circulate throughout the Round host's blood system, and the vast majority of the eggs that the liver doesn't neutralize float in the bodily fluids. They probably can't be filtered out of the blood because the eggs take refuge in the white blood cells. Removing the infected organ doesn't help. If the source secreting the incubation-inhibiting substance disappears for some reason, some of the eggs will hatch and will go through the same life cycle, eventually shutting down the reproductive function of one sexual organ."

"And a new parasite will lay eggs all over again."

"The parasitic machine wasn't made to kill any of the Rounds but to eliminate one of their sexual functions. It's likely its eggs will enter any unborn child by way of the placenta."

"But wouldn't artificial insemination prevent the fetus from being infected?"

"Karina must have thought of that," said Tei. "No, we think

that an unborn child will be infected, no matter what the method of insemination."

"How does it affect Monaurals?"

"It doesn't affect Monaurals, though Monaurals can be carriers."

"What sort of contact does it take?"

"Any direct or airborne contact. Inside a Monaural host, the larvae keep their wings and do not transform past the first stage. Instead, they multiply inside the lungs and are transmitted via coughing or exhalation. By running around the station, Karina was herself another vector for infection. We should assume most of the station staff are already carriers. And the security staff."

"What are you getting at?"

"Unless we come up with a treatment to fight this parasitic molecular machine, the Monaurals won't be able to resume the Round experiments. The Vessel of Life must have the data on the parasitic machine and could be plotting to inflict the same type of damage on Jupiter-I all over again. Even if we resumed our research with an entirely new staff, an unsuspecting Monaural carrier from the planets might come to the station and transmit the parasites to the vulnerable Round population. Karina may well have succeeded in wiping out the bigender community on this station. At the very least, our gender-free society is no more."

Shirosaki thought he could hear Karina laughing in his ear. "What are the chances the Rounds will regain their bigender functions?"

"That depends on how far the research on the parasitic machine continues to develop and how quickly we can keep up to find a cure. Our battle with Karina has only just begun. But someday we will become bigender again. If we make the most of humanity's knowledge and technology, I know we'll see a day when we can defeat the parasitic machine."

"Have you been infected, Doctor?"

"Yes."

"And your sex?"

"I am male. But that doesn't mean I self-identify as male. The Monaurals don't suddenly become something else when they lose their sexual function, do they? That goes for us too. We were raised in a society where being bigender is a natural fact of life. My generation has matured inherently identifying as both male and female. Even though we have lost one of our sexual functions, we remain bigender. Karina may have destroyed the Round physiology, but she hasn't destroyed our souls. No doubt Karina knew that, but she had to do it to save Europa's biotic community." Tei produced the St. Gerard medal from eir coat pocket and placed it in Shirosaki's palm. "I hope you bring the people responsible to justice. For the sake of all the people who've died here."

After eir condition stabilized, Fortia sent Album for Calendula and Tigris.

Calendula did not put up a fight when Album arrived. In fact, ey seemed to expect what was coming. Tigris quietly followed.

After bringing Calendula and Tigris back to the residence, Album helped Fortia sit up in eir bed. Fortia rested eir back against the pillow. "Do you know why I've asked you here?" ey asked Calendula.

Calendula nodded once.

"Emotionally, I can understand what you did, having given birth and raised children myself. But right now, I am the leader in charge of this community. Anyone who disobeys an order must be punished, or there will be others. Otherwise, this tiny community will fall apart. Do you have any idea what a liability that would be when we embark in space? If we are going to confront the unimaginable hardship that awaits us, our solidarity must be strong and unshakable."

"I understand," said Calendula, contrite. "I acted rashly. I'm sorry."

"I order you to have your sex surgically fixed," said Fortia.

The words made Calendula's body go stiff.

"I suspect the parasitic machine has already fixed your sex. But even if a treatment is found, you are forbidden to become bigender again. You will remove the reproductive organs of one sex and work among the Monaurals of this station as a Monaural yourself. That's your punishment."

"So I am to leave the special district? You're banishing me?"

"You can think long and hard about what you've done. Your crime isn't that you attempted to kill Karina, but that you led the others in a revolt."

"I did it for the Rounds," said Calendula, eir voice trembling.

"I know that, which is why I can't allow you to remain here."

Album had been poised to jump in if Calendula tried to put up a fight, but that proved to be an unnecessary concern.

"Tell me one thing," said Calendula. "What will become of my children?"

"They'll remain in the special district. Don't worry. I promise they'll be cared for. Do you acknowledge and accept your punishment?"

Calendula retreated from Fortia's bedside.

"Answer me, Calendula. I gave you a direct order."

Calendula did not answer. Cocking eir head upward, ey glared straight ahead as ey walked out of the room.

"You're to remain here," Fortia said to a dumbfounded Tigris. "You will raise your and Calendula's two children. If you ever need a hand, Album and I will be here to help."

When Tigris came back to emself, ey shook eir head. "If Calendula has to go, I'm going with em."

"And the children?"

"They'll come with us, of course."

"Isn't that being selfish?" muttered Album. "You're depriving your children of the right to live as Rounds."

"They've already been infected by the parasite. What point is there now to living here?"

"When a cure is found, the Rounds will reclaim their bigender bodies," Fortia said gently. "And your children too. You're free to go with Calendula, but leave the children here. Album and I will raise them. While you may be their parents, you have no right to rob them of their futures."

A hush pervaded the room. Tigris let the tension out of eir shoulders and bowed toward Fortia. "I know they'll be in good hands in your care. Please look after them. The kids will have the support of the entire community, but Calendula has only me to look after em. I have to go."

"I know," answered Fortia. "Go on."

After Tigris left, Album tried to help Fortia lie down on the bed. Fortia refused and asked Album to bring em a work tablet.

Album asked if ey was sure ey was well enough to work, at which Fortia smiled. "Everything has changed—the Rounds, the special district…We need a new plan, Album. There's no time to waste."

When Harding regained consciousness, Shirosaki gave him a status report on the station.

Then Harding received a lengthy explanation of his medical condition from Wagi.

Nothing Wagi told him was surprising, considering that Harding's survival was a mystery even to himself. Wanting to look after his affairs with the time he had left, Harding requested to be transferred from the sickroom into an individual room.

Once in the privacy of his own room, Harding recorded messages to every member of his family with his wearable device—to his wife, his children, and to his elderly parents.

As he lay in bed after completing the task, Veritas came into the room.

"I hear you're going back to Mars," ey said with a frigid look, after sitting in the chair next to the bed. "What do you have to say for yourself?"

"Which have you become? Man or woman?"

Veritas shot him a disgusted look. "A woman. But that doesn't mean I think of myself as one."

"I know," mumbled Harding. "Veritas, I've been too afraid to tell you until now—"

"Stop it," interrupted Veritas. "I was born and raised in the special district, brought up embracing my bigender identity. Even though I've lost part of my sexual functions, I will always be both man and woman. I am the same person as when I was healthy. Even though only my female sexual organs function, I am not the same as a Monaural woman. Half of me still remains male, and I don't for a moment regret wanting you as one. Can you really bear to love the male half of who I am? If you're thinking of indulging me out of pity, you can forget it. I refuse to be some savior to ease your conscience or to absolve you of your sins."

"I'm going to die soon," said Harding, letting slip a smile. "So I'm trying to wipe the slate clean. Are you still upset about what happened?"

"Of course I am. You have no idea how much. What a relief to know I won't ever have to see your face again," said Veritas. "Go back to Mars and die in front of your wife and kids for all I care."

"I'm relieved to hear you say that."

"Don't patronize me," said Veritas, choking out the words, as if ey were desperately trying to fight back the anger whirling inside em. Ey raised a fist and brought it down on the edge of the bed so hard that it startled even Harding. The force might have broken two or three ribs had Veritas hit him.

Veritas turned eir back as if to spurn Harding. Eir slender shoulders trembled.

"Look, maybe this isn't my place to ask," said Harding, "but I'd rather you not see me on my deathbed, so why don't we make this your last visit. It's probably better that way for both of us."

Veritas offered no response. With eir back still turned, ey answered, "I have no intention of putting you at ease. You'll have to suffer my wrath until the end."

"Hell, then. Do what you want." Suddenly overcome with exhaustion, Harding closed his eyes. He thought of Miles and all the others who'd fallen in the line of duty, as well as the children of the special district. How they must have suffered in those dying moments. Would he be able to die suffering in a way that would be commensurate with his sins? He wouldn't be able to bear dying an easier death than the others. He had been the one to falter in his duties. It was he that deserved to be slowly raked over the coals.

Harding felt something cool and soft touch his face. A familiar touch he'd felt many times before. That supple sensation that had aroused in him unspeakable feelings of intoxication and guilt and had awakened his passion. He did not have to open his eyes. This was Veritas's hand. Eir cold, slender fingers. Palm. Cheek. Eir lips.

Harding swallowed the feeling of calm that began to rise up inside him. But he did not open his eyes. Pulling his lips taut, Harding said nothing and gave himself over to Veritas's gentle caress.

After Shirosaki's condition improved, Arino informed the commander of the punishment that had been handed down to Barry Wolfren.

"Since he can't be tried by planetary laws, Wolfren will remain in solitary confinement here for the rest of his life. Of course they'll put him to work so he's earning his keep, perhaps in observation or data entry. But he'll be denied all contact with the staff and Rounds. He'll be given the necessary furnishings and computer to complete his assigned tasks, but will never be allowed to leave his quarters."

"What about meals and exercise?"

"A tray will be delivered to his quarter every meal, but there's to be no human contact whatsoever."

"So he's essentially a prisoner. What's Wolfren have to say?"

"He seems surprisingly unperturbed about it. He told me that while he may be alone now, there will be others like him soon enough. Eventually Jupiter-I will have to create a second special district, a place to lock away those who identify as neither Round nor Monaural. The human race is constantly evolving. Just as Monaurals created the Round subspecies, a new race is bound to emerge from the Rounds. Wolfren said that he was merely a progenitor of that race."

"And what did you tell him?"

"I told him he was fortunate to have something to believe in," Arino said.

A faint smile came across Shirosaki's lips. "Why? Don't you?"

"I'm not entirely sure if we've accomplished anything here, sir," Arino said. "What exactly have we achieved?"

"Karina Majella is no longer a threat. That's our greatest prize."

"Do you think so?"

"It's what you should believe," insisted Shirosaki. "If you know what's good for you."

Once Shirosaki was well enough to get out of bed, he took a walk around the station to look for Kline. He found her in the observatory where an image of Jupiter filled the omnidirectional screen. Kline was reclining on the sofa, staring at the gas giant.

Shirosaki walked across the room, careful not to look down at the black void displayed on the floor screen.

Kline turned off the floor screen as soon as she noticed Shirosaki's arrival.

Shirosaki breathed a sigh of relief. "Staring at the eye of Zeus?" he asked.

"Actually," answered Kline, "I was admiring Io."

Shirosaki caught a glimpse of Io's shadow against the face of Jupiter. Jupiter's volcanic and lava moon. Staring at that fiery altar that had swallowed Karina, Shirosaki said, "It's likely I'll be demoted when I return to Mars."

"You're taking the blame for what's happened?"

"I may have to resign my command with SSD."

"I should have killed Karina when I had the chance," Kline said. "After all, I was the only one who had a legitimate reason to kill her."

"There's something you can tell me," said Shirosaki. "What was Dr. Tei's name in the special district?"

"Why do you want to know?"

"Just curious, I suppose."

"Lanterna. It means 'light.' You know, the kanji character 灯," explained Kline, tracing the kanji character in the air with a finger. "In Chinese, it's pronounced *tei*."

"How did the doctor come by that name?"

"One of the female staff, who was Japanese, gave em the name years ago. It was when the doctor was still young. Ey was terribly sad when eir good friend had ended her assignment here and went back to Earth. Ey had sulked and kept eir distance from the staff for a while, but ey was soon back to eir sunny self. That's the kind of person the doctor is. Which is probably why I chose Tei to become an intermediary. Perhaps it's because ey recognized the differences between Round and Monaural that the doctor put emself in the middle—no, gray zone where ey was neither."

"Light..." Shirosaki mused. "If the doctor is true to eir name, maybe the world will change for the better."

Perhaps Lanterna was too small to light humanity's way into space. But any amount of illumination was better than nothing. Much better.

Would there ever come a day when Monaurals and Rounds together journeyed past the eye of Zeus and saw what lay ahead?

The answer was nowhere yet to be found.

AFTERWORD AND ACKNOWLEDGEMENTS

It is my belief that anyone involved in the arts, not just novels, feels compelled to address issues of gender and sexuality sooner or later. For a long time, ever since I began writing novels in fact, I have wanted to write something focused around this theme.

Given that opportunity, I was both stunned and elated at having opened a secret door to yet another fascinating world. Although I've rendered that world in a very stylized science fictional form with this novel, I hope to explore these themes again in general fiction form. The more I write, I am impressed by the depth of the vast world I've yet to explore.

I am indebted to the staff at the Kadokawa Haruki Corporation and many others for their help during the publishing process. I wish to express my gratitude to editor Takeshi Muramatsu who offered many invaluable suggestions via phone and email.

Sayuri Ueda
October 2004

ABOUT THE AUTHOR

 Born in Hyogo Prefecture, Sayuri Ueda is one of the more innovative science fiction authors in Japan. She won the 2003 Komatsu Sakyo Award with her debut novel, *Mars Dark Ballade. The Cage of Zeus*, her second novel, was originally published in 2004. Her recent short fiction collection, *Uobune, Kemonobune* (Fish Boat, Animal Boat), was highly acclaimed in the SF community and was nominated for the 2009 Japan SF Award. Also nominated for the Seiun Award in the short story category was "Kotori no haka" (The Grave of the Bird) from the collection. Her latest novel, *Karyu no miya* (The Ocean Chronicles), won the first prize of Best SF 2010 in *SF Magazine* and was one of the most noteworthy books of the year in any genre.

HAIKASORU

THE FUTURE IS JAPANESE

GOOD LUCK, YUKIKAZE BY CHŌHEI KAMBAYASHI

The alien JAM have been at war with humanity for over thirty years...or have they? Rei Fukai of the FAF's Special Air Force and his intelligent plane Yukikaze have seen endless battles, but after declaring "Humans are unnecessary now," and forcibly ejecting Fukai, Yukikaze is on her own. Is the target of the JAM's hostility really Earth's machines? And have the artificial intelligences of Earth been acting in concert with the JAM to manipulate Yukikaze? As Rei tries to ascertain the truth behind the intentions of both sides, he realizes that his own humanity may be at risk, and that the JAM are about to make themselves known to the world at large.

ICO: THE CASTLE IN THE MIST BY MIYUKI MIYABE

A boy with horns, marked for death. A girl who sleeps in a cage of iron. The Castle in the Mist has called for its sacrifice: a horned child, born once a generation. When, on a single night in his thirteenth year, Ico's horns grow long and curved, he knows his time has come. But why does the Castle in the Mist demand this offering, and what will Ico do with the girl imprisoned within the Castle's walls? Delve into the mysteries of Miyuki Miyabe's grand achievement of imagination, inspired by the award-winning game for the PlayStation®2 computer entertainment system, now remastered for PlayStation®3.

TEN BILLION DAYS AND ONE HUNDRED BILLION NIGHTS BY RYU MITSUSE

Ten billion days—that is how long it will take the philosopher Plato to determine the true systems of the world. One hundred billion nights—that is how far into the future Christ and Siddhartha will travel to witness the end of the world and also its fiery birth. Named the greatest Japanese science fiction novel of all time, *Ten Billion Days and One Hundred Billion Nights* is an epic eons in the making. Originally published in 1973, the novel was revised by the author in later years and republished in 2001.

VISIT US AT WWW.HAIKASORU.COM